SNOWBIRDS OF PREY

A HORROR COMEDY MYSTERY

FREAKY FLORIDA BOOK 1

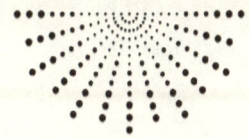

WARD PARKER

MAD MANGROVE MEDIA

CONTENTS

OF POT BELLIES AND PICKLEBALL

issy Mindle wrapped a blood-pressure cuff around the vampire's pale, scrawny arm. She was blissfully unaware of the two dead humans on the beach. Had she known the bodies were completely drained of blood, and were mere yards from the condo tower, she might have been nervous about being in a community full of vampires. For her, however, it was a typical night as a home-health nurse. Her primary job responsibilities were medical screenings and basic care for seniors. It just so happened her patients were vampires, werewolves, and other supernaturals.

She had a touch of the supernatural herself: budding powers of magick she was still trying to understand and develop. But they didn't matter tonight. She had the vampire curmudgeon Leonard Schwartz to deal with.

His blood pressure was a healthy (for a vampire) forty over fifteen, and his resting heart rate was an admirable five beats a minute. He was, however, overweight.

"What do you mean I'm fat?" Schwartz asked in his gruff Brooklyn accent, sitting on a dining room chair in his third-floor condo.

"I didn't say you're fat," Missy replied, glancing at Schwartz's protruding pot belly. "I said it would be good if you lost a little weight."

She had to be careful. Schwartz was known for easily flying into a rage, and you don't want to be alone with an angry vampire.

"I don't understand how I could be fat. I'm on a liquid diet, for crying out loud. I had this," he slapped his belly, "for years before I was turned. Couldn't get rid of it no matter what. Then, when I was turned, I said to myself, 'Schwartz, look at the bright side of being a vampire. You're going to be better looking and much stronger.' What a joke. I got the looks and the strength, but a hundred years later I still got this." He slapped his stomach again.

Schwartz had a shiny, bald dome fringed with tufts of white hair. Additional tufts served as eyebrows. His jowls were prominent, and his nose was a force to be reckoned with. If he considered this good-looking, she couldn't imagine what he looked like before.

"Belly fat is especially difficult to lose for older men," Missy said. "I guess that's the case for vampires, too."

"But there's no fat in the blood I drink. And I play pickleball four times a week. There's no reason I should still have this gut. It lowers my confidence with the ladies."

He was showing some vulnerability here, but Missy couldn't bring herself to say whatever words would bolster his sexual self-image. She simply couldn't.

Schwartz lived at Squid Tower, an oceanfront condominium community in Jellyfish Beach on Florida's Atlantic coast, among other elderly vampires enjoying their golden years for eternity. Vampires can't just show up at a doctor's office to get their healthcare like the rest of us. Primary care physicians have daytime office hours, and they ask awkward questions when they observe death-like symptoms. Missy had to take on that role with her home visits.

Now, you'd probably assume an immortal creature would never have health issues. And you'd be wrong. A seventy-five-year-old like Schwartz was still a seventy-five-year-old, regardless of the supernatural power gained when he was transformed into a vampire. His age when he was turned into a vampire would be his age forever.

Being turned does give you some extra pep, more than any senior vitamin supplements could ever provide. However, you still have to deal with your human, pre-vampire health concerns. Vampirism gives you powerful wound-healing abilities, but it doesn't automatically remove plaque from your arteries, or reverse your arthritis. True, your hearing becomes better than a human's, but it would still be diminished compared to a younger vampire's. Missy had several vampire patients with hearing aids.

In short, dying and being reborn as a vampire does wonders for your health. And immortality is a handy thing for sure. But being a vampire can't fully reverse the physiological damage aging does to your body. That truth is the business model of Acceptance Home Care, Missy's employer. A company that lacked a 401K retirement plan because it didn't expect its employees to survive long enough to need one.

Unfortunately, diet, exercise, and a healthy weight were touchy subjects, even for the undead.

"I'm concerned about your blood-test results," Missy said. "Your glucose level is dangerously high. You could develop Type 2 diabetes."

Missy had drawn Schwartz's blood the week before and her home-health company sent it to a special lab that handled "unusual patients," as they put it. Getting the blood tested was easy. Drawing the blood sample was a different story. Schwartz had whined and complained when she poked him with the needle. And seeing his hungry expression as he had watched the tubes filling with his blood made Missy fear for her life.

"Vampires can be diabetic?" Schwartz asked.

"Who would have thought? But that's what I learned in my training with Acceptance Home Care. Now, do you have a sweet tooth? Have you been feeding on prey with high sugar levels? If they eat a lot of sugar, their glucose levels remain high for up to an hour before their insulin lowers it. Which means their glucose goes right into your own blood."

Schwartz muttered something under his breath. He clearly didn't want a lecture on his feeding habits.

"There's always the Blood Bus for an easy, healthy meal," Missy added.

"I'm not drinking any freaking donated blood. I need the thrill of the hunt. It's part and parcel of the dining experience for me. It's the essence of being a vampire. I'll never be one of these folks who sit around waiting for the Blood Bus to show up every night. I am an alpha predator, a master of the night."

"It's really simple, Mr. Schwartz. If you see a guy eating an ice cream cone, don't hunt him. Or at the very least, wait an hour after he's done eating before you attack. Okay?"

He grunted. But at least it wasn't an obscenity.

"And I hope you don't hunt close to home," Missy said.

"Nah, I don't do that." Schwartz wouldn't meet her eyes.

"There are rumors about you."

"I told you I don't. It's against the rules, anyway."

"And you know why," Missy said. "If the police are involved, it would endanger the entire community."

"I don't kill my prey. Well, usually I don't. And I always mesmerize them, so they forget about the attack."

"Sometimes their memories come back. And what if there's a witness who sees your attack?"

"I don't need a human to lecture me."

"If you insist on hunting, why not get away from the city, go out west into the countryside? That would be a perfect way to get more exercise."

"I'm late for my pickleball game," Schwartz said, buttoning his shirt and getting up. He retrieved a duffel bag from the closet. "Don't mean to be rude, but . . ."

"Don't pretend we're finished, Mr. Schwartz. There's one more thing I need from you."

"I'm *not* peeing in a cup."

"And don't pretend this is the first time you've had to do this."

"Look, I only pee every other day. I'm not even technically alive—what value is there in my pee?"

"Do you want me to list all the valuable data we get from your urine? Granted, many of them are different from when you were alive, but some are even more critical now. Low levels of creatinine can be fatal in vampires."

Schwartz gave a big, theatrical sigh and held out an open hand. Missy placed in it a plastic cup with a lid. He took it and retreated to the bathroom. Three hours later, he emerged and slapped the almost-empty cup on the dining room table.

"I've got to leave," he said.

"I'm sorry I made you miss your pickleball game."

"No, I was lying before about being late. The game begins in a half hour. Goodnight," he said, opening the front door and waiting for her to take her tote bag and leave.

Missy didn't have any more appointments that night, so she looked forward to getting home and relaxing. She started her ancient Toyota in the visitor lot and drove past the pickleball courts, where vampires in white tennis outfits, only slightly whiter than their skin, were assembling. She exited past the gatehouse, where the overnight guard smiled and waved at her.

She was certain he was a human, with plenty of Neanderthal ancestry. But the way he looked at her creeped her out more than monsters did.

THE VAMPIRE who wanted to kill him really sucked at pickleball. From his post in the gatehouse, Bernie watched Schwartz flail about on the court in a doubles match. Schwartz would let the easiest shots pass him by, then go after ones his teammate was hitting, resulting in tangled arms and the thwack of paddles hitting undead bodies. The balls Schwartz did hit, he hammered with preternatural strength as if he wanted to cause bodily injury to the player on the other side of the net.

Every night at midnight, the four pickleball courts at Squid Tower Condominiums filled with vampires playing beneath the bright lights. They didn't need the lights to see but turned them on so humans passing by wouldn't get suspicious. Bernie called the sport tennis for old people, or the lovechild of badminton and ping-pong. Seniors really liked pickleball. Vampire seniors, especially. As vampires, they could move a little faster than their human counterparts, leap an impressive distance (at times), and sometimes make shots that actually impressed Bernie.

But, still, if one of players fell it was a big production. Frantic clucking like vampire hens, and if the vampires couldn't help their friend get up, Bernie would have to leave the gate-house to help. He shuddered at the thought of the withered hands, cold as death, gripping his hand and arm as he pulled the fallen warrior to his or her feet.

Sometimes, when there was shrieking about a possible broken hip, he would have to call the private medical service to come out since dialing 9-1-1 was a big no-no in a community of vampires trying to hide what they truly were. Fictional vampires were supposed to have magical healing powers, but try telling that to the geezer flailing around on the court like a turtle on its back, threatening to sue every entity he could think of. It wasn't pretty.

Schwartz's game on the court nearest the gatehouse didn't last long. An unfortunate possum wandered by, and two players chased after it for a late-night snack. Schwartz sat down on a bench beside the courts, wiping his face with a towel, even though vampires don't sweat (it must have been an ingrained habit). He put his paddle away in his duffel bag. Then he trudged back toward the building.

However, he made a point of passing by the gatehouse. He stopped just outside of Bernie's window.

"Hey, numb-nuts," Schwartz said to him. "It's good to see you're not sleeping on the job for once. Never let your guard down anymore. Because I'm coming for you. You can count on it. I'm coming for you."

Schwartz laughed and walked away.

This was the kind of abuse Bernie had to deal with every night. Bernie Burdine was the new overnight gate guard at Squid Tower. And his prospects for survival were not good.

2
GONE FISHIN'

Just hours earlier, a different tale of predation took place a few hundred yards away as two shark fishermen waited for a bite. Jellyfish Beach had an ordinance against fishing for sharks from the beach. Partly, it was for public safety. Depositing chum made from pieces of dead fish just off the beach to attract the sharks wasn't a good idea when there would be surfers and swimmers in those same waters as soon as the sun came up. Chumming was recently made illegal statewide for shore-based shark fishermen, though most did it anyway.

And partly, the city's ordinance was to protect the sharks, which were often killed by the stress of their long fight once hooked and pulled up onto the beach to be the subject of selfies with their captors. By the time the shark was pushed back into the water, it was often too late.

Billy Ray and Nubb were not concerned about the welfare

of sharks, or about the ordinance. They loved the adrenaline rush of catching giant sharks at night, taking selfies with the dying sharks, and then forgetting to post their photos on social media. And, of course, they enjoyed getting good and wasted while they were at it.

"It's your turn to drop the bait," Billy Ray said.

"What the hell? That ain't fair. I did it last time," Nubb said.

It was long after midnight and they hadn't caught anything but a meager buzz. Nubb was enjoying himself, but he knew Billy Ray would get abusive if they got skunked with no catches. Billy Ray was large and, despite his giant belly, very strong, while Nubb was small and wiry. He'd been on the receiving end of Billy Ray's fists before and didn't want to repeat the experience. Such was the price of friendship.

"You didn't paddle out far enough," Billy Ray said, finishing off a candy bar and draining the last of a can of beer down his throat. "So, it don't count. This time, go out another twenty yards at least. And dump some more chum."

Billy Ray obviously thought Nubb was stupid enough to fall for this logic, but the fact was Nubb was smart enough to avoid making Billy Ray angry.

Billy Ray put a large bluefish on the giant hook and handed it to Nubb, who placed it in the rear tank-well of the kayak. He pushed the kayak into the surf, jumped on, and paddled furiously to get through the waves without dumping. Shark baits were too big, and the sinkers above them were too heavy, to cast out with a fishing rod from the beach. They had to be delivered by boat.

Nubb paddled farther this time. He figured he was about a hundred and fifty yards out, farther than last time. But Billy

Ray waved him to keep going. He was well past the second sand bars and the water was probably deep here. He looked back at the beach and Billy Ray waved him on. Finally, after more padding, Billy Ray gave him a raised fist.

Nubb opened a plastic container and poured the foul mix of fish heads and guts into the water. Then he dropped the baited hook and watched it sink. Time to head back. He hoped his kayak wouldn't get rammed by a shark as he paddled back toward shore.

On shore, which seemed to Nubb awfully far away, Billy Ray was reeling in some slack line, then pulled another beer out of the cooler. They weren't supposed to be fishing for sharks or drinking beer on the beach, but neither the cops nor Fish & Wildlife ever patrolled at this hour. So, they figured they'd be safe.

A flare or Roman candle arced in the sky just inland of the beach. Whoever launched that wasn't cool, Nubb thought. It could attract Johnny Law's attention to their location.

Nubb entered the surf zone and had to be very careful not to dump. He used the paddle behind him like a rudder, switching it from side to side to keep the kayak straight and surfing the waves. He looked up and thought he saw someone talking to Billy Ray, but the kayak dipped into a trough and his view was blocked by a wave. When he went over the crest, he didn't see anyone where Billy Ray had been standing, not his friend nor the dark figure speaking to him.

Had Billy Ray been arrested? Nubb felt anxious and began paddling hard. As the kayak slipped through the wash and onto the sand, there was no sign of Billy Ray. He quickly pulled the kayak up onto the beach, away from the encroaching tide.

"Billy Ray?" he called with a quaver in his voice.

He didn't receive an answer. It was quiet except for the growl of the surf. The beach was totally empty of people. Billy Ray's rig, an expensive fiberglass rod and Penn reel, lay carelessly on the sand. There's no way Billy Ray would have willingly placed it there because sand could get into the gears of the reel.

"Billy Ray?"

Maybe he was taking a leak in the sea grapes beyond the dunes. Nubb approached a gap in the dunes where the stairs to the dune crossover of a condo complex began. On either side were sea oats giving way to dense thickets of sea grape trees with their large, round leaves. It was easy to hide in there when you had to pee.

Then came the oddest noise. It was a slurping, a lapping up of something liquid. It sounded like Billy Ray was drinking beer out of bowl like a dog. And, to tell the truth, Billy Ray had been known to do that more than once.

Nubb stopped suddenly. It wasn't Billy Ray he had heard. Because Billy Ray lay on his back in the sand within the sea grapes, unmoving, his giant stomach as prominent as a sand dune. Nubb knelt to see if he was all right.

He wasn't. He was dead, mouth open, skin pale white in the moonlight. There was blood smeared on his neck and inner forearms.

"Holy Moses on a cookie," Nubb said.

Then someone whispered in his ear, someone right behind him. Silky, soothing words he couldn't understand but which sounded reassuring.

Nubb stood. But before he could turn around, the pain hit him in the neck, sharp and intense. He was wrapped in a smothering embrace of thin, but steel-like, arms while a powerful jaw worked at his neck. He struggled to break free, yet the arms squeezed him until he couldn't breathe.

The loud, throaty growl of his attacker in his ear faded along with his consciousness.

3

SUSPICIOUS MINDS

Missy arrived at Squid Tower after sunset for a patient visit and then the weekly creative writing class she taught for a little extra income. As she was parking in the visitor lot, someone rapped on her car window, startling her. Her first instinct was to clutch the vampire-repellant amulet she wore around her neck. Her second instinct, which should have been her first, was to fumble for the pepper spray in her purse.

Instead of a vampire gone rogue or a mugger, it was a lanky guy in a white Jellyfish Beach Police polo shirt, wearing sunglasses despite the darkness. She lowered the window.

The man introduced himself as a Detective Affird and asked if she had seen a couple of men shark fishing nearby on the beach the night before.

"No, I was inside the entire time," she said.

"Do you live here?"

"No, I'm a home-health nurse." She showed him her business card. "I come here to visit patients."

"And you're just arriving now?" he asked. His dark glasses made him appear as skeptical as his tone.

"A lot of seniors keep odd hours," she said. "They have sleeping disorders and other ailments."

The greatest concern of her patients, aside from feeding and complaining about their ailments, was keeping their vampirism secret. As multicultural as society might be, there was no tolerance for supernatural creatures, or "freaks," as they ironically called themselves. The police, especially, would frown upon the undead who took blood from the living.

And on the rare occasion the police did find a vampire, certain cops summarily executed the creature. It was an open secret among police departments, definitely not a policy. But Missy knew for a fact it happened.

"You come here regularly?" the detective asked.

"I do."

"Do you ever come across any unfamiliar men or women on the property who are too young to live here? Late-teens to twenties-thirties, maybe riding in a car with a resident, or walking in from the beach?"

"I honestly haven't. Why?"

"There's been several who have gone missing, or have been found murdered, over the past couple of months. Many were last seen nearby. Have any residents here shown any suspicious behavior?"

They all did. They were freaking vampires, okay? But she couldn't say that.

"Sorry, I haven't noticed anyone here other than seniors,

and none have acted strangely. I haven't been working here very long."

The detective appeared annoyed. "Where do you live?"

"In town," Missy said. "A few blocks off Jellyfish Beach Boulevard."

Affird looked her and her car over again, assessing her.

"If you observe anything, call me," he said, handing Missy his card before walking away. She accepted it, though she knew she couldn't call him. *He suspects someone living here is a murderer*, she thought.

For vampires, living together in a community was great for their personal safety and avoiding loneliness, but it also carried great risks. If one vampire was discovered, the entire group could be revealed as well.

And that meant they would all be forced to flee. Or all be killed by staking, burning, or decapitation. The public would never know about it. But Missy would be out of a job and lose a lot of patients she had grown quite fond of.

Missy visited the Planktons, a couple who were in their early sixties in body age. This was a second marriage for both. George had outlived his first wife and then became a vampire after being preyed upon in a city park. Barbara was turned into a vampire at a particularly wild office Christmas party, and either her husband didn't want to be turned as well or she refused to do it for him. When her husband's mortal life came to its natural end, she searched for a new husband, preferably a vampire.

Barbara moved to Florida to escape the Upstate New York

winters and ended up at Squid Tower. So did George. They met through the vampire canasta club, fell in love, and moved in together in her larger three-bedroom condo. George sold his unit, and they got married in a recent ceremony Missy attended as the only human invited. It was a beautiful event, held in the oldest cemetery in Jellyfish Beach, catered with warm pints of fresh, whole blood by the company that ran the Blood Bus.

Missy gave them each a brief checkup. As she was about to leave, George took her aside. He had a long face, thick, white hair, and the air of a college professor.

"A police detective was down by the lobby and asked me questions," George said. "I saw him talking to you, too."

"Yeah, there have been murders or disappearances near here. I hope no one from Squid Tower was responsible."

"That would be horrible. Since you're not one of us, I wanted to ask you if humans suspect vampires live here?"

"I have never heard anything," Missy said. "The people here easily pass for human seniors. The only suspicious thing is so many of you leave your hurricane shutters closed during the snowbird season."

"But they keep the daylight out so well," George said. He tried to have a joking tone, but it didn't mask his anxiety.

You're not one of us. The words festered in her mind after she left their condo and headed downstairs for her writing class.

GLADYS FINISHED READING her short story to the group. It was a romance, involving an elderly woman vampire from Rhode Island, like Gladys, who was tall, slender, and stunning, unlike Gladys. The vampire had a torrid affair with the pool boy, who happened to be a werewolf. He never wore a shirt while cleaning the pool and had a hairless chest (despite being a werewolf) with chiseled pecs and a six-pack like the men on the covers of romance novels.

The story ended after an embarrassingly graphic sex scene, and there was no plot or character development. It was basically porn written by a centuries-old woman in a seventy-year-old body. But Missy couldn't be a harsh critic. This class wasn't part of a Master's program in creative writing; it was meant to be fun and inspiring for retired people.

"Gladys, I'm very impressed by your realistic dialogue," Missy said.

The author smiled. If she were human, she may have blushed, but vampires don't do that.

The creative writing group went one-by-one around the circle, making comments about the story. The women enjoyed it and the few men in the group criticized it for technical errors about pool cleaning. But then the conversation strayed from the story to the werewolves living in the community next door.

"They never clean up after their dogs. There's dog poop everywhere along the sidewalk in front of our building."

"Maybe it's werewolf poop."

"Wouldn't surprise me."

"And their loud parties, night after night."

"Horrible music."

"I hate those electric guitars. Why doesn't anyone play lutes anymore?"

"A bunch of them were drinking on the beach the other night, right at the bottom of our boardwalk. I wouldn't be surprised if they came onto our property."

Elderly werewolves were yet another set of creatures that

wintered and retired in Florida. Missy had a few of them as patients. They weren't immortal like vampires, and they aged at a normal human rate. In fact, their monthly transformations brought on by the full moon took a heavy toll on their aging bodies. Their ability to hunt was greatly diminished by age as well. It's hard to chase down a deer or a man when you use a walker. They rarely turned into wolves on demand anymore, simply enduring the involuntary transformations during the full moon. So, they lived fairly normal lives as retirees, except for their fascination with 1970s classic-rock bands and heavy partying.

"I hope the police are investigating the werewolves for the murders and disappearances," Gladys said.

"Seems like the cops have only been looking around at Squid Tower," said Sol.

"Well, it would be just like those werewolves to kill people and make it look like we vampires did it," Gladys said.

The class murmured in agreement.

"Why can't it simply be a serial killer who's human?" Bill asked. "This is Florida. We have serial killers out the wazoo."

"Class," Missy interjected, "let's stay focused on Gladys' story. Did you find her werewolf character to be convincing?"

"He's not like the low-class werewolves next door," Sol said.

"Or like any man I've ever known, to be honest," said a woman named Doris.

4

AN ANGEL, A DEMON

Taylor couldn't remember how she ended up here on the beach. All she knew was how intensely she was tripping. Did she take too much Reboot?

Who cares? She felt awesome, and she had wanted so badly to forget.

She lay against a sand dune and stared at the stars. They were blazing like in the famous Van Gogh painting. The ocean sounded like a million soothing whispers telling her to relax. Everything would be all right. The stalks of sea oats rustled around her head in the gentle breeze. She was thirsty but didn't care.

The Reboot made her feel like she was a good person after all. And that she would make the right choices in the end.

How *did* she end up here? She remembered being at a party with Ashley and Cindi. Jerkface had been there with his new girlfriend. That had hurt like a punch to the stomach. Why did it still bother her to see him with someone else? All she wanted was to forget about him. And the rest of the night was about forgetting.

She remembered getting too drunk at the party. Her friends dragged her out of there just in time before she said something to Jerkface she'd regret, or the police showed up and created news that would embarrass Taylor's mother.

There was a bar afterward. No, maybe two bars. A motorcycle ride. Oh, yes, and the Reboot.

The Reboot.

The purring surf.

The soothing breeze.

The briny scent of the sea.

The stars burning in the sky above.

And nothing else.

One of the stars noticed her looking at them. It twinkled at her.

And now the blazing star was descending from the heavens toward her, coming to say hello. Swooping down like an angel, coming closer.

She could feel its power. It was real.

Yes, it was an angel in all its glory, landing before her on the sand.

No. It wasn't an angel.

It was a demon, she realized too late.

A demon that came to destroy.

WHEN PHILOMENA, the day guard, showed up to relieve him, Bernie told her it had been a typical, uneventful night manning the gate. No signs of Schwartz, and no accidents dropping the gate arm on cars as Bernie occasionally did. He was happy to have gotten a glimpse of a meteor or something—a tiny ball of fire flying by in the sky over the beach—but nothing else memorable occurred.

He was just about to hand over the post to Philomena when the police car pulled up to the booth and demanded to be let in. No problem, that happened from time to time even at a place where residents avoided calling 9-1-1. But the officer told him to expect more emergency vehicles to follow.

Sure enough, another cop. Then an ambulance followed by a fire truck. Then a sheriff's deputy. Later, the crime scene investigators' SUV pulled up. Finally, an unmarked car driven by Detective Affird showed up. The cop had come by at least twice before during Bernie's short tenure as a gate guard.

"Detective, what's going on?" Bernie asked.

"Crime scene on the beach," Affird said, the rising sun glinting off his shades. "Did you see anyone coming or going over the dune crossover in the last few hours?"

The only view of the crossover was from one of the security monitors. He had seen a couple of really old vampires hobbling home before dawn but wasn't going to mention it.

"Sorry, nope," he said.

After Affird drove through and parked behind the other official vehicles in a fire lane near the dune crossover, Philomena shook her head with disgust.

"That cop has been asking too many questions," she said. "The vampires here aren't stupid enough to feed right on their doorstep, are they?"

"No way," Bernie said, though he couldn't stop thinking about Schwartz.

"This used to be such a safe town," Philomena said with

sadness. "And a safe country, America. But no more. Makes me miss Martinique. There, you could swim at night naked, and no one would bother you. Here, if a rapist doesn't get you, the vampires will."

She stroked his arm, as if to comfort him, but her hand lingered a bit too long. Bernie felt a tingling in his nether regions he didn't welcome. He stepped away from her. She was not bad-looking for her age and her dark-brown skin was still smooth and shiny with barely a wrinkle. But no, no, no, he was not into older chicks.

She searched his face after he stepped away from her, so he gave her a big, reassuring smile to avoid hurt feelings.

"I'm heading home now," he said. "You stay safe, Philomena."

"WE'RE Ten-Fifty-One for a Code Five. Victim reported on the beach on the Seventeen-hundred block of North Ocean Boulevard. That's a Code Five."

The voice crackled over Matt's police scanner early in the morning. Ten-Fifty-One meant "en route." Code Five indicated a possible homicide. Murders weren't very common in Jellyfish Beach. Matt Rosen, staff reporter for the *Jellyfish Beach Journal*, was especially interested, however, because there had been a string of disappearances and dead bodies found of late. The victims and missing were generally those who slipped through the cracks of society: homeless, runaways, and addicts who were kicked out of their sober homes. And though it had never been released publicly, he knew the cause of death of many of these victims was exsanguination.

That's right, they bled out. Or, more accurately, were drained of blood.

Matt finished getting dressed and locked up the cottage. It was just after 6:00 a.m., and this time of year the sun wasn't up yet. But there would be early risers on the beach already and he wanted to get to the scene before the police set up a perimeter. Fortunately, the crime scene wasn't far.

The first responders had apparently gained access via a gated condominium community named Squid Tower, so he pulled over in front in a no-parking zone on State Road A1A. He recognized the car in front of him as belonging to the local TV affiliate. They had beaten him there, but at least the news van hadn't arrived yet.

Matt cut through the parking lot of the nondescript residential high rise. It looked like a typical fifty-five-plus senior community. He walked around the building and over the short boardwalk that crossed the dunes. A young newsroom intern from the TV station was talking on her phone near the stairs.

Four officers stood around chatting, waiting for a detective and crime-scene techs to arrive. The body lay nearby in a grassy clump of sea oats where the dunes flattened out into the beach. Matt approached nonchalantly, flashing his newspaper I.D. when the cops looked up at him even though he knew them. He didn't go any closer to the body than where the officers were standing.

The victim was a young woman, lying on her stomach. She wore white shorts and a blouse that were casual but chic enough to be clubby. Her feet were bare.

There was no blood on her clothing or on the sand. From where he stood, Matt couldn't see any signs of violence to the body or on the starkly white skin.

"Is this a homicide or an overdose?" Matt asked.

An African-American cop, Bill Jensen, answered. "Homicide. Looks like she was possibly strangled, but also bled out from some wounds on her neck. Where the blood went is anyone's guess."

"Another exsanguination murder? Wasn't there one just last week?"

"Yeah, I don't know what the deal is," Jensen said. "You'll have to talk to a detective. But there's plenty of kooks out there who like to pretend they're a vampire."

Or they actually are one, Matt thought.

"Are the wounds on her neck puncture wounds?" he asked.

"Yeah, but they could have come from any variety of sharp instruments."

"Like fangs?"

"Hey Rosen, I got a scoop for you," said the sheriff's deputy, a high-school classmate of Matt's named Dawn. "This vic is the mayor's daughter."

"Are you serious? How old is she?"

"Twenty-two. Old enough to get into bars, but too young to know she'd met the wrong guy."

The mayor's daughter. Matt knew this would expand the investigation beyond concerning only the invisible members of society. He waited until Detective Affird showed up.

Fred Affird spoke to the medical examiner, a portly man who was sweating already in the morning warmth. Affird knelt beside the body and looked it over briefly. He scowled when he stood and walked over to the officers.

"Detective," Matt said, "has the mayor been notified?"

As usual, Affird ignored him.

Matt rattled off questions about the "vampire killer." And, as

25

usual, when Affird did finally look at him through his mirror shades, he only smiled without answering anything.

"I thought we had a good relationship, detective."

"It would be much better if you'd just leave me alone and wait for the press release from the department," Affird said.

"But what about transparency and accountability?" Matt said, without hiding his sarcasm.

"I'm accountable to the chief, that's it. And I'm certainly not accountable to reporters."

At least he talked to me this time, Matt thought.

AFTER BERNIE GOT HOME, he turned on the TV to the morning news as he ate a bowl of cereal in his dingy studio apartment. He shoveled the generic-brand sugared flakes into his mouth at his small table, inches from the twenty-four-inch monitor. Below the closed curtains, the window-unit air conditioner chugged desperately. The news anchors gushed breathlessly.

It turned out it was the mayor's daughter who had been found murdered on the beach. She looked young and hot in the photo they showed. Bernie wondered what she had been doing on the beach at night.

After he tossed the empty bowl into the sink, he fired up his clunky computer and went to the *Jellyfish Beach Journal* website. An article about the murder had just been posted. It was straightforward and laid out the same basic facts he had heard on TV. But it already had a few reader comments attached below it. One of them wondered if the body had neck punctures and if it had been drained of blood.

Most people would laugh at such speculation. Not those who worked at Squid Tower.

He replayed in his mind the night's migration of residents' cars in and out of the tower's parking garage and rolling past his guardhouse, wondering if any of the occupants had been responsible. None of the residents looked like savage killers. They looked like his grandparents, except their complexions were whiter and their eyes tended to glow red. He couldn't imagine them dining on anything other than raccoons, rabbits, possums, and stray pets. Maybe, just maybe, on the occasional homeless person. And there were just as many residents who didn't hunt at all and relied instead on the nightly visits of the Blood Bus. He realized he had begun to feel protective of these people whose gate he guarded.

But he remembered Schwartz exiting the gate, pausing to fix a hate-filled glare upon him. Bernie had to find something to improve their relationship. Before Schwartz gave in to his instincts and killed him.

Had Schwartz returned to the property in time to kill the woman?

5
NOT IN MY BACKYARD

M issy was feeding her two gray tabbies, Brenda and Bubba, when her doorbell rang.

It was Affird. He had tracked down where she lived.

"Sorry to bother you, Ms. Mindle. I needed to ask you a few more questions."

She didn't like the feeling of being investigated when she had done nothing wrong. She didn't like the man, either. He had thick black hair going gray, a hollow, pockmarked face, and wore sunglasses despite the fact it was dark out. His khaki trousers and navy-blue polo shirt with the department logo hung loosely from his bony frame. The shirt was tucked in, making his holster quite conspicuous jutting out from his hip.

"I'm rather busy right now."

"No problem. I respect your time." He had inserted himself into the doorway so she couldn't close the door without pushing him out of the way, made more difficult by the fact Florida hurricane codes require exterior doors to open outwards. "This won't take long."

Missy sighed. "Go on."

"Another person was murdered last night, on the beach in front of Squid Tower."

"Oh no, that's horrible."

"I need you to try again to remember if you've seen any strange behavior by the residents."

"No, I haven't. The people who live here are old retirees. Why would you suspect one of them?"

"I'm not saying I do. I want to rule it out, though. And it's too much of a coincidence that there have been so many incidences at or near the property."

"Near? How near?"

"Easy walking distance," he said.

"Well, there are several other buildings within 'easy walking distance,' including a convenience store and an ice cream shop. And why would a murderer kill people right in his backyard?"

"It happens all the time. Murderers are impulsive. Especially serial killers. Very few of them make careful plans beforehand."

"Have you checked out the other buildings in the area?" Missy asked.

"I have, including the retail property. Right now, I'm talking to you about Squid Tower. Why is the place so deserted during the daytime?"

"The seniors don't enjoy being out when it's hot."

He frowned. "That doesn't seem to be the case with seniors in the neighboring buildings. Even in cooler weather, I've seen Squid Tower residents outside only at night. Why is that?"

"They're avoiding melanoma? You'd have to ask them. I don't know their habits. I just give them health screenings."

"I sense antagonism in your tone," he said.

"Detective, I'll let you know the instant there's anything suspicious," she said, signaling she wanted to close the door. "May I get back now to my to-do list?"

"Of course. Thank you for your time." He smiled without the least trace of sincerity and backed out of the doorway.

She peeked out the window and watched him get in an unmarked SUV and drive away. Then she checked the local news app on her phone and learned the mayor's daughter was found murdered on the beach. The story didn't mention Squid Tower, but Affird said that was where the most recent victim was found. She suddenly had a stress headache.

She wondered if someone at Squid Tower truly was the murderer. If so, maybe she should reconsider her job. She doubted that was the case. But even if they were innocent, the residents—her patients—were at grave risk of being revealed as vampires with Affird snooping in their lives. It meant, at the very least, they would have to abandon their condos and flee to other cities. At worst, it meant they might be murdered by law enforcement or vigilantes.

How could she help them? Should she try to find the actual killer? The idea seemed ridiculous. She was a nurse, not a sleuth. She didn't have the knowledge or the personality to hunt down a murderer. Besides, the police were already working on it. Once the police found the actual culprit, the residents of Squid Tower would be safe.

Her rationalization didn't make her headache go away.

"ALL IN FAVOR?"

The seven men and women seated at the folded table raised their hands and responded in the affirmative. All were vampires. At one point, both humans and vampires shared residency at Squid Tower. Somehow, the vampires kept their secret through it all until the human population aged out or passed away, but the vampires took over the homeowners association board long before that. Even with two dozen residents in the audience, Missy was the only human in the room tonight.

"The special assessment for crypt cleaning passes," board president Agnes, a tiny, wizened bleach-blonde at the center of the table, said in a raspy accent that was vaguely European but impossible to place. "Now on to open discussion. Does anyone have any matters to bring before the board?"

Schwartz, sitting at the table with the board, raised his hand.

"I do. The gate guard on weeknights—I want to get him fired."

"Is he a vampire?" a male board member asked.

"Nope," Schwartz said. "But more important, he's a major idiot. An incompetent loser."

"Perhaps you are unaware," said the raspy-voiced president, "but it's almost impossible to hire a vampire for that position. No vampire young enough to hold the job would want to spend his or her waking hours sitting in a tiny booth, unable to go out and hunt. What able-bodied vampire would want to just sit around for hours on end, reacting to others and not instigating action?"

Murmurs of agreement spread through the room.

"Does he know about us?" the male board member asked.

"According to Rudy at the security company, he doesn't," Agnes said. "So his being an idiot is actually in our favor."

"I don't care," Schwartz said. "He left a big oil stain on my parking spot."

"It's not your spot," another board member said. "It's a handicapped spot, and you just took it as your own."

"I happen to have mobility issues," Schwartz said.

"You don't on the pickleball court."

"Leo, if you park there, you'd better have a handicapped permit," Agnes said. "Let's move on. Any other issues?"

"Is the association going to pay to clean the oil stain?"

"Next topic," Agnes said in a tone that shut Schwartz up.

Missy stood from her folding chair at the back of the sparse audience.

"I would like to alert the board about a potential legal issue," she said.

"Go ahead," the bleach-blonde president croaked.

"A police detective has been poking around here. He said people have gone missing or been found murdered on the beach nearby. In fact, someone was found just this morning."

"I heard about that," Agnes said.

"The detective seems to believe a resident here is responsible."

An awkward silence as people exchanged worried and quizzical glances.

"Just a heads-up," Missy said.

"I wish to remind everyone the condominium bylaws expressly forbid hunting or killing on or near the property. Discretion is demanded of everyone," the president said. "We have a nice existence here at Squid Tower. Let's not mess it up and expose us all by acting selfishly. Please spread the word to your neighbors."

"What if none of us is responsible?" Schwartz asked. "We're not the only predators in the food chain. What about the were-wolves next door?"

"Doesn't matter," the president snapped at him. "We still have to behave responsibly and avoid attention."

She motioned for adjournment and the board agreed. They and the audience dispersed to enjoy the remaining hours before dawn. Some went to change for the water aerobics class or to soak up some moonlight on the beach. The hardcore canasta players headed for the card room. And a large contingent flocked to the pickleball courts.

But a few stragglers lingered in whispered conversations. The numbers dwindled until two groups remained: Schwartz and two other men, and, on the other end of the board table, Agnes and three women. Both groups whispered and gesticulated passionately, although, as vampires, they could probably hear what the other group was whispering. Missy felt hostility and mutual distrust simmering in the air between the two groups.

Politics, she thought. Who needs that nonsense? At least she warned them about Affird. It was all she could do.

WHEN MISSY GOT HOME, she made a pot of tea and fed Brenda and Bubba. Turning on the local morning news, it was quickly apparent the big story still was the murder of the mayor's daughter. They abruptly cut to live coverage of a news conference.

It was a typical affair. But since Jellyfish Beach was such a small municipality, it didn't have a fancy, high-tech media center to serve as a backdrop. Instead, the authorities had to use the space where they held city commission meetings, namely the high-school auditorium. This venue happened to have its stage occupied at the moment by the set for the Wizard of Oz production the student theater club was currently performing.

So chief-of-police Rick Tooey, Detective Fred Affird, and the grieving Mayor Janet Donovan, dressed in black, gave their briefing loomed over by a giant rainbow and a two-dimensional Munchkin Land behind them.

Chief Tooey droned on about how the murderer was a cancer on the reputation of our city, so beloved by tourists and retirees alike. How the killer must be stopped. How evidence suggests other murders might be the work of the same culprit. How the department has some promising leads that cannot be revealed to the public at this time. How a person of interest has been interrogated by police. How the crime hitting our very own mayor's family did not add any urgency other than the same diligence any other grieving family would receive. And how the mayor will continue with her duties but did not wish to speak at this press conference.

Then the questions began.

Reporters from the local NBC and CBS affiliates asked perfunctory questions and received evasive answers from the chief. Missy paid little attention while she poured her first cup of Earl Grey and the cats brushed against her legs. Then she heard a voice that wasn't distinctive but had a pleasant vibe, making her glance at the television. It was a bookish man with a beard who identified himself as Matt Rosen from the *Jellyfish Beach Journal*.

"Was a weapon ever found?" he asked.

"No," the chief replied. "The wounds indicate it was an icepick-like instrument."

"Can you comment on the fact that the corpse was drained of blood?" Matt asked quickly, before another reporter could get in a question.

"It's common for victims with wounds to their arteries to exsanguinate," the chief said.

"Yes, to bleed out," Matt said. "But I meant *drained*. As in the blood was purposefully removed from the body. It's my understanding there was very little blood found at the scene, certainly not the amount an adult body holds. Where would the blood have gone?"

Buzzing of conversation broke out in the room off-camera.

The chief appeared to find his uniform too tight in the collar. "I don't know where you got your information. We have no such evidence."

"Can you comment on the fact that other victims have also had similar wounds and had been drained of blood?" Matt asked. "Do you believe this was a ritual killing? Or that it was committed by a vampire-like individual, or someone pretending to be a vampire?"

Someone laughed very loudly, and the crowd buzzed. The chief, red-faced, said into the microphone, "I'm only taking serious questions. If there aren't any, then we're wrapping up."

There were more questions about the person of interest and about other victims. But it was clear by their reactions the "serious" reporters found Matt's inquiries to be a joke.

The problem was, the word "vampire" was out there now. And it truly looked as if a vampire or vampires were responsible for the killings.

This is really bad, Missy thought. Her patients at Squid Tower were especially vulnerable now. Even if the public didn't believe in vampires, the police and reporters were on the lookout for a killer behaving like a vampire while committing murders near Squid Tower. Its residents were in great danger of being revealed. And their very existence was in peril.

6

THE OLD, THE ILL, THE UNDEAD

You don't belong.

George Plankton's words drifted into Missy's mind while she drove to Squid Tower for patient visits. And the words still hurt, more now than when she had first heard them. True, she wasn't a vampire and had no intention of becoming one. But she felt like she was part of the communities of Squid Tower and Seaweed Manor, the werewolf enclave next door. Her life revolved around learning the vampires' and werewolves' special needs and idiosyncrasies while trying to keep them healthy. Not to mention preserving their secrecy from the normal outside world.

Plus, she was sort of a freak herself. There were powers inside of her she didn't understand. She considered herself a witch, but more of a hobbyist than a supernatural creature. She dabbled in Wicca and in her own brand of Florida Cracker magick, though she sensed she had access to powerful energies residing in the earth and, even, deep inside of herself.

She was friends with Luisa, the owner of a botánica where Missy worked part-time, who knew quite a bit about magic— though Luisa insisted she herself wasn't a *bruja*, a witch. She had been encouraging Missy to learn more about witchcraft and to seek out other practicing witches, though Missy didn't know any and had no idea how to join a community of them.

Missy's previous job as a nurse had made her part of a tight-knit community at her hospital, particularly her coworkers in the Intensive Care Unit. She loved working and hanging out with them. But each year in the ICU took a toll on her. The extreme emotional ups and downs—the stress, the heartaches, the impact of the patients she lost as well as those she helped save—began to turn her empathy into a hardened shell.

Caring too much would break her. But caring less would be a betrayal to all she believed and worked for. It became time to move on.

She had been divorced for years and had no children. The overnight work schedule put a damper on any social life she might have had. Her birth parents had died when she was too young to remember them, and her adoptive parents had moved to Tennessee when they retired. Her father lost his long battle with cancer, and she only saw her mother during holidays. She had an eccentric aunt in Florida whom she avoided. That was it when it came to family.

She was pretty much alone, except for her two cats. The communities of "freaks" she cared for was all she had.

The independence of a home-health nurse had sounded appealing. She found out about an opening for a nurse on the overnight shift. She had worked this shift in the ICU for years, so her body clock was used to it. But she was very surprised a home-health service would need staff to work overnight, aside from the live-in aides.

She found out why on the second round of her job interviews.

"Like we told you before, your experience working in the ICU is a real plus," Deborah, the human resources director of Acceptance Home Care, had said. She was rather young to be in charge of HR, with her copious tattoos and piercings. "We need someone who is compassionate, yet strong. You seem to have a thick skin."

"You need to have one when you work in the ICU. It was a rollercoaster of emotions."

"You can't tell from the stock photos of attractive seniors on our website, but we have a highly unique clientele."

"How so?" Missy asked.

"Are you strictly religious, or more open-minded?"

"Don't tell me your clients are nudists. Or swingers? I wouldn't feel comfortable . . ."

"No, no, nothing of the sort," Deborah said. She was performing the delicate ritual of a sales job.

"To answer your question, I'm not really into conventional, established churches," Missy said, trying to indicate she was still interested. "I'm a bit of a pagan, actually."

Deborah perked up. "Okay, so you're not opposed to the concept of the supernatural?"

"No, I'm not, but . . . why do you ask?"

"Our clients have special needs, and some people might be frightened by them, or offended by their needs."

"Is this about something illegal?" Missy asked.

"Not as it pertains to us. It's just that our clientele is often shunned by society."

"Are you talking about circus freaks?"

"I'm talking about vampires. And werewolves. Fauns, ogres, trolls, etcetera, etcetera. Some fairies and elves, but elves tend to retire in Arizona rather than Florida. They hate humidity."

Missy forced a laugh. "Arizona? Good one. But seriously."

"I'm serious. Look, supernatural creatures get old, too, and there's something in the laws of the universe that mandates when you get old you move to Florida. And later, after years of complaining about Florida, you move to North Carolina."

"Vampires get old? I thought they were immortal."

"Yes, but if they happened to be old when they were made into vampires, that's the age they remain. So they come down here as snowbirds every winter, or they live here full time. I'm pleased you appear to be accepting of what I've told you."

"I knew a vampire once, briefly. Years ago," Missy said, fighting the sadness accompanying her memories.

"People say, 'vampires in the *Sunshine* State?' Well, old creatures don't like the cold. And it doesn't matter how many sunny days we have, because they only come out at night. And we have werewolves, too, who age like mortal creatures. Other supernatural creatures age very, very slowly, but do eventually get old. And that's where Acceptance Home Care comes in. We care for them with the respect and compassion they deserve. Without judgement."

Missy thought of her grandmother, a victim of elder abuse, her assets stolen before dying in a horrible nursing home. This painful memory, along with her dad's cancer, was one of the main reasons Missy went to nursing school, vowing to build a career by helping others.

"We're all God's creatures," Deborah said, "even those whom you might think are on Satan's team. They're not really. Only demons are. And divorce lawyers. And we don't have any demons as clients."

"What about divorce lawyers?"

"Um, we have a few."

"How can you ensure my safety?"

"The rules are very strict. If any of our clientele violated the safety agreement, they'd be banned from their community and forfeit their savings. Besides, they're all so grateful to be cared for. They would never bite the hand that feeds them. Oh, I shouldn't have said 'bite.'"

Missy accepted Deborah's job offer. And then signed a very, very extensive non-disclosure agreement.

It took some time afterwards for her to realize why she took the job. She didn't want her empathy for patients to dry up. And if she could empathize with supernatural monsters, it meant she still had a heart after all.

SHE PULLED up to the gatehouse of Squid Tower. The creepy guard stuck his head out of the door of the booth, saw the cardboard visitor's pass on her dashboard, and gave her a creepy smile before raising the gate arm. She parked in the same spot she always used. The residents here didn't get many visitors.

It was during the gloaming, after sunset, but not fully night. Watching the last vestiges of light slip away always made her melancholy. The orange glow faded from the sky and its reflections in windows not covered by shutters died. In less than an hour, the Blood Bus would arrive, and elderly vampires would line up beside it. Others would start their cars and drive out through the gate, seeking prey in town or going to Mega-Mart.

None, she hoped, would be hunting for humans on the beach or along the jogging path beside A1A.

She entered the lobby with her tote bag filled with medical supplies and a few charms and amulets. While she waited for the elevator, a woman using a walker hobbled over from one of the common rooms.

"Oh, Missy, I'm so glad I ran into you," the lady said.

"Hello. Have we met?"

"No, but I know all about you from some of your patients. I've been meaning to set up an appointment with you. My name is Victoria, but everyone calls me Vicky."

"Of course, Vicky," Missy said. "I have an appointment now, but I can meet with you right afterwards. Do you need screenings, or is anything wrong?"

"My knees, heavens to Betsy. They've been killing me lately."

The elevator arrived. Missy got on, followed by the lady sliding her walker, and punched the button for the eleventh floor.

"What floor are you going to?" Missy asked.

"I've got nothing to do. I'll just ride with you. As I was saying, my knees. I was turned only two years ago and becoming a vampire definitely improved them. I could barely walk before and suddenly I'm able to chase down prey half my age! But whenever a weather front comes through, I'm in agony and have to use this darned thing."

"Sounds like osteoarthritis," Missy said.

"My doctor said the same thing. Before I was turned."

What was left unsaid was that she could never see her doctor again now, in her undead state.

The elevator beeped as it reached the eleventh floor.

"I'll let you go," the lady said. "I'll be down in the card room waiting. Thank you so much!"

As she walked down the hallway, Missy thought about Vicky's predicament. Missy would have referred Vicky to a specialist for knee replacement surgery to end her chronic pain. If she were still a mortal human. Now, as a vampire, Vicky didn't have that option.

There were a few physicians in South Florida who specialized in vampires and other supernatural creatures, but they worked under the radar of the American Medical Association. They were all unlicensed, backroom practices that didn't have the resources to perform major surgery like a knee replacement. And there's no way a hospital for humans would accept and comprehend an undead patient, let alone understand their special requirements. Maybe someday a secret hospital will exist for freaks, but in the meantime people like Missy would bear the responsibility for their healthcare. Vampires don't need much of it, thanks to their supernatural healing abilities. But those abilities simply can't transform a sixty-something's damaged knees, whose cartilage has worn away causing bone spurs, into the knees of a twenty-something. A vampire's body can heal a bone that breaks in an accident, but not repair damage to a body that occurred over a period of decades when it was human.

Before she reached her patient's door, Missy briefly considered the therapies she would recommend for Vicky. Surely magick could help the vampire's suffering somehow. Missy decided that as she learned the art of witchcraft and watched her latent powers grow, she would develop spells, charms, and potions to aid vampire medicine.

She could bring untold benefits to these geriatric creatures. And the werewolves next door, too.

Missy realized she might not belong here, but she was needed. Anyone who needed her—the sick, the infirm, the helpless—deserved her full dedication and commitment. And she was making a big difference in their existence.

With this sense of responsibility, she vowed to do whatever she could to find the murderer, whether it was a resident or an outsider. If it were the latter, she would make sure the police knew it.

7

PARTY ANIMALS

The condo complex next door where the werewolves lived was a pair of low-rise buildings that were not as luxurious as the vampires' building. It was called Seaweed Manor. Perhaps not coincidentally, every time Missy visited, the distinct smell of weed drifted through the hallways.

The folks here were the proverbial animals who loved to party. Morning, noon, and night. In fact, it was not long after sunrise, after her patient visits of the vampires in Squid Tower had wrapped up. It wasn't by any measure close to happy hour, no matter what kind of creature you were. Nevertheless, bass thumped behind many a front door along with moaning guitar riffs from forgotten '70s jam bands. Raucous laughter and shattered glass erupted in the condo next to her destination.

She knocked. A tall woman with gray hair in ponytails answered. She wore a psychedelic Grateful Dead T-shirt, cutoff jeans, copious beads, and a large bronze crucifix. Many of the werewolves living here were aware they had a colony of vampires next door and the Joint Cooperation Agreement between their two condo associations banning predation upon each other wasn't enough to assure the werewolves they were safe.

The feeling was mutual. The vampires kept their distance from Seaweed Manor on nights with a full moon, and Missy avoided patient visits there. No sense taking extra risks. The few normal humans living here were supposedly clueless about any supernatural creatures, even though one or two would pass away under mysterious circumstances every season. Which goes to show how well the Joint Cooperation Agreement was enforced.

Cynthia Roarke warmly welcomed Missy and offered her tea while Missy went into the master bedroom to examine Harry.

"Hey sweetheart, how are you?" he asked, sitting on a chair facing a TV.

He was a hulking specimen of lupine masculinity with a big beard and long silver hair. A retired contractor from New Jersey, he had found Jesus, got infected in a near-fatal werewolf attack in the Pine Barrens, became a werewolf, lost Jesus, and then found Satan. After he walked away from the dark lord when the allure faded, the Roarkes took up surfing, and that's where their passions now resided. They particularly enjoyed surfing during a full moon in werewolf form and, remarkably, have managed to avoid being seen by the public while doing it.

When in human form, Mr. Roarke was also on the condo board. He had a reputation for hostility against the vampires, often filing frivolous lawsuits against the board of Squid Tower. Residents of the two communities coexisted peacefully, but the two condo boards feuded with more bitterness than the Hatfields and McCoys.

"I'm good, Mr. Roarke. How are you?"

"Oh, it's horrible to grow old. You should avoid it. Aside from the usual aches and pains, I've been okay lately, just some constipation."

"Have you been eating enough roughage?"

"I eat bones sometimes."

"That's not roughage. Roughage is fiber, like grains and vegetables. Mr. Roarke, you can't survive on raw meat alone."

"I like to say I have a vegetarian diet. I eat vegetarians whenever I can catch them."

"Which reminds me," Missy said, wrapping beefy biceps with a blood-pressure cuff, "do the werewolves who live here hunt close to home?"

"Nah, we have rules against that."

"Have you heard about the people who have been found murdered nearby?"

"Yeah. Everyone figures the freaking vampires are doing it."

"Why do you say that?"

"Because the bodies were drained of blood, of course."

"One-fifty over ninety. Kinda high, Mr. Roarke. Have you been taking your blood-pressure medication?"

"Yeah."

"Let me check it again. Have you had any disputes with the vampires lately?" She squeezed the bulb to inflate the cuff.

"No. I've been a perfect angel."

"Has anyone else here had problems with the vampires?"

"Not that I know of."

"One-seventy over a hundred. Am I stressing you out?"

"No. I just don't like talking about the vampires. Bunch of pretentious snobs who think they're better than us."

"Maybe their snobbishness led someone to frame them—make it look like the vampires killed those people?"

"Exactly what the vampires would have you believe," he grumbled.

"I'm serious. A lot of werewolves live here and some of them are ... how do I put this?"

"Rough characters?"

"Yeah. Maybe one of them killed some people and then drained their blood to make it look like a vampire did it."

"Werewolves don't kill people for the fun of it," Roarke said. He was getting annoyed. "We do it to eat them. Or out of uncontrollable rage. So, the bodies would be missing a whole lot more than blood."

"Did you fast today?" Missy asked as she unpacked her blood kit and checked his arm for prominent veins.

"I haven't eaten anyone since the last full moon."

"You know what I meant."

"Yes, I fasted. And, by the way, we eat animals, not people. Most of the time, at least."

As she drew his blood into a specimen tube, he watched her and then turned his head away.

"How anyone could survive on blood alone is beyond me. Vampires are sick fiends," he said. "As for me, when I'm not in wolf form, the sight of blood freaks me out, to be completely honest."

WHEN MISSY WALKED across the Seaweed Manor visitor parking lot, a man was leaning against a car near hers. He watched her approach. Although she should be safe in broad daylight, she reached into her bag for the pepper spray just in case. She was fortified against supernatural creatures thanks to charms and protective spells, but pepper spray was still the best potion for repelling men.

"Hi," the man said. He wore shades and a shy smile. "Are you a nurse?"

She stopped in surprise. "Yes. What's wrong?"

"Uh, nothing. I saw you leaving the building next door and then going here, carrying a large bag, and I tried to figure out what you were doing. You don't look like a cleaning lady. Then it occurred to me, with all the seniors living here you might be a healthcare worker."

"What do you want?" she asked without hiding the suspicion in her voice.

He took off his shades. "I'm Matt Rosen with the *Jellyfish Beach Journal*. Can I ask you some questions?"

Now she recognized him. He was one of the reporters in the televised press conference about the mayor's daughter's murder. He was the one who made a big deal about the victim's exsanguination.

"No. I'm in a hurry." It was true. She needed to get home and sleep a little before she had to put in some time for her part-time job at Luisa's botánica.

"C'mon, it'll only take a minute." Tall, with dark, curly hair and a trimmed beard, he had a bit of a surfer vibe and was actually kind of cute in an intellectual way. He looked better in person than he had on TV.

"Let me ask one," she said. "Why are you stalking me?"

49

"I'm a reporter. That's what we do. We stalk, hunt, surveil, observe. Sometimes we just ask questions."

"You sound like a tabloid reporter. Have you mistaken me for someone famous?"

"Funny," he said in a tone meaning she wasn't funny. "What's your name?"

"Missy. I'm not giving you a last name because you're a reporter."

He followed her until she reached her ancient silver Toyota Corolla. She didn't have one of those key fobs with the emergency button on it. In fact, she didn't have a key fob at all. She fished her keys from her bag and unlocked her car manually. Then she grabbed the pepper spray again, keeping it out of view in the bag.

"A young woman was murdered a couple of nights ago," the reporter said. "The mayor's daughter, if you haven't heard. Her body was found on the beach between these two buildings. So, for lack of any leads, I was hanging around, checking out what kind of residents live here."

"Old people. You must be new to Jellyfish Beach."

"No. I grew up here, on the mainland side. And over the years, I've noticed more and more strange things going on."

"Like what?" Missy was beginning to get concerned about his knowledge of those she vowed to protect.

"Other murders like these over the years in which the victim was drained of blood. And lots of second-hand stories of weird stuff. The kind of things that start rumors about vampires and werewolves and such."

"Are you sure you're a reporter and not a novelist?" Missy asked.

"Yes, I prefer to make money with my writing."

"Well, if you were really a reporter, you wouldn't waste your time with rumors. Just because the victim bled out—"

"And no blood was found on the ground or anywhere."

Missy was frustrated. "Don't you think the sensible course would be to find out if anyone had a motive for murdering the mayor's daughter?"

"I'm working on it."

"Well, you go do that. I have to leave now."

"I seemed to have hit a nerve," he said.

"Many of the residents here are my patients, and I truly care about them. You show up and imply one of them is the murderer, then you mention wacky claims about vampires and werewolves. How am I supposed to react? You're obnoxious. Don't treat seniors like they're oddities. These could be your parents or grandparents."

"I'm sorry," he said, genuinely chagrined. "I'm just trying to understand the environment of the murder scene."

"Condos filled with old retirees. If that wasn't obvious to you. I have to go."

She got in her car and after a few engine shudders, she drove off, leaving the reporter standing there.

8

FLORIDA MAN
INVESTIGATES MONSTERS

M att thought Missy had a kind of hippie, folksy
way about her that would have been inviting if
not for her hard edges. And she was beautiful.
Her long brunette hair had a few strands of gray. He liked that
she didn't try to hide the fact. She had a slender face with delicate features, a bit of an elfish upturn at the tip of her nose, and
narrow, though sensuous, lips.

There was a toughness to her, he thought. He had seen the
pepper spray in her hand when she got in her car and dismissed
him. And she was stonewalling him for a reason. He could
understand why she'd be protective of the communities where
her patients lived. But he was talking about murders, not
parking violations.

He strolled over to the Seaweed Manor gate and knocked on
the door of the guard booth. A short Hispanic woman
answered. She smiled as if he had brought her a present. He

introduced himself and asked general questions about if anything suspicious had been going on.

"The police already talked to me," she said, happy to continue the conversation. "I said there ain't never anything suspicious here because everything's too dang weird."

"Um, in what way?"

"These old folks party like there's no tomorrow. No matter what shift I'm working, there's music blaring with drunk and stoned oldsters wandering about, playing frisbee on the beach, skinny-dipping in the pool, hitting golf balls into the ocean. Usually, the police come here for noise complaints, not murder investigations."

"You ever notice young people here?"

"Only when their grandkids are visiting. Though, between you and me," her voice dropped to a loud whisper, "a couple folks here—and I don't know who they are—sell pot and pills and stuff, so they get a lot of younger visitors."

Matt figured the guard knew who the drug dealers were, but didn't want to upset the apple cart. And if the mayor's daughter had been clubbing before she was killed, there was certainly a possibility she had been here to buy drugs.

He thanked the guard and went next door to Squid Tower. A concrete wall separated the two properties, but there was a narrow gap where the wall had crumbled away. It was partially hidden by a cocoplum hedge, but a footpath worn into the grass indicated many feet had used it. Matt decided not to. He didn't want to look like a trespasser. Instead, he entered through the gate.

The property was immaculate at Squid Tower with carefully manicured tropical landscaping and not a single beer bottle on the ground, unlike next door. The gate guard was an older, dark-skinned woman named Philomena with braided hair. She spoke in a melodious Caribbean accent.

"Yeah, there are weird happenings all the time here," she said to Matt after the introductions. "But I don't see them myself because I work the day shift. And this place is dead during the day."

She snickered at some private joke.

"What kind of weird stuff?" Matt asked.

"The folks here are old. *Really* old," she said, snickering some more.

"And?"

"Man, I can't say bad things about the people who live here."

"I'm not asking you to. I just want to know if you've seen anything suspicious."

"No. Most of the residents here sleep all day." Philomena gave a knowing wink, which was uncomfortably close to a promiscuous leer.

This woman really wants to tell me something, Matt thought. She just needs permission.

"They sleep all day?" Matt asked. "I thought seniors got up really early in the morning and went to bed early at night."

"Not these seniors."

"What are they, vampires or something?"

Philomena's face brightened. "If they are, you didn't hear it from me," she said, smiling.

"'If they *are*?' But vampires don't exist." Matt, of course, suspected otherwise.

"I'm just a gate guard. What do I know? But I've got eyes and ears and so do the other guards. That's all I'm saying."

"Do you think residents here are responsible for any

murders? There was a young woman found on the beach nearby, drained of blood."

"I heard. The police questioned me."

"Well? What do you think? I don't care what you told the police, I want to know what you really think. Off the record, do you believe someone here did it?"

"C'mon, I work for these people, you know? But I'll say this: You better think twice about wandering around here at night."

Vampires, Matt thought. I knew it!

MATT DROVE to the office to file some stories when he almost ran into the riding lawn mower. It was cruising along north-bound I-95 in the center lane at five miles per hour. Which actually was a rapid clip for the rear-engine style of mower. It was causing constant near-collisions as cars whipped into the adjacent lanes rather than be stuck in the long line of brake lights behind it. It was still rush hour, after all. Driving the mower was a man, a naked man. He drank from a twenty-four-ounce can of beer, even though it was not yet 9:00 a.m.

Matt maneuvered his pickup truck into the lane to the right of the man's lane and slowed down until he matched the speed of the mower. This caused more brake lights and dangerous swerving by the cars behind him. Surprisingly few people honked their horns at him, disproving the notion that South Florida was full of rude people. Matt lowered his window and took a picture of the spectacle with his phone.

"Good morning, sir," he shouted to the naked lawnmower driver. "What is your name?"

"Lance Jenkins!" the man shouted back. "And good morning to you, too."

Matt wrote the name in his reporter's notebook propped against the steering wheel.

"Why are you driving your lawnmower on I-95?"

"I got a dentist appointment," the man answered.

"But why a lawnmower? Don't you have a car?"

"Because I'm drunk, and I don't want to get a DUI."

Matt was pretty sure the man's logic was flawed, and that there were many tickets in Mr. Jenkins' immediate future.

"Forgive me if I'm being too personal," Matt shouted, "but why are you going to your dental appointment naked?"

The man looked down at his lap and seemed surprised to find he was, indeed, naked.

"No comment."

Matt decided to drop his follow-up question about why Mr. Jenkins was going to his appointment drunk. Besides, the flashing lights of Florida state troopers had erupted behind them, and Matt knew his interview was over.

It took the two black-and-brown Highway Patrol cars a few miles to cajole and escort Mr. Jenkins across two lanes of traffic and then to stop on the shoulder. Matt pulled over ahead of them and walked back to witness the arrest and ask for statements from the troopers.

"It's just another Tuesday morning in South Florida," one of them said.

Matt got from Mr. Jenkins the name of his dentist. He called the office to let them know their patient wouldn't be arriving for his appointment and they were actually very lucky that this was the case. Then he drove to the newsroom to file this classic

Drunk-Florida-Man-Does-Something-Criminal-and-Stupid story.

Matt liked to quip that he covered the Florida Man beat. But bizarre tales of idiocy occupied only a small portion of his time. He specialized in crime reporting. The problem was, aside from the latest string of murders, Jellyfish Beach had very few crimes. Normally, there were just the usual burglaries and petty theft. He spent a lot of his time stuck in county commission meetings or ribbon-cuttings at shopping centers and reporting politicians-bribed-by-developer stories.

When he wasn't stuck with those assignments, he pursued his Quixotic passion: trying to get someone else to believe South Florida's spicy melting pot culture was peppered with monsters. That the place attracting all the freaks too weird for the rest of the country also attracted those too strange for reality itself.

And he was convinced there were monsters right here in Jellyfish Beach.

Now, Matt thought, comes the difficult part: a visit at night. If there were vampires at Squid Tower, now would be the time to observe them. Then again, would he be able to tell that a vampire was a vampire? Or, on the other hand, would he end up as a vampire's dinner?

He drove past the community around 8:00 p.m. There were some people (or vampires) walking around, but keeping with the flow of traffic at thirty-five miles an hour was too fast to observe them. A mile or so down A1A, he parked at a small strip center with a convenience store and an ice cream shop. Then he walked along the paved pathway that ran beside the road.

He passed other condominium buildings bathed in exterior lights, but there wasn't anyone out and about. When he reached Squid Tower, it was a different story. The pickleball courts were crowded with seniors in tennis whites barely whiter than the players' complexions, save for two African-American doubles partners who nevertheless appeared unusually pale.

A shuffleboard court further back in the property had a few occupants. A group of residents chatted beside the building. Cars streamed out from the gate. The place was positively hopping compared to the dead zone he had visited during the day.

Matt walked up to the guardhouse with exaggerated confidence to lend himself some authority. He knocked on the glass door that faced the inbound traffic lanes. The guard wore a uniform and had slicked-back dark hair. His head was shaped vaguely like a Neanderthal's. He appeared to be in his forties or early fifties.

The guard opened the door, surprised that someone had approached him on foot.

"Hi, my name is Matt Rosen." Matt smiled and offered his hand. "Have you worked here long?"

The guard shook his hand with a limp grip. "Not long. How can I help you?" He had a Long Island accent.

"I just have a few questions."

"Are you here to visit someone specific?" the guard asked suspiciously. "I'm not supposed to chit-chat while I'm on duty."

"I'm a reporter for the *Jellyfish Beach Journal*. I'm looking into the murders on the beach," Matt said. "Have you noticed anything out of the ordinary?"

"The cops already questioned me. I haven't seen squat."

"Any odd stuff about the residents here?" Matt gave a reassuring grin.

The guard looked even more suspicious now. "Like what?"

"I spoke to the day guard today. I think Philomena is her name? She had a lot to say about this place."

The guard visibly relaxed. "Yeah, she's worked here a long time."

"I'm sorry. What was your name?" Matt asked.

"Bernie Burdine. But don't quote me in any article."

"Of course not. This is just background. So, you've got a bunch of night birds living here, it seems."

"Yeah. When I was hired, I thought I'd have nothing to do and could focus on writing songs. But it turns out this is the busiest shift."

"But why?" Matt asked. "Most seniors go to bed early. Why is this crew so different?"

"I wouldn't know."

"Philomena said these folks are really old. Like *inhumanly* old."

"She's from Martinique. They exaggerate a lot."

"C'mon, Mr. Burdine. This is totally off the record. You can trust me."

Headlights flooded Matt as a car pulled up to the gate. He stepped onto the platform of the gatehouse to get out of the way. Bernie stuck his head out to search for the proper decal on the windshield, waved nervously, and reached inside the booth for the switch that opened the gate.

A grimy silver Lexus with New York plates rolled slowly through. It stopped before the gate arm and the driver's window slid down.

"Don't drop the gate arm on my car, okay moron?" the driver said, a toad-like man with an enormous nose and a ring of white hair surrounding a bald dome.

"Of course not, Mr. Schwartz," Bernie said.

The old man looked at Matt in his awkward perch outside the gatehouse. His expression was malign.

"Is this your drug dealer?" the driver asked.

"No, this is my . . . cousin Matt," Bernie replied.

The driver laughed, a phlegmy bark. "Stupid runs in the family."

The car's engine revved as it sputtered past the gate with a belch of burnt-oil smoke. Matt made a note of the car and its vanity license plate: "Snowbyrd."

"Nice fellow," Matt said.

Bernie shook his head. "Mr. Schwartz. He's constantly busting my chops. I think he wants to . . ."

"What?"

"Nothing."

"Has this guy ever threatened you?" Matt asked.

"He wants to get me fired. Or worse."

"Bernie, let me cut to the chase. Have you ever heard any rumors, or seen any evidence, that vampires live here?"

Bernie's eyes popped open along with his mouth. Then his mouth closed. He had appeared close to giving an honest answer before discretion took over.

"I'm not supposed to talk about the residents," he said.

"I understand. Mind if I take a walk around the grounds?"

"Sorry, man, but you can't. Only residents and their guests."

"I'll be your guest," Matt said.

"I don't think that's a good idea. It's much safer if you come back during the day. Trust me."

Matt accepted defeat and thanked Bernie before walking back to his car.

Another non-denial about vampires.

9

LIFE ON THE GRAVEYARD SHIFT

After the reporter left, there was the customary lull between the rush of cars leaving after the vampires woke up and when they returned as the night waned. Bernie stared at the dark façade of Squid Tower looming over the guardhouse. Most of the condos had their accordion hurricane shutters closed, covering the windows.

In perennially warm South Florida, if you needed to remember what season it was, look at the condos along the beach. If the hurricane shutters were closed, that meant it was May through October when the snowbirds were up north. The few with shutters open were the homes of permanent residents.

There's a rule of nature: When the weather starts getting nippy in New York, New England, Quebec, and other points of the Great White North, the entire elderly population is stirred by some primal urge and flocks southbound across the Mason-Dixon Line, eventually arriving at the gates of the thousands of trailer parks, subdivisions, and condominium complexes along both coasts and the vast interior of the Sunshine State. Then, you'll see the shutters cranked open everywhere.

Unless a building was occupied by vampires. They, of course, aren't impressed by the beautiful Florida sunshine.

Bernie didn't have anything against snowbirds in general. He wasn't surprised old vampires migrated to Florida in the winter or lived there year round. When you're old, it's no fun to slosh around in snow and slush, and he supposed it was no different for folks who happened to be elderly when they became vampires. But trying to navigate the over-crowded roads during tourist season with confused eighty-year-old drivers was bad enough. Imagine trying to avoid fender-benders with 800-year-olds.

Bernie still had difficulty processing the fact that vampires really existed and didn't all look young and sexy like those in the movies. There were plenty who glided about on mobility scooters, had hair growing out of their ears, and complained about the blood being too spicy from the Latino landscaper they just fed upon. He learned the age you were when you were turned is the age you'll remain forever, no matter how many years of AARP dues you'll have to pay.

Bernie didn't move to Florida because he was old. He came looking for a better life. After failing to break into the New York music scene as a lounge singer, and then getting fired from his job at Pete's Piano and Organ Emporium in Glen Cove, Long Island, Bernie moved here, thinking, as so many people do, that somehow life would be easier in Florida, as well as cheaper and warmer. He believed his shortcomings would matter less outside of the Big Apple, such as his voice's tendency to break like he was going through puberty, or his sloping forehead, wide nose, and other features the mean girls in high school mocked.

He was wrong. His shortcomings did matter. He couldn't get a single gig at the piano lounges in the big resorts. He played at some Italian and Greek restaurants and the occasional senior center. There, the clientele of oldsters and tourists wasn't as discriminating as long as he sang their favorite songs. He even dusted off his guitar and learned a bunch of Jimmy Buffett tunes. He managed to get some work in the tourist seafood joints, mostly for tips.

In the meantime, he had to support himself with a real job. He wanted one with privacy and plenty of time for practicing, so he first got hired as a drawbridge tender. Not only was the pay lousy, but he had a bad habit of lowering the bridge before the boats got all the way through. It only took a few sailboats with broken mainmasts and one sunken cabin cruiser before his boss told him he should look for a job that was a little less demanding.

He thought he found one, an easy gig involving no stress and very little actual work. He answered a listing for a company that provided security for condominium associations. The owner, a German dude named Rudy, seemed only moderately sleazy and promised Bernie he would pass the state exam and get his security guard license without a problem. Not long afterwards, Bernie ended up here at Squid Tower. On the graveyard shift.

And the stress-free existence he had imagined turned into a constant battle for his job. And his life.

BERNIE'S CONFLICT with Schwartz began shortly after he started the job. He often saw Schwartz taking a stroll on cooler nights, a short, pot-bellied man who always wore colored socks with Bermuda shorts and sandals. Even after Bernie learned the residents' secret, he couldn't believe this man could be a vampire.

Of course, if Bernie had known this from the beginning, he would have been more careful not to get on Schwartz's enemy list. He got there on only his third night of work. His internal clock hadn't yet adjusted to working overnight, so he was sound asleep when a loud rapping shook the glass door of the gatehouse. He jumped and wiped the drool from his chin. Schwartz glared in at him through the glass. His eyes appeared to be glowing red.

"We don't pay you to sleep at the job," he said in a gruff Brooklyn accent when Bernie opened the door.

Bernie mumbled an apology.

"Is that your car over there?" Schwartz demanded.

"Where?"

"There by the palm trees. That's a reserved space. It belongs to me. You've got to move your car now."

"It's a handicapped spot," Bernie said.

"And it belongs to *me*."

"But who—"

"My name is Leonard Schwartz. I'm on the homeowners association board of directors. Now move your car or I'll have it towed and then banned from the property. I used to work in city government, and I know how to get things done."

Bernie raced outside to his lovingly restored Pacer. The ignition ground fruitlessly.

"C'mon, I don't have all night," Schwartz said, glancing at his watch.

"Sorry," Bernie said after he rolled down the window. "She's very temperamental."

"I don't care, you moron. A piece of junk like this, it shouldn't even be allowed in here."

"Hey, I got rights," Bernie murmured.

Suddenly he was out of the car and hanging two feet above the ground with Schwartz's right hand clamped around his throat.

"You also have a job you're going to lose if you don't get this heap out of here."

Bernie couldn't help but notice Schwartz's canine teeth were awfully long and sharp. There was also a small bloodstain on the front of his shirt, almost lost among the floral patterns. Maybe Bernie wasn't the quickest wit around, but none of these observations added up to any sort of vampire conclusion at the time, not even the fact that a guy with a physique shaped like Mr. Peanut's was holding up Bernie's 170 pounds with one scrawny arm. He was much more concerned about being able to breathe again.

Just as Bernie was seeing large dots in front of his eyes, Schwartz put him down. He was looking at the faint glow appearing in the eastern sky. He stroked his chin nervously.

"She'll start, don't worry," Bernie said hoarsely. "I just need to do a little tinkering under the hood."

He glanced at the Pacer and then back at Schwartz, but he was gone.

Eventually, he was able to start the car and move it to another spot in the visitor lot. The problem was, his car had left a giant oil stain in Schwartz's space. He didn't think this was a big deal until Schwartz paid a visit the following night.

"You moron," Schwartz said.

"Good evening to you, too, sir."

"If it weren't so hard for the security company to hire people for this shift, I'd have you fired on the spot. What, you think you can leave your oil stains on our asphalt just like that and walk away from it? Huh?"

"Sorry, sir. I'll clean it up tomorrow. There's this stuff you can buy, this powder—"

Schwartz disappeared. He was simply gone, with nothing but the building's lobby doors swinging shut to assure Bernie that Schwartz hadn't just vaporized right in front of him.

THERE HAD BEEN plenty of clues pointing to vampires. The strange patterns of all the residents heading out after sunset, when most geezers would normally be getting ready for bedtime. The parking lot and garage filled with cars all day. The utter lack of tanned complexions on every resident he saw. He should have figured it out right away, but logical deductions were not his strength. Even after finding the grave dirt, he still had doubts.

What happened was early one evening before sunset, not long after first meeting Schwartz, Bernie had been making a quick patrol of the grounds before relieving the day guard. The parking lot was still full. He walked past the cars, through steam rising from hot asphalt, wet with a just-ended rain. He was whistling a Barry Manilow tune when he noticed the car in Schwartz's spot had its trunk partly open.

It was a rusty, silver Lexus with New York plates, and the doors were all locked. Schwartz must have accidentally hit the trunk release when he got out of the driver's seat. Just as Bernie was about to close the trunk, a rat popped its head out, a fat, oily rat like you'd find along the waterfront in Brooklyn. It squeezed through the crack, looked at him nonchalantly, and dropped to the ground, waddling away beneath some cars.

Why Bernie did it, he didn't know, but he opened the trunk all the way. The smell walloped him. It was the smell of mold, mildew, and rotting things—the smell from beneath a porch where the light never shines. The trunk was filled with dirt that was clay-like and covered with fuzzy mold, packed hard like something had lain upon it. When he noticed a large human-like bone protruding, he slammed the trunk shut and took off for the gatehouse.

None of this made any sense until Philomena, one of the day guards, brought up the bodies on the beach.

"Bernie," she had said, "ever notice how this beach has gone to the pits?"

He asked her what she meant.

"This is no place you'd want to live, with all the undesirables here."

"You mean the Red Sox fans?" Bernie had asked.

She studied his face for a moment and scratched her long chin. He had only recently learned she was from Martinique, or some other Caribbean island originally settled by the French—he couldn't quite remember. She seemed old to be a gate guard, but in Florida lots of seniors had to work after they discovered their retirement nest eggs wouldn't be enough.

"No, I mean *them*." She pointed to Squid Tower rising above them, dark and ugly in its 1960s concrete architecture. "Do you believe in vampires, man?"

"Get out of here. Are you still into that superstitious stuff from the islands?"

"Say what you want," she said with a patronizing smile. "But they found a couple of bodies on the beach the other night. A young man and woman."

"Yeah, a detective was asking around. I didn't know anything about it."

"He didn't tell you *how* they died. My friend's brother works at the coroner's office. He said the dead people didn't have a drop of blood in their bodies. Not a drop. No marks on them either, except for two little holes in their necks. Just like in the movies."

"You're making this up," he said.

"This building used to have humans in it. You know, normal seniors who stay in at night. They used to own half the units in the building, but now none of them are left."

"What happened?"

"They sold out. Or they died. No one asks many questions when an eighty-year-old dies."

"You're actually telling me they were killed by vampires?"

"No, they're smart enough not to feed on their own neighbors. There's a rule against it. They go out for dinner instead. Man, with all the homeless folks and runaways in this town, it's like a vampire's all-you-can-eat buffet out there."

It suddenly occurred to Bernie why a blood donation bus showed up at the community every night. He had assumed the residents were simply generous and altruistic.

"If you're so sure they're vampires, why don't you do anything about it?" Bernie asked.

"Who's gonna believe me? Besides, it's good pay and I can sit around all day watching the soaps with no one to bother me. They're all inside, asleep. No, they're not going to hurt me. I guess I got the best shift."

She laughed as she walked away. Bernie had the whole night alone to think about what she'd said. It didn't take long before he learned Philomena was right.

The next night, Unit 742, the vampire from Scarsdale, called and said her sink was leaking. He told her he was just the gate guard, but he promised to call the management company. Their answering service reached a manager who tried to find a plumber willing to make a call so late at night, while the woman in 742 kept calling and demanding that Bernie fix her pipe. Finally, two hours later, the plumber showed up. Bernie let him in and went back to the love song he was composing on his tablet.

He happened to look up at the security monitors and saw the plumber waiting at the elevator in the lobby. There was something moving in the background. He zoomed in on the camera just as a shadow lunged at the plumber. The plumber wrestled with something and suddenly the screen was empty. Then the plumber's face popped back into the picture. He was screaming silently, his eyeballs bulging out, and his head had been twisted around like a doll's. Something was holding him up, chewing on his grotesque neck.

The thing looked up and stared at the camera. It was Schwartz, his fat nose, and his mouth all covered with blood. Fangs protruded over his lower lip. He obviously knew he was being watched. He bared his fangs like a rabid dog, and something flew at the camera. The screen went dead. Just then, Bernie realized he was sitting in a pool of urine.

He called the security company he worked for, because the most important rule of working here was that he wasn't supposed to call the cops himself. Ever. He sat in his wet pants for twenty minutes until Rudy arrived. Bernie told him about

Schwartz, only for Rudy to smile and say Schwartz would never attack anyone here because it was against the condo association bylaws.

"But I saw him on camera," Bernie said, pointing toward the bank of security monitors.

"Let's say you did see him," Rudy said in his German accent. "What are you proposing we do about it? Our job is to keep the residents safe. Not cause trouble about vampires' natural feeding habits."

"You never told me vampires lived here."

"Well now you know. You want to resign?"

"Rudy, please put me on the day shift, bro. At any property. *Please*." Bernie tried not to cry in front of him.

"Sorry," Rudy said, turning away. "Can't do it. We need you here at Squid Tower."

Bernie would have quit on the spot except for the fact he was completely broke. He needed to collect a couple more paychecks, then he'd be out of there, he promised himself. He'd heard the piano lounges were booming up in Orlando. All the European tourists just loved that stuff. Or he could play guitar at the bars along the Florida coasts. He knew enough Jimmy Buffett and Eagles songs to pull it off easily. Or, if he had to, he could even get a gig with a cruise line. He tried to believe his skills had improved and that this time he could kick-start his music career.

He arrived the next night to find a surprise waiting for him: a dead rat with its head chewed off lying on his chair. He immediately threw the chair along with the rat outside. Then he found the note lying on the desk. In elegant, old-fashioned script it said, "Too bad the bloodstain on your chair is so small compared to the stain you left on my parking spot."

So, in the meantime, he had to make it through each night, which was never easy, even under normal circumstances. The worst hours were those nearing dawn when the vampires were all back in their condos and there was hardly a car along A1A. The only sounds were the wind and surf. He tried to sing old John Denver songs, but his voice seemed hauntingly hollow against the silence. All the songs on his playlist sounded like the saddest, loneliest tunes ever written.

So, he just sat there, praying for morning, his mouth dry, his eyes sore, listening to the buzzing of the fluorescent bulb above his head. Sitting alone in his glass booth, a tiny oasis of light in the blackness of the dead hours.

Thinking about Schwartz.

10

INTERVIEW WITH THE VAMPIRE

The vanity license plate said, "Snowbyrd." It caught the eye and was easy to remember.

The plate helped Matt recognize the grimy silver Lexus parked right in front of the Mega-Mart in a handicap spot, although it was readily apparent in the bright lighting of the parking lot that the car lacked a disabled-person plate or permit hang tag.

The car belonged to the obnoxious old man at Squid Tower who was giving the gate guard a hard time. Schwartz was his name, if Matt remembered correctly.

The Mega-Mart was the only store open at this late hour, aside from convenience stores, and Matt was here to pick up a few groceries. He decided to first try to find Schwartz in the store, scope him out, and see if there was anything vampire-like about him.

It didn't take long. Schwartz, with his blindingly shiny bald head, was in a checkout lane arguing with the clerk about a

73

coupon. Matt got behind him and pretended to select a brand of chewing gum from the impulse-buy rack. He studied the alleged vampire. Schwartz wore a moth-eaten sweater, a pair of cheap white tennis shorts, and sandals with black dress socks that didn't quite grip his skinny calves.

In short, he looked like any other retiree in the store.

"How could it be expired?" Schwartz said in a heavy New York accent. "I told you it was in today's newspaper. It's not my fault if there was a misprint."

"How do I know it was in today's paper?" asked the clerk, a cherub-faced young man with a pencil neck.

"Because it was," Schwartz replied.

"I mean, it could be from months ago."

"Are you implying I'm lying?"

The clerk's face turned red. He stammered without getting any words out. Schwartz's stuff was lined up on the checkout counter ahead of the scanner: more cheap white tennis shorts, several pairs of dark dress socks, swimming trunks, mothballs, nose-hair clippers, and a large bottle of laundry detergent. The detergent was the cause of the coupon clash.

"I'm not implying anything," the clerk said. "I'll be happy to get the manager if you'd like."

"You could just give me the benefit of the doubt and honor the coupon," Schwartz said in a low, angry voice.

"Sir, I've already pointed out this coupon expired two weeks ago."

"You're a good man. You know the customer is always right." Schwartz's voice took on a strange, musical lilt. It was hypnotic. "You want to be kind, don't you?"

The clerk had a blank look on his face. He nodded and stared off into space.

"You will honor my coupon. Tell me you will honor my coupon."

"I. Will. Honor. Your. Coupon." The clerk sounded like he was in a trance. He robotically moved the detergent over the scanner and then swiped the coupon, which was rejected. He manually entered a code and then continued scanning the other goods on the counter as he stared blankly into space.

The clerk's left hand attempted to place each scanned product into a plastic bag on the carousel at the end of the counter, but merely dropped them in between the bags. The nose-hair clippers bounced off an arm of the carousel and fell onto the floor.

Schwartz calmly paid with a credit card, bent over with a grunt, and put the goods into bags. As he gathered them in one hand, he held the other hand close to the clerk's head and snapped his fingers.

The clerk regained his senses. "Thank you for shopping at Mega-Mart," he said.

Schwartz hadn't given Matt any strong clues he was a vampire until he appeared to have hypnotized the clerk. Matt followed Schwartz outside.

"Excuse me, sir," Matt called after him.

Schwartz stopped and turned around, glaring at Matt with suspicion.

"Mr. Schwartz?" Matt asked with a smile.

"What do you want?"

"I'm Matt Rosen. I work for the *Jellyfish Beach Journal* and I'm doing a story about the murders on the beach. Do you have a moment for a couple of questions?"

"No," Schwartz said, turning and walking away.

Matt followed him. "Are you a professional hypnotist? That was an impressive job with the clerk."

"I don't know what you're talking about," Schwartz said, continuing to walk.

Matt hurried after him and got ahead, walking backwards so he faced Schwartz. He decided to go all-out with his questioning.

"There are rumors vampires are responsible for the murders. Do you agree?"

By now they had reached Schwartz's car. Matt stood with his back to the driver's door, blocking Schwartz, who stopped uncomfortably close to him. Matt studied the man's face. It was unnaturally pale, but that didn't prove anything. His ears were a bit elongated. His nose was large and did, indeed, need nose-hair clipping. In all, he looked like a normal male of his generation.

But then something odd happened in his eyes.

His pupils expanded until they eclipsed his gray irises, and his eyes became black discs with only a ring of white around them. Red light, like glowing embers, appeared in the center of each eye.

Matt suddenly felt scared.

"Vampires don't exist," Schwartz said in a flat, tight-lipped voice as if he were trying not to let his teeth show.

"Someone is making the murders appear like a vampire did them," Matt said, worrying he was pushing Schwartz too far.

"That's none of my concern," Schwartz said. "Now get out of my face."

"I will. But please, one last question."

Matt was in the air.

Schwartz's car passed beneath him, followed by a row of

other cars, and then Matt landed hard on his butt on the asphalt next to a minivan.

A harried mother with a kid in her shopping cart was loading groceries into the van. She looked at him with disgust.

"Get a job," she said.

He stood, pain flooding his back and buttocks. He hadn't even seen Schwartz move, but Matt's shirt was torn with two buttons missing, and deep scratch marks crossed his upper chest. Somehow, the guy had grabbed him and tossed him halfway across the parking lot. Matt must have pressed one button too many with an old man who had poor anger-management skills.

Make that an old vampire. Matt had encountered his first vampire, and he was both giddy about finding out they were real and awestruck by the incredible strength being undead could bring to an old man. And, Matt had to admit, he was embarrassed at being treated like a Frisbee in public.

He reminded himself the fact that vampires lived in Squid Tower didn't prove one was the murderer. There was still a lot of shoe-leather journalism he had to do to learn more.

It occurred to him he ought to disinfect the scratch marks on his chest. You never knew what germs a vampire carried on his nails. Matt drove straight home without buying any groceries.

11

OF BINGO AND BOTÁNICAS

Bernie's twelve-hour shift, four days a week, required more than adopting a new sleep cycle. He also had to retrain his bladder. There wasn't a toilet in the tiny gatehouse, so he had to leave to use the restroom. And who wants to do that when vampires are out and about? They might not recognize him and want a little nibble. Plus, if anyone had to wait too long for him at the gate while he was in the bathroom, they complained.

But thinking about Schwartz made him nervous and being nervous made him need to pee. He always used the closest men's room, which was past the lobby elevators and next to the community room. As he was about to push open the restroom door, he was surprised to hear voices coming from next door. After all, it was getting close to sunrise.

"I sank my fangs into Gerta's neck," said an elderly woman's voice with a Boston accent, "and drank my fill of the nasty old busybody's blood. Then I gnawed through her neck until her head popped off and landed on the tile floor—the brand-new Mediterranean tile she loved to brag about."

Bernie detoured from the restroom door and looked into the community room. It was filled with seniors sitting in a circle of chairs. One held up a sheaf of papers as she read.

"As I expected," the lady went on in a flat voice like a school kid reciting her homework, "Gerta's blood left a nasty aftertaste. The flavor of bitterness and jealousy."

"Talk about purple prose," a man uttered. "I've never drank blood that tasted like emotions."

"Let's stick with constructive comments, folks. Okay?"

The woman who said this was the only person in the room who wasn't ancient. She was attractive, probably in her forties, with straight brunette hair and bangs. A few freckles were scattered on her cheekbones. She saw him standing in the doorway with his mouth hanging open in confusion. Humor crinkled her eyes.

"Just a creative writing class," she said. "The violence is fictional."

"No. You told us to write what we know," the author said. "I know from experience how nasty Gerta and her blood were."

By now, everyone in the room was looking at him. Not with curiosity. With hunger.

He gave a quick wave and headed for the bathroom, broke a world speed record in relieving himself, and then dashed back to the relative safety of the gatehouse.

IN TIME, Bernie learned more about the comings and goings of the undead residents of Squid Tower. Most of those who still hunted for their meals went out for one nightly feeding; others went out for their "breakfast" as it were, then returned home before heading out for another feeding before dawn. Those who had their blood delivered left immediately after their meal to get some shopping in before the stores closed. They apparently loved chain discount stores, because the stores were open late or because the vampires were cheapskates.

Bingo Night was on Wednesday, an event everyone apparently attended. Cars streamed into the complex all at once, creating backups in the lane for residents that required a clicker or keycard to open. The lane closest to the gatehouse was for visitors and vendors, and Bernie had to open the gate manually for them. Many residents entered this way to avoid the backups in the other lane.

One night, he made the mistake of stepping out to use the restroom right before the bingo crowd began showing up. The horns began honking outside just as he flushed the toilet. He raced outside.

Guess who was waiting at the visitor gate. Schwartz, of course. His horn blared without pause as Bernie hurried into the booth and opened the gate. Then Schwartz started yelling.

"Why did you abandon your post, you idiot?" he screamed.

"Sorry, sir, I was using the restroom."

"We don't pay you to take a dump. We pay you to man the gate. It's Bingo Night."

"Sorry, I'm only human."

"Yes, and that's a big problem. You keep getting deeper and deeper on my crap list, Burdine. You'd better start looking for another line of work. Something you can't screw up. Like rodeo clown."

That comment bothered Bernie. He had a childhood friend

whose dream had been to move to Montana and become a rodeo clown. It took natural talent and years of training for someone to achieve success in the rodeo-clown world. But Bernie wasn't about to inform Schwartz.

After Schwartz's car pulled forward, Bernie manually lowered the gate. And heard a "clack" as it clipped the rear edge of the trunk. Schwartz slammed on his brakes.

Dang, Bernie thought, I'm falling into my bad habit from my drawbridge days.

But this time, it could get him killed.

Schwartz opened his door to get out and see if his car was damaged, but already horns were blaring from impatient drivers lined up behind him. He closed his door and drove off. Sometimes it seemed like old vampires loved bingo even more than blood.

After the flood of bingo attendees dried up, it was quiet again. Schwartz hadn't walked to the gatehouse to yell at him, so Bernie assumed his trunk wasn't damaged by the gate arm. He started to relax. Until a white BMW pulled up to the visitor's gate. It was Rudy. After he was let in, he parked and returned to the gatehouse. It was too confining inside for both of them, so Bernie stepped outside to greet him.

"Hi Rudy," he said. "Why are you here at one in the morning?"

"I come here to knock your head," he said in his thick German accent.

Then Bernie remembered his initial job interview with Rudy had been at night.

"Are you one of . . . them?" Bernie asked.

"Yes. How do you think I won the contract? All my clients have special needs. I thought you knew that."

Bernie should have figured it out. No wonder Rudy was always so quick to defend the vampires.

"What about the other guards?"

"Most are mortal humans. Everyone on the day shift is. And no one wants the night shift at Squid Tower. It's the only reason you have a job, Burdine. And if you keep antagonizing Mr. Schwartz, you won't have it any longer."

"It's not my fault. He hates me. He watches me like a hawk looking for any excuse to get me fired."

"He watches you like a hawk because he's a predator, Burdine. And you're the prey."

"I know, bro. That's why you've got to protect me somehow."

"It's in our contract with the owners' association that my employees are off limits."

"You're not making me feel any safer."

"Just focus on your job, Burdine. And stop pissing Mr. Schwartz off."

AT FACE VALUE, Bernie's job was perfect. Sitting around all night with time to write songs and practice guitar or keyboards. Three days off each week. In reality, though, he felt like a big chocolate cupcake sitting unguarded in an employee lunchroom. And his weekends, away from the protection against predation in the condo bylaws, were like the cupcake bearing a sign saying, "please eat me."

Who's saying Schwartz couldn't get to him when he was off the clock? And no one would know Schwartz did it.

At last count, Bernie had seven crosses and crucifixes

hanging in his apartment and on his front door. Two hanging from his neck. Bulbs of garlic everywhere, often around his neck as well. He didn't know if they would work. With all the vampires in movies and novels, you would think there would be some practical and consistent advice on vampire repellants, but no such luck.

The Jellyfish Beach Mystical Mart and Botánica was in a bad part of town, which meant it was near Bernie's apartment. With all the people in Florida from Latin America and the Caribbean, botánicas did brisk business catering to their ancestral beliefs and folklore, from Santeria to Voodoo to Obeah. Philomena, the day guard, told him about the store. If anyone sold vampire repellant, this would be the place.

A bell above the door tinkled when he entered, and a strong cloud of incense hit him. The store was a small, cluttered space filled from floor to ceiling with statuettes of saints, baggies and vials containing ground herbs and powders of many hues, bottles with unknown liquids, packets with crudely printed labels. Bernie was overwhelmed by all the objects before his eyes. A curtain covering a doorway into a back room parted, and a woman emerged.

"Can I help you?" she asked.

She looked very familiar. It was the woman who taught the vampires creative writing.

"It's you!" he said.

"It is, indeed, me," she said. "And who the heck are you?"

"Bernie Burdine. I work at Squid Tower. I'm one of the gate guards. I saw your class the other night."

"Oh, yeah, now I remember. You had this look on your face like you just stepped in a pile of dog doo. Let me guess, seeing a classroom brought back terrible memories for you?"

"I was confused. I'm new on the job and don't fully under-stand the fifty-five-plus, active-adult vampire lifestyle. Who knew that vampires would be interested in creative writing?" He stopped himself from asking the question, then let it out anyway. "Are you a vampire?"

"Do I look like one?"

"Uh, no. Your skin isn't as pale."

"Do you not realize it's daytime right now? These windows are kind of dirty, but there's plenty of sunshine coming through. It should have been your first clue."

"Okay, I get the point. But I don't understand why you're working with vampires."

"I work with seniors. I'm a home-health nurse and I run the class to help them stay mentally active. These seniors just happen to be afflicted with vampirism."

"You make it sound like some kind of disability."

"In a way, it is."

"I'm sorry, but those seniors scare the heck out of me. I'm a sitting duck in the gatehouse every night. I'm serious."

Her face became a little more sympathetic.

"No one would attack an employee," she said.

"Schwartz would. Leonard Schwartz. He's on the board and freaking hates me. He's threatened to kill me. And I know for a fact he's broken the rules and attacked a plumber on the property."

"I didn't know that. Yes, he's rather . . . difficult. And he has a serious sweet tooth. Try not to eat a lot of candy while you're on the job to avoid tempting him into snacking on you."

"That's the reason I'm here—to see if you can help me. Do you have any potions or spells or charms or anything to repel vampires? I mean, I've got these," he pulled out from under his shirt the two crucifixes he wore on chains. "But I'm not convinced a Jewish vampire would care about them. Besides, I'm Jewish, too, so they probably won't work, anyway."

She frowned. "I'm sure I can put together something for you. I don't know if Schwartz would be more influenced by the lore of European heritage or of the Americas." She smiled. "I'll figure something out."

"I thought you'd be wearing some sort of protection yourself."

"I have this," she said, withdrawing an amulet on a leather cord from under her blouse. "Yours will be similar, but customized more for you and for repelling Schwartz in particular."

"Does yours work?"

"I think so. But they would never hurt me, anyway. I care for their special needs. They depend on me."

"It's your life," Bernie said.

"Next time I'm at Squid Tower, I'll drop off your amulet," she said. "No charge for this one."

He thanked her enthusiastically and said goodbye.

"I'm Missy, by the way. My creative writing classes are Tuesdays at two in the morning," she said. "You're welcome to join us if you can get a break."

"Uh, I think I'll pass," he said. "I can only leave the gatehouse to use the bathroom and I'd rather not be in the same room as vampires. Besides, I'm not much of a writer. My passion is music. And staying alive."

1 2

IT'S MAGICK

After Bernie left, Missy opened a box of magnetic car statuettes and placed them on a recently cleared shelf. Missy was constantly impressed by the variety of goods in Luisa's botánica. The customers here sometimes wanted potions or charms to give them luck, love, or money. But other times, they were on a more religious-like quest to receive blessings from a number of saints and religious figures that combined African-based religions with Christianity. Sometimes they came seeking spiritual advice or Tarot-card readings from Luisa. Across the gray borders between the magical and the spiritual, the botánica probably had what you were looking for.

She put a hand-painted, five-inch-tall Saint Anthony figurine right next to Elegua, an orisha, or spirit, of the Yoruba tradition from Africa. Next to him went the Holy Infant of Atocha. He was flanked by Papa Candelo sitting cross-legged. He was a powerful loa, or voodoo spirit, from Haiti and the

Dominican Republic. And he was the perfect accessory for your car dashboard or end table at home.

A few years ago, if you had told Missy she'd be working as a home-health nurse caring for vampires, she would have called you crazy. If you had told her she'd also work part time in a botánica in a slightly dangerous neighborhood, she would have called someone to have you institutionalized.

Missy hadn't considered herself a serious witch. Sure, for most of her life she'd dabbled in Wicca and the traditional pioneer spell craft she called Florida cracker magick. She became more interested in it after her marriage ended, but never had the time to fully dedicate herself to the mystical arts.

Once she realized her career as a nurse in the Intensive Care Unit had burned her out to a crisp, she quit her job at the regional hospital and began working as a home-health nurse. But the pay was a fraction of what she had made at the hospital, even though, considering the patients, it was hazardous duty. She had needed to find additional, part-time, work. She had a mortgage to pay, cats to feed, and magick ingredients to buy.

But a botánica? Really? What happened was she had been searching for some potion ingredients—dried frog livers, nightshade, Florida Water, Four Thieves Vinegar, and such things that were rarely a good idea to order online. There was a New Age bookstore not far from her house, but the store sold only books, crystals, and incense. She'd found the botánica almost by mistake. It was in a strip center between a convenience store and a takeout seafood joint that had bars on its windows.

The botánica was like others she'd been in before, but this one had, besides the Santeria merchandise, a large inventory of Voodoo, Obeah, and Hoodoo products. She also found occult supplies and several obscure ingredients for various kinds of witchcraft that were hard to find anywhere.

She became a regular customer. Until one day, when the owner, an Afro-Cuban woman named Luisa, asked if she could help out a few days a week. She negotiated late-afternoon hours that ended in the early evening after sunset when she began her nursing visits.

The supernatural had always been on the periphery of Missy's life. She was an orphan, and her adoptive parents were loving and permissive. They had never been devoutly religious themselves, but they opened a door for various forms of spiritualism to enter Missy's life. In fact, her adoptive mother was a college professor of comparative religion, so she instilled in the household an acceptance of all belief systems.

The one exception was witchcraft. Even though Missy's parents were open to all sorts of spiritual exercises, they forbade anything to do with witches and, at the time, never gave a satisfactory reason why. Her more conservative father, in particular, discouraged witchcraft almost as if he were afraid of it, which was odd for him. They weren't obnoxiously strict about this ban, because doing so would have made Missy rebel. They simply steered her away from it. And if she ever left a book about witches lying around, it would mysteriously disappear.

Despite this, they did allow her to hold a seance for a dead pet parakeet when she was only eight. A used Ouija board found its way into her playroom, and she loved to freak out her friends by summoning ghosts.

Her parents believed it all was the product of a rich childish imagination. It wasn't. These were genuine ghosts, including those of a killer clown and his killer-clown-in-training who had been killed by his killer-clown mentor. The two ghosts did not get along, to put it mildly.

In addition to her communicating with ghosts, Missy believed she might have other psychic abilities, with all her heart, in her early adolescent years, when kids yearn for something to make them special. She played with tarot cards, though her fortune-telling abilities were not impressive. She often had strange hunches, premonitions, and feelings of brushing up against forces not quite of this world. But she couldn't make sense of them, let alone harness them for practical use.

Her one ability showing true potential was telekinesis. She could visualize a book sliding off a table, and it would happen. A pen she dropped on the floor would return to her hand. She couldn't do anything much more dramatic than that, but it was a start. As she entered adulthood and became consumed by its pragmatism, she lost her enthusiasm for her psychic side, though her telekinesis would occasionally prevent a drink from spilling or a shopping cart from rolling into her car. However, she rarely used it in a premeditated way.

Then, one day, Luisa noticed something about her for the first time at the botánica while they were unpacking boxes filled with potions in tiny glass bottles. When the shelves were jostled, a bottle on the top shelf tottered and then fell.

With her mind alone, Missy slowed its plunge and set it gently on the floor.

"Wow, you've got some power in you, *chica*."

"What are you talking about? What I did with the love potion, or whatever it is?"

"The Better Business Oil. I meant more than telekinesis. You know, I've always liked your positive energy. And just now I felt something more."

"What do you mean?"

"It's hard to say. More than just energy. More like *power*. Yes, power. A true sorceress or priestess needs power to control the spirits," Luisa said, tapping the ceramic head of some saint Missy didn't recognize. "And you got it, *chica*. I don't know what you can do with it, or if there's enough to do anything with. You know what I'm talking about?"

"No. I think you've been sniffing too much incense. What makes you believe this?"

"I can just feel it, *entiendes*? Do you understand?"

"I've always had an affinity with the spiritual world and the paranormal. That's why I got into Wicca."

Luisa snorted. "Wicca's fine, but you got the power to do a lot more. I'm a businesswoman, not a *bruja*, but I have a strong connection to the spiritual world. And I've got a feeling about you."

"What do you mean by 'do a lot more'? You mean other kinds of witchcraft?"

"Call it what you want. We just need to figure out how to tap into what you got. I know a gentleman who might be able to help."

"I'm sorry, Luisa, Santeria is very interesting, but I don't know if it's my thing. Nor is Voodoo or Obeah."

"Of course not, *chica*. You got to stay true to your heritage, your traditions. It's in your blood, your memories, and dreams. It's what you know deep down whether or not you realize it."

"My parents were into spiritualism, but they didn't follow any traditions regarding magick."

"I didn't mean it literally. I'm just saying your best path is to follow the traditions from the part of the world your ancestors came from. I assume yours are not from Africa and the Caribbean like mine."

"My adoptive family was in Florida for generations. True Florida crackers," Missy said. "I've been reading lately about cracker folk-healing potions and practices. It's really interesting, a combination of pioneer remedies from the 1800s and Seminole herbal medicine. I figure I can combine those traditions with witchcraft spells and such."

"Bo-ring," Luisa said. "All that stuff is fine and has its uses, but I'm talking about *power*."

"To be clear, I know a few good spells. I have a truth-telling spell which works every time I've tried it. It's pretty powerful."

"That's nothing compared to the kinds of things you could do with the power you have inside of you. You got to talk to this guy I know. I'll set you up soon."

Missy didn't say no. Because, although she was afraid to admit it, she had recently sensed something long dormant inside of her was waking. Some mighty force she didn't understand.

13
A PRIEST WALKS
INTO A BOTÁNICA

Father Marco Rivera Hernandez insisted on being called Father Marco, even though he admitted he was a defrocked priest.

"I was the only priest in the diocese who could do an exorcism," he told Missy in the back room of the botánica, where readings and ceremonies were performed. "Most of the time, the afflicted had mental illness. But every so often, I'd come across a real possession. They're seriously scary, I tell you."

Father Marco had an aristocratic face with a well-trimmed beard. He looked like a Spanish nobleman from the conquistador era. He might have been in his forties or fifties with brown hair untouched by age, but his beard was fully white. They sat across from each other at the fortune-telling table in the dimly lit room.

"I was assigned to this one case," he continued. "It was approved by the diocese and the archdiocese. And the moment

I saw the subject, a thirteen-year-old girl, I could tell it was bad. There was something seriously evil and powerful in her."

"How could you tell?" Missy asked.

"Well, aside from her talking to me in a voice that sounded like James Earl Jones, and already knowing my name, and telling me she was going to mess me up big time if I didn't leave right away—aside from that, you could say it was a gut feeling. I could sense the power."

"But how?"

"Maybe it's a gift I have. It's not a thing you can learn. I just feel it, maybe because I have a little myself. Can you sense it in me?"

She cleared her head and stared at his intense brown eyes. Then his aura appeared, in a pulsing reddish black. A troubling color. She rarely saw auras except those of people with exceptionally forceful personalities. The kind of people she avoided. She also picked up the feeling of energy humming within him, radiating outwards.

"Yes, I can," she said.

"Good. I can sense power in you as well. A great deal of it. I felt it the minute I first saw you. You need to be careful, because your power could attract unsavory characters who want to tap into it or who see you as a threat. Like other witches or wizards." He sipped from a glass of wine Missy hadn't noticed before.

"I'm not sure I understand," Missy said.

"I should explain what we mean when we speak of power. Power can be generated from the natural energy of the earth, from electromagnetic power, ley lines, fault lines, and power points. Non-dark forms of magick work in this way, and many people can harvest it directly and keep it within themselves, holding it like an electrical charge.

"Then there's power that comes from forces beyond this earth. At the risk of sounding trite and simplistic, this power can come from good or evil supernatural entities. Some people with no power inside themselves can leverage this supernatural power, like the tales of sorcerers summoning demons to perform actions.

"And there are people like you, who naturally have power inside you. You were born with it. Regardless of whether you know it. Regardless of whether you use it. You can also tap into the energy of the earth as a temporary force multiplier or do the same with supernatural power. People born with power inside them, and who can combine it with these external kinds of power, are the mightiest people of all."

"How does this relate to me?" Missy asked.

"You need to understand the strength and nature of the power within you. Learn how to access and control it. Find ways to enhance it using the power of the earth. Then, someday, you can learn how to use the power of the supernatural world as well. My advice, though, is to stay away from dark power." He gave a mordant laugh.

"You know this from personal experience?"

"It's why I was de-frocked. The exorcism I attempted of the thirteen-year-old girl? I never finished the story."

"Please do."

"The demon claimed he was Asmodeus, but I don't know if it was true. Demons lie more often than politicians. Anyway, it was the most difficult, dangerous exorcism I had ever attempted."

"That's the second time you said 'attempted.' Do you mean you didn't succeed?"

He sighed. "Yes, and no. I won't go into a blow-by-blow account of what happened, but there were times when I feared for the girl's life and my own. You could say I was in over my head, but it's not as if there are lots of more experienced exorcists out there nowadays. Anyway, it got to the point that the demon and I were bargaining with each other. I agreed to host the demon if he would leave the girl. He did. So, in one sense, you could say it was a success."

"Oh my, you mean you were then possessed?"

"Yeah. But I was probably a disappointment for the demon. Adolescents have tons of crazy hormonal energy, which is why poltergeists often manifest themselves in homes with kids going through puberty. So, this demon enjoyed possessing her. I, on the other hand, was boring. I mean, I was a *priest*. What would a demon find exciting in my life of writing sermons, hosting bingo, and having tea with old ladies? He didn't even do anything to me for weeks, so I almost forgot about him. Of course, he chose to show up one Sunday when I was celebrating mass. I have no memory of it, of course. But apparently my performance emptied the church of parishioners, half of whom vowed never to come back. I even defiled the altar. It was bad."

"Yeah, I'd say."

"I was put on sick leave and given every drug test and psychological evaluation in the world. I explained about the deal I made with the demon to save the girl, and the monsignor of the parish said I had no right to do it without prior authorization. As if I could stop the exorcism and ask the demon to wait while I routed paperwork through the bureaucracy. I appealed to the bishop, and it turns out he didn't even believe in demonic possessions. He allowed exorcisms solely for public relations reasons. I was upset, so I used the demon for dark purposes."

"What did you do?" Missy asked in a low voice.

"I discovered and exposed the embezzlement scheme the bishop was involved in."

"What you did doesn't sound evil to me."

"Well, it sure did to the archdiocese. I was defrocked, kicked out of the church, and here I am today."

"How did you finally get rid of the demon?"

"I didn't. He's still in me."

"Oh," Missy said.

"Yes, 'oh.' It's kind of awkward when I reveal it to people. Now that I'm no longer a priest, I can date women, but who wants to date a guy possessed by a demon? Men can be bad enough without being possessed by demons. And my old friends from before the seminary don't want to hang out with me because I can really ruin a party when the demon takes over. He always chooses the most inappropriate times. He won't even let me play golf."

Missy would never admit it, out of politeness, but she suddenly felt very uncomfortable being alone in the room with ex-Father Marco Rivera Hernandez. She tried to change the subject.

"How do I learn more about my power?" she asked.

"I will gladly train you."

"That's very kind of you, but I'd like to try some exercises on my own at first. You know, get warmed up before I have any training, so I don't pull any mental muscles. I'm already able to do a little telekinesis here and there."

"Ah, yes, the ability to move objects through mental power.

Also called psychokinesis. I'm very impressed," he said. "Why don't you begin by exercising your brain and seeing if you have any other gifts? Then we can explore methods of amplifying your power."

"Sounds good. I'll start with the exercising and get back to you."

"Start with exorcising instead, you stupid wench," the ex-priest said in a voice identical to James Earl Jones'.

"I beg your pardon?"

"Sorry," he said with an embarrassed smile in his normal voice. "Asmodeus is sticking his evil nose in my businesses again."

"Are you sure you don't have Tourette Syndrome?"

"Quite sure. Just ask the people at the church picnic that was rained upon with pig excrement last weekend. Only a demon could have done such a thing. A demon with a wicked sense of humor."

Missy thanked ex-Father Rivera Hernandez profusely for his help and left the shop as quickly as she could, thankful to put distance between her and the demon-possessed dude.

14
REBOOT

I t was time for Matt to focus his investigation on what happened to Taylor Donovan. He would do the most delicate part first: speaking with the victim's parents.

Mayor Janet Donovan consented to the interview if it would be brief. And she insisted it be at her home rather than her office in City Hall since, her assistant told Matt, it was a personal topic. No questions about city business, the assistant warned.

The mayor's home was more mansion than house and was right on the Intracoastal Waterway. She did not buy the home on a mayor's salary. She and her husband were developers and obviously did quite well. So did their developer friends who needed the city to approve their projects. He was surprised when the mayor herself, instead of a servant, answered the door.

"Come on in. We'll be in here," she said, directing him into her study on the first floor. "My husband is away on business, so he won't be able to join us."

The room was white with sophisticated, classical furnishings. Half the walls were lined with built-in bookshelves and the others had Eighteenth-Century oil paintings of horses and riding scenes. There was one window with blinds closed. Matt was disappointed there wasn't a view of the water from this room. He figured there was probably a huge boat moored alongside the house.

Mayor Donovan sat behind a delicate writing desk set diagonally in a corner where she faced the room and two guest chairs in front of the desk. He sat in the left chair. She offered him a bottled water which he accepted but didn't open, perching it awkwardly between his knees as he hit play on his phone's voice-recorder app, placing it on the other chair. He opened his narrow reporter notepad to take notes.

"Again, I'm so sorry about your daughter," he said.

The mayor put her hands on the desk, fingers touching, and swallowed as if girding herself.

"Taylor was a brilliant young woman," she said. "She was doing well in college—she was attending Gulf Stream College locally, studying business. But it's no secret she had gone through a long battle with substance abuse. She spent years in therapy. It wasn't easy, but she was a real trooper. She was clean and sober for over a year now. I'm so proud of her." She wiped her eyes with a tissue. The mayor had a wide, pleasant face, framed by well-coiffed dark hair, but she also had a sharpness signifying she didn't suffer fools.

"You should be proud," he said.

It would be weeks before an autopsy report came back, but Matt would not be surprised if it revealed drugs in her system.

The search for drugs often brought good people into contact with bad ones, which rarely ended well.

"Did she have a boyfriend?"

"Of course, the police asked about that," the mayor said. "It was their first question, actually. She was serious with a boy named David, but they broke up a while ago. Since then, she's been on dates, but no one serious."

"What kind of social group did she hang around with?" Matt asked, writing notes about his next questions.

"A group of fine young women from some of the best families in the county."

"I see. And what did they do for fun?"

"Taylor loved serving the community. Taylor and her friends did a lot of volunteering and liked to go to charity events."

"But what did they do for *fun?*"

Mayor Donovan gave him an icy stare. "I want this article to be a tribute to Taylor. Not salacious trash trying to blame her for her murder."

"I would never write that."

"But the questions you're asking sound like you're trying to solve the crime. That's what the police are for. I've already answered dozens of questions like these. I truly believe Taylor wasn't in the wrong place with the wrong people. She wasn't doing anything improper. I believe my sweet girl was attacked by some pervert or psycho who'd probably been stalking her for a long time."

"Do you suspect an ex-boyfriend like David?"

"There you go again asking police questions."

He wanted to remark that the police hadn't had much luck in solving the murders of the other young people who weren't children of the rich and powerful, but he managed to edit himself.

"Sorry for offending you," he said. "I'm a news reporter, not a feature story writer. It's my instinct to ask questions like those. We'll switch back to more legacy-building topics, I promise, if you'll just tell me what she was up to before . . . on the night in question."

"She was at an event for the Junior League."

"Thank you," Matt said, defeated. "Now tell me more about what Taylor was studying in college and what she hoped to do when she graduated."

The mayor went on in great detail about Taylor's good grades, her athletic prowess, and other achievements. The main gist of it all was that Taylor's passion was to make the world a better place. Of course.

He walked out of the house with little useful information, but at least he knew she had been at a Junior League event on the night she was killed.

THE LIFESTYLE SECTION of the *Jellyfish Beach Journal* wouldn't be printed until later in the week, but on the newspaper's internal network, he found the layout. Photos from the Junior League's Casino Night were on the front page. The event's purpose was to raise money for a local gambling addiction organization.

The photos were all of attractive young women in cocktail dresses smiling at the camera like celebrities. Taylor Donovan had a wide, warm face like her mother's, with long, dark-blond hair. She looked earnest and fun-loving. There were no traces of psychological scars from substance abuse in her eyes. She posed with her arm around a petite young woman the caption identified as Cindi Stockton.

As Matt expected, Cindi had a robust presence on social media. He sent her messages with his phone number through several sites, asking if he could speak to her about Taylor. He was pleasantly surprised when she called him the next day.

"I'm calling you because you're a reporter and the world needs to know how great Taylor was. She was, like, the most wonderful person I've ever known," Cindi said in a squeaky voice. "All she cared about was making the world a better place."

"Yes, I heard about making the world a better place," Matt said. "And I'm sorry for your loss."

After enough polite conversation eulogizing Taylor had taken place, Matt began carefully digging.

"Do you know where she was on the night she lost her life?"

"After the Junior League event, she was with me and a bunch of friends at a party in a house on the beach," Cindi said. "Later, we stopped for some ice cream. And then *he* came in."

"Her ex-boyfriend, David?"

"No. David was at the party earlier. And that's another story."

"What do you mean?"

"They went out for years, from the end of high school and into college. He went to Gulf Stream, too. But then, you know, she got into drugs, and he broke up with her. When she was in recovery, she hoped they could, like, get together again. But he has another girlfriend now. She was at the party. Taylor was not at all happy to see them together. It was like, you know, really awkward."

"Does David have any bad feelings for Taylor? Anger or resentment?"

"No," Cindi replied. "I think he was happy to be free of her. She was a real mess back then, and he told me he just wanted her to get clean and find happiness. There's talk he and his girlfriend might get engaged."

"Okay," Matt said, mentally crossing David off the list of potential suspects. "So, who's the 'he' who came to the ice cream shop?"

"Kyle. He's, like, really bad news. Some dude Taylor met at the recovery place and had a fling with. But he's back to using. Or dealing. Or both, I don't know. And Taylor was so upset about seeing David with his girlfriend, she just went off with Kyle. On his motorcycle. She wanted him to get drugs for her. Some Reboot."

"Reboot? What's that?"

"Some new drug showing up at clubs and parties lately. I know nothing about drugs, but Reboot is supposed to make you hallucinate, and it really messes up your mind. We tried to stop her, but she was too upset. If we had stopped her, she'd be alive today." She began sniffling.

"Don't blame yourself. If she wanted to relapse, no one could stop her."

"She was upset. If we took her home that night, if we, like, got her away from Kyle, she would have gotten over the cravings. I just know it."

"You did all you could. Did you tell all of this to the police?"

"Yeah, some detective. But he didn't sound very grateful. Maybe he knew about Kyle already."

"Do you think Kyle killed her?"

She didn't speak for a while. Then sighed. "I don't know, but he would be my first choice if I had to guess."

"Was he ever violent with her?"

"I didn't see her much when she went out with him, but I heard she had bruises on her face and arms more than once."

"Do you know how I can find Kyle?"

"I don't know his last name. But he hangs out at the nasty surfer bar on Pelican Avenue downtown. He's really fat and tall and hairy."

"Hairy?"

"Long hair, huge beard. He's gross. You can't miss him."

Matt thanked her and said goodbye. He wondered who the police's suspect was. He called, texted, and emailed Detective Affird, who responded as he usually did: crickets chirping.

THE "NASTY" surfer bar on Pelican Avenue was actually a place Matt enjoyed drinking at from time to time. In Jellyfish Beach, it was hard to find a bar where the clientele was under seventy and The Ripped Tide was one of them. It wasn't particularly nasty in Matt's opinion, just old, funky, and a bit dirty. Okay, yes, he would concede the bathrooms were nasty, Matt thought as he went in after consuming his second beer. He'd been waiting at the empty bar, hoping for Kyle to show up. The bartender, a young surfer chick with dirty blonde hair and more ink and piercings than he could fathom, said Kyle was there most nights unless he was in jail or in the emergency room.

Sure enough, while Matt was standing at the urinal, the flimsy wall of the bathroom vibrated from the roar of a Harley pulling up outside. He hoped it was Kyle. When he returned to the bar, the bartender caught his eye and nodded toward a large man who looked like a cross between a grizzly bear and the Swamp Thing. Scary, hairy, and in the mood to kill.

This dude ought to be the primary suspect, Matt thought. He was the last person known to have seen Taylor, and he looked like he wouldn't hesitate to kill someone. Anyone.

Being a general-assignment reporter in a small, affluent market such as Jellyfish Beach did not normally involve the risk of getting disemboweled while seeking a source. Matt hoped he wouldn't be the first at the *Journal* to achieve this distinction.

"I'd like to buy him one of whatever he ordered," Matt whispered to the bartender.

The bartender poured a shot of tequila and a shot of Jagermeister. When she put them both in front of Kyle, Matt cringed. Cindi was right, this man really is gross, he thought.

The bartender leaned over the bar and said something to Kyle. The gross one looked over at Matt.

"What are you in the market for?" Kyle asked.

"What do you mean?"

"Pot, coke, opiates, what? I'll warn you the heroin has been full of fentanyl lately, so you buy at your own risk. Lots of opiate-heads OD-ing, so stuff like coke and meth are back in fashion, if you aren't already addicted to opiates."

"All I want is a little information," Matt said.

"Weirdo." The gross one gulped down the tequila, quickly followed by the Jagermeister.

Matt felt nauseous just watching. "What happened to Taylor Donovan?"

"Are you a cop? No, you look too dweeb-ish to be a cop." Kyle stood and moved next to Matt, standing too close with his enormous bulk and ripe unwashed body odor, breathing his unholy cocktail of alcohol breath in Matt's face. "I'll tell you the same thing I told them. Taylor called me and asked me to pick her up at some ice cream place on the beach. I picked her up. We went for a ride. Got into an argument. And she jumped off at the beach. I left her there. I had no idea she'd get killed."

Taylor really dated this lowlife? Matt wondered.

"I was told she wanted to buy drugs," he said.

"Yeah. Reboot. The new kind of LSD going around. I don't deal with any of that garbage. She wanted me to drive her to a dealer I know, the only one around here who sells it. It's one of the reasons we argued. I was giving her a hard time about the Reboot, so she asked for the name and address of the dealer. Then she jumped off my bike near his place, and I figured she walked there. That's the last I saw her."

"Where did you go afterwards?"

Kyle cocked an eyebrow. "You sure sound like a cop. I came straight here and the bartender that night can back me up."

But you still had time to kill her before you got here, Matt thought.

"Do you know if Taylor took Reboot often?"

"She never took it with me, and she never talked about it," Kyle said. "Maybe she found out about it after she got clean."

"Is it the kind of drug that lowers your defenses?"

"Never took it myself, but I'd think you'd be pretty helpless while you're tripping your brains out."

"Did you tell the police about this guy with the Reboot?" Matt asked.

"I'm no narc, dude. I just told them she was looking for drugs from some dealer on the beach."

"Can you tell me how to find him? All I want is information about Taylor."

Kyle's eyes squinted with suspicion, but Matt quickly pulled some cash from his pocket. It was around $100, all he had left until payday, but he thrust it into the monster's giant hands.

"I just want to find out who killed her," he pleaded.

Kyle shrugged, then nodded. "I used to be really into her. For a while."

He pulled his phone from his jeans pocket and scrolled through his contacts.

"He goes by the name of Chainsaw. He's in unit A-305 in Seaweed Manor."

Those condos were near where Taylor's body had been found, where he had met the nurse, Missy. They were right next to Squid Tower, where other bodies had been found.

"Is this guy violent?" Matt asked.

"Getting cold feet about visiting him?"

"No. But do you ever wonder if he killed Taylor?"

"Yeah, I wondered. Chainsaw is an animal."

Kyle, the beast, can say that with no irony? Matt wondered.

"But I don't think he's stupid enough to kill a rich girl," Kyle continued. "At least not near his own apartment."

"Chainsaw's not one of those goth dudes who pretend they're vampires, is he?"

Kyle laughed. "Hell no. He's a biker like me. But I can't vouch for any kinky stuff he does in his free time."

Matt thanked Kyle and left the bar. He drove to an ATM to get a cash advance from his credit card to buy some Reboot he would not use.

15

FANGS WITH A SWEET TOOTH

During the nights Bernie had off, he kept the same graveyard-shift, waking-sleeping schedule. It was the only way to keep his body trained to sleep during the day. On one of these nights, he drove past the small strip of shops on A1A near Squid Tower. A convenience store, an ice-cream shop. And a vampire.

Schwartz. He was lurking in the shadows near a handicapped parking spot, watching two young women eating ice cream cones just outside the door to the shop. They didn't appear to notice him.

Bernie slowed down. Should he warn the women? Didn't Detective Affird say some people who had gone missing or turned up dead were last seen here?

Schwartz never took his eyes from the women. He remained in the shadows, unmoving, his posture giving the air of a cat about to spring at a mouse.

Bernie did a U-turn and pulled into the strip center. How

was he going to warn them without Schwartz going berserk and decapitating him? He backed into a nearby parking spot.

Just then, an SUV stopped in front of the ice cream shop and the two young women got inside. It drove away, leaving Schwartz standing there, red eyes burning. Missy had told Bernie that Schwartz had a sweet tooth. Did he prefer victims who had just eaten sweets and had a high blood-sugar level?

Well, he was going to have to loiter here a lot longer if he wanted dessert tonight.

As Bernie drove away, Schwartz stared at his car. God, he implored, please don't let him recognize it.

Then again, he drove a GMC Pacer that leaked oil. How many other Pacers were there in this town?

He was doomed.

He searched his pockets until he found Detective Affird's card. Should he call him? No, Rudy had told him the Squid Tower residents' privacy was just as important as their security in this job. If he found out that Bernie ratted out Schwartz, Bernie would be fired in an instant.

There was nothing he could do.

THE NEXT NIGHT, Bernie was back at work. From the moment he started his shift, he worried about the inevitable confrontation with Schwartz. But the old vampire didn't pass through the gate. By three in the morning, the last of the vampires were returning to the parking garage. It was hours before dawn, but this was considered staying up late for the geriatric residents of Squid Tower. The ones who dined right after sunset when the Blood Bus arrived had been tucked away in their coffins or on their memory foam mattresses for hours already.

Bernie peered out of the condominium's gatehouse, counting the last-of-the-night's cars as they inched past him through the residents' automatic gate. All had elderly drivers hunched over the steering wheels, and most had pulled into the palm-lined entrance using their left turn signal to turn right. There were Cadillacs, Mercedes, BMWs, and plenty of Toyotas. Lots of New York, New Jersey, and Massachusetts plates.

Schwartz's Lexus was not among them. He must have stayed home tonight. Just the thought of him made the hairs on the back of Bernie's neck prickle. He looked around at the parking lot, the landscaping lights, the dark, looming bulk of the high-rise, his haggard reflection in the gatehouse window. Nothing out there or on the security monitors. Nothing but palm fronds quivering in the wind.

Bernie was a goldfish in a tiny, illuminated tank, on display for all hidden predators lurking in the darkness. Especially the one with a vendetta against him.

When was Schwartz going to confront him about the ice cream shop?

THE FOLLOWING NIGHT, when the headlights of the first vampires to return home struck the windows of his booth, Bernie woke up and wiped the drool from his chin. When Schwartz's grimy Lexus approached the gate, Bernie took a deep breath, leaned out of the gatehouse, and waved, sporting a huge smile.

Schwartz drove past him, a look of annoyance on his face.

But annoyance was better than hatred. And both were better than hunger.

Later, after midnight, Schwartz came shuffling past, carrying a small bag of trash to deposit in the dumpster. (Since they don't buy and cook food, the undead don't generate as much trash as living humans.) Bernie popped out of the gatehouse.

"Hi, Mr. Schwartz! Allow me to throw that away for you."

Schwartz stopped, confused. Then angry. "Your job is to stay in the booth. You're a gate guard, you moron."

"You're absolutely right, sir. Sorry about that!"

"I see you've heard I'm trying to get you fired. Being a little brown-nose won't help you at all."

"No, sir, but I hope my improved work performance will not go unnoticed by you."

Schwartz laughed. "Fat chance."

"And rest assured, I would never, ever, talk to anyone about your eating habits. Your secrets are safe with me."

"Your mouth is moving, but only nonsense is coming out."

"Your hunting. I would never mention it if anyone asked. Like the police."

Schwartz growled, sort of like a Rottweiler but sounding even more scary.

"Yes, you saw me at the ice cream parlor," he said in a low voice. "Were you following me?"

"Of course not!"

"Look, you feeble-minded, Long-Island jackass. If you're trying to blackmail me or something, I'll kill you before dawn. If you're expecting praise for not giving the police false information about me, then you're more stupid than I thought. You signed a non-disclosure agreement when you were hired, insisting on absolute secrecy. So don't expect a pat on the head for obeying it. And don't ever threaten me."

Bernie sputtered various sounds without managing to utter an actual word from the English language.

"Killing you would be just like swatting an annoying mosquito. Don't tempt me."

He walked away toward the dumpster, his tall dress socks gradually sinking down to his skinny ankles.

Well, that didn't go very well, Bernie brooded. So much for trying a charm offensive.

MISSY HANDED Bernie a pouch made of heavy black felt, tied shut with a leather cord long enough to wear around the neck. Bernie sniffed its pungent ingredients.

"Whew! Is there garlic in there?"

"Yes, of course there's garlic," she said. "As well as aloe, wolfsbane, blessed thistle, and other ingredients I will not divulge because I'm applying for a patent."

Bernie had a strange attraction to her. Which surprised him, because she appeared to be in her forties, a bit younger than him, and he'd never been attracted to women older than twenty (which might explain why he hadn't had a girlfriend since he was twenty-one). And he'd especially never been drawn to the New-Age type of chicks. But there was something about her—a kind of power.

"Did you cast any magic spells over this?" he joked.

Her expression was deadly serious. "No comment."

And he'd never been attracted to witches, either.

"Can I share a secret with you?" Bernie asked.

She frowned. "It depends on what kind."

"It's about Mr. Schwartz."

"I don't think I want to hear any of Mr. Schwartz's secrets."

"No, this is important," Bernie insisted. "Did you hear about the woman they found on the beach? The mayor's daughter?"

"Yes, of course. It's sad and horrible."

"Well, the other night I saw Mr. Schwartz hanging around outside of The Cone of Uncertainty, the ice cream shop. It looked like he was stalking some girls there. Good thing someone they knew picked them up in an SUV."

She stared at him for a moment. "But that doesn't mean—"

"You told me about his sweet tooth," Bernie said. "He wasn't there jonesing over ice cream. He was hungry for someone with high blood sugar. We've had young women disappearing or showing up dead, and we have Mr. Schwartz stalking young women. And don't say he wouldn't break the rules and feed close to home, because I've seen him do it."

"You mean the plumber?"

"Yeah. My boss told me to shut up about it. Just something to keep in mind."

"Yes, I will. Thank you, Bernie," she said as she left. "Be sure to wear your amulet every night, even when you're not here."

"I sure will," he said, straining to give her his best smile. "Thanks for making it."

16

THE RACE

A be jogged down the beach at 3:00 a.m., along the firm stretch of sand just above the highest reach of the waves. No one was on the beach to get in his way at this hour. He had to work out so early to get in enough miles before it was time to leave for the office.

He had already run five miles. Now it was time to swim a few. He plunged into the ocean. The water was cool but not chilly. The surf was a little too rough to swim through, but he pushed on anyway, waves pounding his face.

Abe was training for . . . well, he was training just for the sake of training. He'd evolved from 5Ks to 10Ks, to half-marathons, to a couple of full marathons. Then it was the Iron Man competition and other triathlons. Next it was Spartan races and events where you tortured yourself ankle-deep in mud. He recently won a competition in which the entrants wore backpacks filled with bricks, hauled telephone poles, and ran for twenty miles while a man yelled and threw water balloons at them.

Note: He *won*. He kicked butt, in fact.

Abe was solid muscle without an ounce of fat. So, it no longer was a question of getting his body in its greatest possible condition. Now it was all about competition. Abe liked to win. Or, more accurately, he liked beating other people and his own records.

He knew he'd become unbearable to everyone in his life. Having reached his twenty-eighth year, he believed no romantic partner was good enough for him, and the few he lowered his standards for couldn't stand his constant competitiveness. He didn't enjoy hanging out with people because he had absolutely no interests other than improving his performance. Almost all his leisure time was spent training, at gyms, on tracks, on beaches, in the ocean. Eating was not for pleasure, but only for sustaining his body and improving its performance. He didn't read or listen to music. Forget movies. All he liked to watch were videos of his own races.

At his workplace, he was competitive to the point of obnoxiousness. He didn't care how well his data analytics firm did; he only cared how well he outdid his colleagues. The problem was, he was so obsessed with himself that he didn't have time to focus on his job enough to advance very far with the company. Work was much lower on his priority list, anyway, than his athletic performance.

Somewhere along the way, he had lost sight of any goal in life other than beating performance goals he arbitrarily set for himself.

Once Abe got through the surf zone and the waves no longer broke upon him, he turned and swam parallel to the shore, riding the swells. Occasionally, he looked to his left at the beach to watch for the high-rise condo tower marking the three-mile point.

A shooting star passed overhead. To other people, it may have been beautiful, but he couldn't care less about it, even as it appeared to land in the ocean behind him. He kept swimming freestyle, three kicks per stroke, breathing to his left, opposite the incoming waves.

The star appeared again, coming from behind him and passing over. Though he tried to keep his head down for proper form, he couldn't help glancing up at it. It wasn't a star; it was a fireball of sorts. And it was moving along with him, just ahead.

Abe's oxygen-starved brain couldn't make sense of it other than to conclude it was some organic entity related to the phosphorescent glow he'd seen before in tropical seas.

He didn't really care what it was.

He just wanted to race it!

And race it he did. But every time he caught up to the glowing ball, it increased speed and got ahead of him. This caused his competitive instinct to flare up. He pushed himself even more.

He passed the high-rise that marked three miles but kept going. He was determined to beat this stupid fireball. Suddenly, the ball turned left and cut across his path, heading toward the shore. He turned and followed it.

Plowing through the surf, getting back on his feet, and wading onto the beach slowed him down, but it was as if the fireball waited for him. Then it shot up the beach northwards.

He pursued it at the pace he used for long-distance runs. But as it went faster to keep ahead of him, he sped up as well. Soon, he was nearly sprinting. His lungs and legs were burning, but he refused to give up.

Now he was passing it! Had it allowed him to get ahead, or was he really beating it? He didn't care because he was winning. He glanced back. It was only ten feet behind.

Then it stopped. So he did, too. He was the victor!

"Woo-hoo! I win, sucker!" he shouted, as if the fireball could hear him.

The fireball moved toward the dunes and hovered near the end of a dune crossover belonging to a moderately tall building. The sign at the bottom of the steps read, "Private property. Squid Tower residents only."

As he bent over, regaining his wind, hands resting on his legs above his knees, he looked more attentively at the fireball, which hovered now at a height of a couple of stories. It was perfectly round, with a diameter of four or five feet. It was bright, but not so much that he couldn't stare at it. The surface of the ball was smooth with fiery swirls inside. The luminescence throbbed with varying levels of intensity.

It was a bizarre phenomenon. During the race, he had thought of it only as a competitor to be crushed, but now he wondered what exactly it was. Should he be afraid of it?

As if reading his thoughts, the globe drifted closer to him and dropped to the level of his head. It shrank to the size of a basketball, as if to be less threatening.

Inside the globe, within the fire, were the outlines of a human face. Looking at him and smiling. Abe felt himself smiling back.

Then it all went bad.

The ball disappeared and a hard mass slammed into him, knocking him on his back in the sand. A heavy body lay atop him and weighed him down. Despite all his weight training, he didn't have the strength to push the body off him.

Pain flared in the side of his neck. He tried to twist away from it, but something held his head immobile. The weight on top of him felt like the body of a human and he tried again to push it off him, his hands touching hot, slippery tissue.

He could barely breathe. Sharper pain arced through his neck. The creature had bitten him. And it continued to do so, gnawing at his neck with the sounds of grunting and slurping.

He screamed in agony. With every move he made to slip out from underneath, the creature adjusted and held him immobile with its body and limbs.

He'd never been this afraid before. He'd always been in control of his physical well-being, always confident in his body's ability to persevere. For the first time, he was completely powerless.

More grunting and slurping. Panic amid the burning pain. And then dizziness and helplessness and growing despair.

Abe took a faltering breath as the creature lifted its head from his neck, but all he saw in the darkness was a bloody face with blood-stained, sharp teeth, and eyes glowing with the same color as the fireball he had raced.

I beat the stupid fireball, he reflected with pride.

It was the last coherent thought he would ever have.

And the creature sank its teeth into his neck again, grunting and slurping, until his world went black, and he lost the ultimate contest.

17

A REAL BARBARIAN

When Missy arrived at Agnes' condo, the vampire HOA president was taking a bath with the help of a home-health aid from Missy's employer, Acceptance Home Care. The bathroom door was open, and Agnes invited Missy to take a seat in the adjoining master bedroom.

"Did you hear?" Missy asked. "They found another one on the beach."

"Yes, regrettably I did," Agnes said. "The body was right at the end of our dune crossover. The murderer isn't subtle at all in trying to implicate one of us."

"I heard the victim was a young man," Missy said. "His name hasn't been released yet."

"I know. The police were here questioning us. They're getting increasingly aggressive."

Agnes groaned, and water splashed.

"Sometimes I think being immortal is a curse," Agnes said as the home-health aide helped her out of the bathtub and dried her off with a thick white towel. The aide, a sturdy young Haitian-American woman, was gentle in her work.

Agnes didn't hide her nakedness from Missy, as she was used to being attended to by nurses and servants throughout her human and vampire lifetimes. She was slight and frail, not quite five feet tall, and wrinkled from head to toe. The Visigoth tribal tattoos ringing her neck still maintained their vibrancy on the wrinkled flesh. Similarly, there was a presence inside this tiny body greater than the vessel that held it.

Missy grabbed another towel from a bathroom shelf and wrapped Agnes in it as the aide finished.

"Humans who are old and infirm welcome death as a release from suffering," Agnes said. "I was made a vampire just as I was at the point of looking forward to death. I was quite old for that day and age."

"When were you reborn?"

"In the year 497 of the Common Era. I remember like it was yesterday," Agnes said in her hard-to-place European accent. "It was exceptionally rare for anyone to live into their nineties back then, let alone sixties. The Visigoths were good at war and pillaging. Healthcare was not our strong suit. But I came from a wealthy family, so I lived well and had a servant to help me once I had trouble walking."

"Tell me more, please," Missy said, fascinated. "How did your family gain its wealth?"

"The spoils of war. It was the primary way to get rich in those days. No tech start-ups, vulture capitalists, or hedge funds back then. Though the rapaciousness of humans has never changed. I was fortunate my father was a lord of King Theodoric, and my husband was Mauric."

"Who was he?"

"You haven't heard of him? Everyone knew his name back in the day. He was a top general under King Euric. My husband defeated Romans and Franks alike. After he died, I lived with my son's family, and he had enough wealth to afford a servant to care for me in my old age. She helped me like Jeanette here. Even after I was turned, my son cared for me until he died. I then lived with my granddaughter in Hispania, and then my great-grandson's household until the family was scattered by war. I became homeless. It was not easy to be homeless at my age.

"I was finally taken in by a colony of vampires. After the Moors invaded Hispania, we migrated to France and then Germany. There, incredibly, I was found by the vampire who made me, Portia. She took me to live with her in a convent. I lived there for centuries. I was fortunate. The Middle Ages were a very hard time. I might not have survived otherwise."

"The nuns knew you were vampires?" Missy asked.

"Yes. Some of them were as well. Then, when Protestantism spread throughout Germany, many of us in the order moved to Rome, where we joined a large vampire nest in Vatican City. Life was better for me then.

"There I remained until, once again, humans ruined things. When the Fascists took over in the 1920s, some of us fled to New York City. We had enough money to live comfortably, with nurses for those of us who needed them. After the war, the warmth and palm trees of Florida beckoned. And here we are!"

"'We'?"

"A small group of us, a couple from the convent, a few more from Rome. We've stayed together all along. It's the only way we could survive."

"They live here at Squid Tower? Who are they?"

"I can't tell you who they are. It's up to each of them to tell you their own stories, if they choose to do so."

"Is your maker among them?"

A cloud moved over Agnes' eyes. "No. I lost her many years ago. Which is another story for another time."

Missy patted her shoulder. "It must be much more comfortable for you now with all the conveniences today."

"Yes," she laughed darkly. "But it still is a burden to be very old. When I see younger vampires spending eternity at the peak of their physicality, I admit I hate them."

"But didn't your transformation to vampire improve you?"

"It was thrilling to see at night without carrying a torch. My sense of smell became so sensitive that it was torture living in cities with all the unwashed bodies around you and the excrement on the streets. It's better nowadays, but I'm practically asphyxiated whenever I come across a human senior who wears too much perfume because she can't smell it herself. And I can more easily open jars. Now, does it sound like my existence is excellent? Do I not still need Jeanette to help me bathe and dress?"

She had a hint of a smile. Missy patted her hand and gave her a quick medical examination. Agnes had a host of geriatric medical conditions. In humans, these conditions meant your body was gradually failing you. In a vampire, they meant your body was compromised, but it wouldn't get worse. They were just an irritant and, if you've lived with them for hundreds of years, you almost got used to them. Even if Agnes acted as if she hadn't.

"The vampire who made me was younger than I was. I used to resent the fact she chose someone as old as me. But I shortly realized when you're a very old vampire, the only humans you can catch are the ones who are older than you."

"Fortunately, these days you have the Blood Bus."

"And, since I moved to Florida, lots and lots of old humans are in easy reach."

Missy let that one go. But thoughts of the murders arose in her mind.

"Are you absolutely convinced no one from Squid Tower preyed upon the man who was just found on the beach?" she asked. "Or any of the others?"

"Human murderers make stupid mistakes. Vampires don't. Our instincts are too strong to risk endangering our community. No, I don't believe one of our residents is responsible. A vampire from somewhere else? It's possible, but one of us would have sensed he or she was here, invading our territory."

"I was told that in the early days of the Squid Tower colony, human residents were taken."

"By stupid vampires who are no longer with us."

"No longer with us? You mean killed, or forced to move away?"

"Whatever it took to rid us of them," Agnes said.

"The night gate guard told me he saw Mr. Schwartz stalking young women at the ice cream shop. Some of the people who disappeared were last seen there."

"Leo is notorious for his sweet tooth. But as a board member, he wouldn't be stupid enough to prey so close to home."

"When I binge-eat a tub of ice cream, it's pretty stupid," Missy said. "But I can't help myself. Sometimes I think sugar is a drug."

"Even if Leo ignored his best judgement, I can't believe he

would feed to the point of killing. Vampires aren't monsters, do you understand? We need sustenance just like anyone else. We take as much blood from our prey as we need without killing them and only kill if the victim was a threat to us."

"Only then?"

"I admit when a vampire is near starvation, he might be unable to stop himself from draining prey to the point of death. Often, then, the vampire will use his own blood to turn the dead prey into a vampire. When practical, of course, because it's a great responsibility to re-make someone. You must help them through their transition period. You become, in essence, their parent or guardian."

"Maybe vampires are smarter than humans," Missy said, "but they begin as humans, right? They keep most of their personality, right? Good parts and bad?"

"Yes. Of course. All their personality."

"Well, there are bad people out there, sociopaths and psychopaths and plain jerks. I'm sure it's the same with vampires."

"Yes. There are those who choose an evil path."

"Wouldn't they just kill their prey without guilt? Especially if they don't want a witness who could report them?"

"We have ways of mesmerizing our prey so they don't remember the attack."

"I know. But are you sure the memory is permanently erased?"

"Not necessarily," Agnes said quietly.

"It's something to consider. The vampire could be ignoring the rules. Because he or she doesn't want witnesses and doesn't care at all about the victims. Because he or she is just a bad guy. Bad vampire, I mean."

Missy didn't need to say, because everyone knew the biggest vampire jerk in Squid Tower was Schwartz.

"The gate guard also told me he witnessed Schwartz attack a plumber in the lobby. He reported it, but his boss told him to keep it quiet."

Agnes sighed. "Yes. We had to deal with the incident. The security company passes on that kind of information to the board. Plus, the homeowner kept complaining about the plumber not showing up and then the plumbing company started calling our management company. Fortunately, the plumber wasn't killed, and Schwartz mesmerized him to forget the incident. Schwartz was fined and given a warning."

Agnes made it clear the topic was finished. But when Missy looked into her eyes, she realized they both suspected Schwartz.

18

ENTITIES MOST FOUL, PART ONE

Missy left Agnes' condo around 3:00 a.m. which was nice, since she often didn't get off work until close to dawn. She looked forward to relaxing at home. But as she drove through the gate, Bernie, the geeky gate guard, flagged her down. She stopped and rolled down her window.

"What's up?" she asked, trying to hide her annoyance.

"Hi, miss . . ." he seemed to have forgotten her name.

"Missy."

"Miss Missy, thanks again for the charm. But I'm still worried about Mr. Schwartz. He really wants to kill me."

"Have you asked your boss about working a day shift?"

"There are no openings. I'm working this shift because no one else wants it. Who would? Besides, the owner of the company is a vampire, and he doesn't have much sympathy for me."

"I'm sorry to hear that."

"I just know Schwartz is the murderer everyone has been talking about."

"It's a possibility. But remember, it's our job to protect the residents here, so we can't go spreading rumors that give our residents unwelcome attention. The police are investigating, and we must let their investigation take its course."

"But Schwartz knows I saw him at the ice cream shop. He's going to want to get rid of me. Don't you think I should call the police?"

"If you do, and they question him, then he's going to know who tipped them off."

Bernie scratched his head and swallowed hard. "Yeah, I guess."

She wondered if maybe he should go to the police. Protecting the residents from being revealed as vampires is one thing. Shielding a murderer from justice was another.

"Look, Bernie, it's up to you if you want to speak to the police or not. But the least I can do is cast a protection spell for you."

His face brightened. "That would be awesome!"

So much for relaxing after work, she thought.

She backed up her car and swung around into the visitor lot. She returned to the guardhouse with her tote bag of witchcraft supplies: her oils, charms, essential herbs, and other ingredients, all stowed in Tupperware and plastic baggies. Bernie opened the door for her, but she didn't go in. It was too confining for two in there.

"I'm going to cast a protection spell. It will work in the guardhouse to make you safe when you're inside. I don't know how to do a protection spell that's bound to you personally, so it won't help you when you leave the guardhouse. But hopefully, the amulet you're wearing will do that. Now, get out and let me do my work."

"Just so you know," Bernie said, "I've already tried putting cloves of garlic all over in there, but the cleaning crew always throws them out."

They traded places, and she set her tote bag on Bernie's desk, closing the door. A set of rosary beads with a crucifix hanging from the doorknob rattled. She sat in his chair. She was ready.

Now, if she could only remember how to do this.

She pulled out her notepad and flipped to the page where she had taken notes on casting the spell from a grimoire. It was basically a list of instructions and ingredients—a recipe for magick. She had been getting better at harnessing her power to perform magick mentally, such as moving objects with her mind. Conjuring an advanced spell that lasts for a long time without her attention, such as a protection spell, is something she still struggled with. Earth magick, enhancing her powers with those found in the earth via natural ingredients and incantations, enabled her to do it.

She had been making great progress, but she still had a lot of work to do.

Cinnamon sticks, fennel, bay leaves, garlic, ivy—these were all supposed to offer protection or ward off evil. Using her intuition, she added what felt like the right amount of each ingredient to a small copper bowl, pricked her finger with a sewing needle, and squeezed a drop of blood upon the mix. She stirred it all together and put the potpourri into a sandwich baggie, which she placed on the windowsill above the desk.

She used chalk to draw a magick circle on the floor—a small one, because of the closet-like size of the room—then drew a pentagram within it, its points representing the five elements of earth, air, fire, water, and spirit. Next, she went about the mental exercises required to close the circle, gather her energies within it, and cast the spell.

She cleared her mind and focused on her intent: banning Schwartz or anyone from entering this structure to cause harm. She sat silently, going into an alpha mind-state, being in the zone. Then she began a slow, rhythmic rocking of her upper body to raise energy from the earth, focusing on the doorway and windows, visualizing them permanently sealed against harmful forces and—

"You almost done?"

Bernie was looking in through the opened door.

"I'm a little nervous standing out there," he said. "I'm too exposed."

Her concentration shattered, Missy stared at him before words came to her.

"Do you mind? I'm trying to cast your spell."

"Sorry." He shut the door.

Jeez, where was I? She tried to clear her mind of the angry thoughts about how annoying Bernie was. It wasn't easy. After doing some breathing exercises to relax, she once more reached a meditative state and recited the spell she had created:

"Protect this space from evil deeds," she intoned.

"And give this man the peace he needs,

"Expel all entities most foul,

"Like—"

The door opened.

"Schwartz is out there," Bernie said, breathless. "He's watching me. Are you done yet?"

"Yes. I'm done. I'm so friggin' done." She gathered up her things.

"It's safe in here now?"

"I have no idea. Let me know. I'll be curious to hear."

19

THROUGH VAMPIRE EYES

Missy's spell-casting session in the guardhouse was mostly likely a bust, but it gave her an idea. Could magick find the true killer? No, magick didn't work like that; it didn't give you omniscient God-like powers. Instead, it worked in smaller ways, tied to the physical properties and energies of the earth.

But it could, she supposed, keep tabs on certain suspects. Namely, Schwartz.

She had the evening off and spent it in front of the fireplace of her 1940s-era Florida bungalow, curled up on the couch with the half dozen grimoires she'd collected since becoming interested in witchcraft.

One grimoire was a massive, leather-bound tome with a brass lock and vellum pages. It must have been over two hundred years old, found at a yard sale on a folding table next to super-soakers and old dolls. How it ended up in a suburban home was beyond her. Her other grimoires were more recent reprints, some more useful than others. The spells found in this one for summoning demons probably didn't work. At least she hoped they didn't.

A spell from the old grimoire caught her attention. It was called "The Wandering Eye," but it had a different meaning than the ophthalmological disorder. The spell gave the sorcerer who cast it the ability to see beyond his or her own eyesight by becoming attached to another individual's sight. It was essentially like a GPS tracker, allowing you to see where this individual went.

It called for a variety of herbs and natural ingredients that Missy had on hand or could get in the botanica. One of which, dirt from a zombie's grave, had just been stocked in Aisle Four.

The only difficult ingredient was a lock of your subject's hair. It didn't help that Schwartz was mostly bald, except for the lower hemisphere of his head, and was possibly the most cantankerous subject she could have chosen.

Vampires' hair doesn't grow, so she couldn't swipe it from his barber. It would be unethical to pluck his hairs during a physical exam. Although it was tempting to pluck those unsightly ear hairs. And just as vampire hair doesn't grow, stray hairs don't fall out as they do with humans, making her task even harder.

She would have to find another way.

An idea came to her while she was wrapping up the latest meeting of the creative writing group. Bill finally finished reading a not-so-short story about a heavily armed vampire—who sounded a lot like him—who single-handedly took on the Chinese army in a plot more far-fetched than the most ridiculous action movie.

Agnes marched into the room carrying a whiteboard.

"Sorry to barge in," she said. "The board of directors has a budget workshop in an hour."

Missy turned to pick up her tote bag packed with the group's printed-out stories, when her eye caught her baseball cap she had shoved in the bag.

Two strands of hair were caught in the Velcro of the cap's adjustable rear closure.

Velcro, she thought. That's the ticket!

Glancing at her watch, she saw that Mega-Mart would still be open. She ran out of Squid Tower faster than if a vampire had been chasing her.

When she returned to the community room after her errand, the whiteboard was resting on an easel, but no one was sitting at the table yet. She removed the package of white Velcro strips from her Mega-Mart bag. The hook-and-loop fastener was backed by self-adhesive tape, allowing her to stick a length of the hook side across the top of the board. You could hardly tell it was there.

Missy took a seat in the small group of spectator chairs facing the Board of Directors' table.

"You really want to sit through this boring nonsense?" Schwartz asked her as he and the others filed in and took a seat at the table.

He was right. Missy nearly fell asleep during the discussion about the landscaping company until Agnes snapped at Schwartz.

"No, we will not impale the landscaping crew for waking you up with their blowers," she said. She finished writing numbers on the whiteboard and sat down. Schwartz grumbled.

Missy decided it was time to act.

The whiteboard was right behind Schwartz's seat. Missy

focused on the top of the board and used her telekinesis to move it.

It tipped forward and fell off the easel, its top edge hitting the back of Schwartz's head, below his bald spot.

"Ouch! Did you do that?" he demanded of Agnes.

"Of course not."

"Stupid, cheap easel," he muttered.

Missy rushed over to him. "All you all right? Let me examine your scalp."

"Don't touch me!" Schwartz waved her off. "I'm going to sue everyone in this room!"

"You'll be fine," Missy said. "You didn't even get a scratch."

No one noticed when Missy reached to the floor and removed the white hairs stuck to the strip of Velcro.

SCHWARTZ'S HAIR had a sharp smell when burned, like human hair does, but his reminded Missy of moldering earth. She pushed that thought from her mind as she continued with casting the spell: tending the fire in the brass bowl with the hair, mint, dried hemlock, and shredded pieces of paper from her previous year's tax returns. The bowl was with her inside a magick circle on her kitchen floor, white tea candles burning at each of the five points of a pentagram.

She recited the words of the incantation, found in the grimoire—a mixture of Latin and Hebrew.

Suddenly, her vision dimmed. Replacing it was the view of someone looking at a television set, the old boxy kind that even thrift stores won't accept anymore. On the set was a woman's beach volleyball match. A hand came into view, holding a remote. It was an old, gnarled hand with white hairs on the backs of the fingers.

It was Schwartz's hand. She was seeing through his eyes. The spell was working.

Night had fallen, and Schwartz would go about his nightly routine, including hunting for a meal. She hoped to see if he would feed on a human, and if so, if it would be too near Squid Tower.

This would be an experiment, like when someone puts a tiny video camera on their cat and discovers the surprising places the feline goes when left unsupervised.

So, Missy watched. And waited. And waited some more.

Apparently, Schwartz spent most of his time planted in front of the TV. With a sinking feeling, Missy realized this experiment could take much longer than she'd imagined. Good thing she saved some hair for future spell castings.

At last, Schwartz rose from his couch and wandered out onto his balcony. There was a nice view of the moon over the ocean, but his eyes were fixated on a balcony two apartments over.

Faint notes of a violin drifted over, barely audible above the drone of the surf.

"Turn that music down!" Schwartz shouted. "Young vamps these days and their crazy music," he muttered to himself. "I hate that hippie Beethoven. No respect for the classics."

He returned inside, went into his bedroom, and pulled on shorts and a shirt that were lying on a chair. Fortunately, there wasn't a mirror anywhere, so Missy was spared a view of Schwartz dressing. He stepped into a pair of sandals, grabbed a key fob from his dresser, and left the condo.

At last, she thought, he's off to hunt.

Um, no. He went down to the mailroom near the lobby and grabbed a stack of coupon books from a table. Now he was flipping through the books, tearing out multiple copies of the same coupons.

Missy was bored already. Was this what retirement was like? How could Schwartz endure this for eternity?

Finally, he shuffled to the parking garage. Now, the adventure would begin.

Or so she thought. Schwartz drove to Mega-Mart, removed a cane from the back seat, and put it in a shopping cart. Which was odd, since she didn't know him to use a cane. She endured forty-five minutes of him shuffling through the store, collecting random items, without using the cane. Adult diapers and a rubber snake? Bubble bath? She cringed at the thought of the old vampire soaking in his tub.

Finally, he paid and left the store. But as he was walking out, his eyes followed a chubby man munching on a candy bar, pushing a cart into the parking lot. Schwartz followed him. Missy tensed, anticipating the predator's attack.

Schwartz avoided the pools of light from the parking lot lights as he stalked the man with the candy bar. With his vampire vision, he saw the man in perfect detail, even as his prey walked through shadows.

Missy didn't want to watch what was going to happen, but she had no choice.

Schwartz pulled the cane from his cart and started using it. With lightning speed, he shot in front of the man, then slowed down, pushing his cart with one hand and tapping his cane on the asphalt unsteadily with his other, until the man caught up.

"Can I help you to your car, sir?" the man asked, his mouth still full of chocolate.

"I'm just a little unsteady on my feet after my surgery," Schwartz said, affecting a feeble voice. "It's the Lexus over there."

Releasing his own cart, the man took Schwartz's and offered his arm. Schwartz clutched it for support. The Good Samaritan led the vampire to his car and continued supporting him as he slowly eased into the front seat.

"Please put my bags in the passenger seat," Schwartz said.

As the man leaned in to place the bags, Schwartz turned toward him.

"You will feel no pain and forget you ever saw me."

Schwartz's head shot forward like a cobra's, and Missy saw a close-up of the man's jawline. Just as quickly, Schwartz pulled away, leaving two bloody puncture wounds in the man's neck.

"Thank you so much, young man."

The victim closed the passenger door and left without a word.

When Schwartz arrived at the gate of Squid Tower, the arm went up, but Schwartz didn't drive through. He rolled down his window and gestured at the gate guard.

Bernie stepped out and approached the car nervously.

Schwartz tossed the rubber snake from Mega-Mart into Bernie's face. The guard screamed like a four-year-old, clawing frantically at the toy.

Schwartz drove through the gate, cackling with demonic glee.

Okay, Missy thought, I know Schwartz hunts his prey instead of using the Blood Bus. But will he attack someone near the Squid Tower property?

Sure enough, after puttering around in his condo, Schwartz

changed into his bathing suit and flip-flops and carried a towel downstairs.

When he reached the pool, he halted. A vampire water aerobics class was in session, and all but the deep end was filled with elderly women in one-piece bathing suits doing exercises with floats. Schwartz muttered a curse and circled the pool, heading for the beach.

The sand, of course, was deserted. He dropped his towel and waded into the surf. Just past the breakers, he paddled around, then floated on his back, his belly protruding above the surface like a white humpback whale. Finally, he left the water and toweled off.

His eyes snapped to a dark object far down the beach. It was a human walking toward him. Missy sensed his predatory instincts coming alive.

Schwartz walked toward the human. It was a young woman dressed in street clothes, carrying her shoes in one hand. As she got closer to Schwartz, it became apparent that her gait was unsteady due to intoxication.

Missy's heartbeat picked up. The woman fit the profile of the recent victims. Was there anything she could do to stop Schwartz? She tried to send mental impulses to distract him.

"Hey, young lady," Schwartz said. "Nice evening, isn't it?"

The woman smiled and nodded, but looked concerned. She passed Schwartz quickly.

He turned and caught up with her.

"What's a lovely lady like you doing promenading along the beach without a fella?"

"I'm meeting my boyfriend at a condo up there," she said in a faint Hispanic accent.

"When I was your age, my sweetheart needed a chaperone whenever we promenaded or went on a buggy ride."

"Leave me alone, boomer. You creep."

Missy tried to interrupt Schwartz's thoughts.

Leave her alone!

Something shifted. Schwartz turned to stare at the water, and Missy's vision faded.

He's aware of me, Missy realized.

"Who's there?" Schwartz whispered.

Her vision faded to a milky fog. Then two burning red eyes appeared in the fog. They grew larger.

"Who are you?"

Missy realized she needed to break the spell, but felt paralyzed. Somehow, Schwartz was mesmerizing her, though she was miles away.

"Do I know you? I think I do."

Suddenly, Missy was back on the floor of her kitchen among the flickering tea candles.

Her cats had wandered into the magic circle, crossing the circumference, and breaking the spell. They were hungry, brushing up against her sides.

"Thanks," she said. "You'll get some extra treats tonight."

THE NEXT DAY, Missy scoured the news in every channel and format, looking for a mention of a woman's body found on the beach. Fortunately, she found nothing.

But in the meantime, she worried if Schwartz knew it had been her spell that invaded his head.

20

WOLVES AT THE DOOR

Agnes sat alone in the clubhouse's card room overlooking the swimming pool. It was designed with floor-to-ceiling windows to maximize the natural light, not that the current residents appreciated it. Agnes knew the room would be empty because it was early in the night and most residents were out hunting or waiting in line at the Blood Bus, which had just arrived.

The large, red, bus-style RV was the kind that showed up in shopping center parking lots or at public events. A banner promised free movie tickets if you donated a pint. After stocking up on the wholesome blood of generous humanitarians, the bus crew would park at a warehouse, killing time until sunset. Then it would head to the beach and pull into Squid Tower, attracting residents like kids running to an ice cream truck.

Henrietta rolled into the room on her mobility scooter. She was Agnes' child, meaning Agnes had turned her into a vampire. It happened in Brooklyn, back in 1974, a time of hunger in the nest, and Henrietta had a leg disability, making her easier for Agnes to catch.

Henrietta brought two bags of blood from the bus for their supper. She warmed them in the microwave in the nearby kitchen area, piercing each one with a straw before rolling over to her maker.

"I got us O-Positive tonight," she said as they each sipped their dinner.

"Was it collected at the strip mall with the Thai restaurant?" Agnes asked.

"Oh yes, you must be right. I detect hints of tamarind and ginger."

"Delicious. So, let's get down to business," Agnes said. "Do you have anything to report?"

Henrietta was not on the condo association board, but as the community's most prolific busybody, she always had valuable gossip to share. She was Agnes' eyes and ears. And the community's undisputed authority on who was shtupping whom.

"Leonard Schwartz is on the warpath," Henrietta replied.

"Isn't he always? Who is the target of his wrath this time?"

"You."

"What did I do now? He wants to be president, I know. But my term isn't up until the end of the year."

"He wants you removed through a recall vote. He blames you for the scrutiny we've been getting since the mayor's daughter was killed and says you haven't done enough to protect us."

"What can I do?" Agnes asked, as her annoyance heated up. "What can anyone do?"

"Well, for one, he thinks you're too chummy with the werewolves next door. He thinks one of them killed the humans and tried to make it look like we did it. And he believes the were-wolves are cooperating with the police."

"He's entitled to his theory but needs to leave us out of it."

"He says we should go to war with the werewolves."

"A vampire-werewolf war? That would be catastrophic."

"Oh, Agnes, dear," Henrietta said, patting her friend on the arm. "You've been reading too many urban fantasy novels. Schwartz means our lawyer should go to war with theirs. Hit them with a big lawsuit over the swain they're not irrigating properly. Threaten even more lawsuits. Basically, intimidate with litigation."

"In my day, 'war' meant swords and flaming arrows."

"You have to adapt to the times, Agnes."

"I know. But every century it just gets harder."

"Well, I think Schwartz is trying to deflect our attention to the werewolves and away from himself," Henrietta said. "The reason he's being so difficult is—and don't tell anyone—but I hear the police questioned him in the parking lot the other night."

"As well they should."

"And he's not happy about it. He wants to know who gave his name to them."

"Oh, I wouldn't know," Agnes said.

Henrietta studied her face for a moment. "Well, if Schwartz drained those people, what do we do? We can't let him be arrested. The police would find out awfully fast he's a vampire, and then what will become of us?"

Agnes hobbled over to the trash can and threw away her empty blood bag.

"We have two choices," she said. "We can look the other way

when he's arrested and hope the police believe he's the only vampire here—hope they don't sniff around and look for more."

No one spoke for a while.

"I've heard," Henrietta said in a low voice, "some police know about vampires—unofficially, that is. But if they've ever responded to a crime in some way involving a vampire, they've never taken one into custody. Somehow, a vampire has never made it to a jail."

"I know. Extrajudicial killings. We can't allow that to happen."

"Then what is our second choice?"

"We can act preemptively and dispose of Schwartz ourselves, so the police never get their hands on him," Agnes said. "It would not be an easy decision to make."

"How would that make us better than the police?"

"Because he is one of us. And if he has broken our code of justice, we have the right to mete out punishment. It's for the greater good of our community."

"Okay. The murders will stop, but the police will still believe the killer is out there. What if they arrest an innocent member of our community?"

"I'm still hoping Schwartz isn't the killer and the police find out who it is," Agnes said, standing with the aid of her four-footed quad cane. "I have a meeting with Harry Roarke about the accusations a werewolf committed the murders and drained the blood to implicate a vampire. Who knows where this trail will lead?"

HARRY ROARKE LOOKED like his anger was only barely contained. He glared at Agnes with a reddened face, which was a little unsettling since he was twice her size. She had her vampire strength, but it only went so far when your body was ninety-two years old and four-foot, eleven inches tall standing straight, and when was the last time she was able to stand straight?

"Who is spreading rumors a werewolf is to blame for the killings?" he asked. "Schwartz?"

"More people than him."

"Vampires aren't people," Roarke said.

Agnes ignored the insult. Yes, vampires were people, though they were no longer human.

"Our human staff members have made comments as well," she said.

"Well, it doesn't make sense. When werewolves kill, we leave bodies mostly eaten or at least badly mauled. The body wouldn't look the slightest bit like the ones that have been found. It really stretches logic to think a werewolf would kill a bunch of people in a completely unnatural way for us, all just to frame a vampire."

"That's not what's being alleged," Agnes said in a firm voice. "Someone living here, while in human form, could have killed those people. Why, I don't know. Maybe it's a psychopath. But this individual did it in a manner to deflect attention elsewhere."

"If he was in human form, why not a random human from anywhere? Why a werewolf?"

"It was someone who knows vampires live in Squid Tower. Only a few humans know that and we're keeping an eye on them. However, a lot of the werewolves living here know about us."

Harry grunted. "What would you want me to do about this?"

"Be vigilant. If you do nothing—if all of us do nothing—the police will intrude upon our lives and endanger us all. It's a barely concealed secret that Seaweed Manor lets in all sorts of outsiders."

"We're human beings who have a disorder. But we still enjoy social lives, having parties, inviting guests."

They were meeting in a large common room in Building B of Seaweed Manor. Two fifty-something women played ping-pong on the other end of the room, drinking beer, and cursing like Visigoth warriors.

"You have drug dealers in your community," Agnes said, leaning toward him, her small fingers laced together on the table. "That's a major security risk. It brings stupid humans here late at night who get high and end up dead on the beach."

"Then you, too, are one of the vampires spreading the rumors blaming werewolves?"

"I have no interest in rumors unless they involve matters that endanger my community. And endanger yours, too. Why do you tolerate drug dealers?"

Roarke sighed. "It's complicated. Our people have always been about tolerance and inclusiveness. We're not a bunch of scolds who judge others."

"Surely your bylaws allow you to kick out residents who break the law?"

"Which would include almost all of us. Yeah, drug dealing is bad, but half our residents are their customers. Plus, we have smugglers, tax cheats, fraudsters, alimony delinquents, bail-skippers, witness protection program members—you name it," he said. "Why are you looking at me like that? Vampires sure as hell aren't angels, either."

"This conversation isn't going the way I had hoped. We need to work together, Harry. If the murderer lives in either of our communities, we need to find out and take action before the police do."

"Fine. Are you doing anything about Schwartz?"

"We've put him under surveillance every night, ever since the mayor's daughter was murdered."

"Really?" he sounded impressed.

"Yes, though we should have started much sooner. We have a couple of residents who are retired law enforcement and military, so they know what they're doing. I help them out myself sometimes."

Roarke didn't hide his smirk at the last part, but he promised to keep a close watch on, and hopefully discourage, the drug dealing. He also promised to order the gate guards to keep lists of all visitors, an area in which they were notoriously lax.

Agnes didn't mention that her helping with surveillance also included monitoring the beach and Seaweed Manor. She didn't trust the werewolves to police themselves. And with her little-old-lady appearance, she could wander about without attracting attention.

In fact, after she left the meeting with Roarke, she walked with the aid of her quad cane down the breezeway of every floor of the two buildings, looking for anything suspicious. Several apparent visitors came and went from condos. She was dismayed by how little privacy the complex had. The following evening would be a full moon. How would the residents shifting into werewolf form keep from being observed?

After Building B, she explored A, which was easy since the lobby entrance was not locked. She walked the breezeways. And on the third floor she found one of the problem residents: a condo with an open door and a line of people standing in front of it.

She listened with her vampire hearing, which wasn't as keen as that enjoyed by a vampire in a thirty-year-old's body but was way better than a typical human's.

"I heard he has Reboot. He better not run out before it's my turn."

"He's the only dealer in the county who has it."

The two people were a man and woman, young adults, a bit scruffy looking. She guessed they may have flunked out of one of South Florida's many drug rehabilitation centers. Agnes hid in the shadows at the end of the hall and waited. Vampires are great at hiding, especially if you're less than five feet tall and weigh under 100 pounds.

The young man emerged from the condo first and lingered nearby. The people waiting in line eyed him hungrily. One asked if the dealer still had Reboot and the man replied that there was plenty. Soon, the young woman exited and headed toward the elevator. The young man caught up with her.

"Hey, want to do a little Reboot with me on the beach?" he asked. "It's safer to have someone with you, you know, when you're really tripping."

"I was going to take it at home with my boyfriend."

The young man wasn't the least concerned about her boyfriend. "You can take it with him later, but can you hang out with me for just a little right now? I don't want to do it alone. I love to take it on the beach. It's such a peaceful rush."

The young woman agreed. Perhaps she didn't have a

boyfriend at home after all. While they waited for the elevator, Agnes hobbled carefully down the stairs, stopping at the ground floor to lean on her cane and rest. When she went outside, the young man and woman were walking over the dune crossover and down to the beach. She followed them only as far as the crest of the dunes and waited there.

It was a beautiful night. The nearly full moon bathed the beach in soft light and glittered upon the lines of surf rolling in. A steady southeast breeze brought a rich saltwater smell and a faint suggestion of the island spices of the Bahamas. With her keen hearing, she listened over the rumbling of the waves as the young couple spoke inanities. She guessed they were lying on the sand just on the other side of the dunes, slightly to the south. Which put them close to Squid Tower. Soon, their voices became slurred and there were long stretches of silence, punctuated by giggles and soft moans of pleasure. How long did effects of this drug last? Agnes wondered.

She sensed a presence nearby. A vampire. A dark figure stood on the Squid Tower dune crossover, roughly the same distance from the beach as she was. Dark eyes glowed as the vampire noticed her.

A bright flash caught her eye. An orb of light like a giant firefly rose from the beach south of where the young couple was and flew by, heading north. She had no idea what it was.

"Whoa!" the young man said. "Did you see that? Totally intense!"

"Was it a hallucination?" his new friend asked.

"Dude, yeah! What else? I hope it happens again."

"Wait, if it was a hallucination, how come we both saw it?" the woman asked.

"Dude, you're messing with my head. Just go with it."

Agnes walked through the Seaweed Manor parking lot and cut through the opening in the border hedge to the Squid Tower property. She passed through the lobby and out to the dune crossover.

Schwartz stood at the top of the steps looking down at her.

"What were you doing next door?" he asked.

"What are you doing *here*? Were you stalking those young people on the beach?"

"I'm taking in the night's beauty," Schwartz said. "Since when has that been against the bylaws?"

"No one said it was. Hunting on or near our property is a different story."

"When is this going to stop, Agnes? Am I going to be accused of breaking the bylaws every time I wander outside my condo?"

"You may choose not to believe it, but I'm trying to protect you."

"No, I don't believe it. You know I want you removed from the board. Getting me arrested on trumped-up charges would be a perfect way to stop me."

Over the course of many centuries, Agnes had learned how to control her temper. But Schwartz was really getting to her. She resisted the urge to call him a barbarian, her most vicious insult because though she was born into a noble family, the Romans used to call her and her people barbarians.

"Listen to me, dimwit," she said. "I don't care about your petty machinations with the board. Go ahead and have me recalled. No one would vote for you as president, anyway."

Schwartz waved a hand dismissively.

She continued, "And if the police catch you, they won't arrest you. They'll stake you. Yes, they'll stake you on the spot.

Some of them know vampires exist and they're executing us with no pretense of justice, killing us like cockroaches."

Schwartz's mouth dropped open.

"It's true," Agnes said. "So even if you're the most innocent vampire walking the earth, you'd better be careful. No more stalking young people. Stay away from the ice cream shop. Lie low until these murders are solved."

"Can't I visit the beach?" Schwartz asked.

"Frankly, I wouldn't advise it."

21

UNDER SCRUTINY

The morning sun slanted between the two buildings of Seaweed Manor when Missy left after completing her werewolf patient appointments. She cut through the gap in the border hedge and entered the Squid Tower visitor lot, where she had left her car. And then she saw him.

Affird was prowling around the property, pretending to be ambling casually while constantly glancing around, looking for something. She walked quickly to intercept him.

"Good morning, detective," she said with a fake smile. "What brings you here today? Any developments in the case?"

He stopped and studied her without a trace of an expression. She observed her reflection in his mirror shades. Her hair looked awful. So did the bags under her eyes.

"I can't discuss the case," he said.

"Can I help you with anything here?"

"No. I was here to talk to residents, but no one is answering their door. No one is around anywhere. It's dead here."

She studied him. Was his double entendre intentional? She couldn't tell; he apparently wore a poker face his entire life. He had probably been the only poker-faced baby in existence.

"There are plenty of cars in the lot and the parking garage," he said. "Do people here really sleep this late? I thought seniors get up early."

"Last night was Bingo Night. I'm sure they're all exhausted."

"When I've come here at night, there were always people around," he said.

"You've heard the slogan, 'active senior lifestyle'? The seniors here really believe in it. They're very active and it makes them young at heart. They're like teenagers—staying up late, sleeping late."

He stared at her. His expression was illegible, but she didn't think he was buying her nonsense.

"And the fact is," Missy said, making it up as she went along, "there really aren't many people here this season. That's why so many of the hurricane shutters are closed."

He glanced up at the tower. "Then why are there so many cars here?"

"Well, the snowbirds fly to Florida and leave a car here to use. The year-round residents, if they're married, have two cars. And some auto enthusiasts have extras."

He shook his head. "Excuse me, I want to find a resident to speak with."

"Let me take you to Agnes, the board president. She's an early riser." A night-owl was more like it. "Please follow me."

"She and I have already met," he said.

He followed her into the lobby and up the elevator to the eighth floor and Agnes' unit on the end. Missy pressed the doorbell. She knew the vampire was checking out her visitors through the doorbell camera.

Agnes answered the door wearing her usual outfit of a conservative dark-gray, matching pants suit. It wasn't exactly typical Florida resort wear. She smiled. Her fangs were retracted and safely out of sight.

"Good morning, Ms. Geberich," he said.

"Detective Affird, to what do I owe this pleasure?"

"Your bad luck, I guess. I was in the neighborhood and decided to poke around."

"Come in, please."

He followed Missy into the apartment. It was dimly lit by a couple of lamps and the heavy curtains were closed. The furnishings were spare but high-end. Though she was the daughter of a wealthy Visigoth nobleman, much of Agnes' time after she'd been made a vampire had been spent in poverty. Somehow, she had clawed her way out of it, and then some. Having an infinite time horizon is definitely an advantage when investing.

"Please sit down," Agnes said, gesturing toward an antique settee. She sat in a Queen Anne armchair. It was low enough to the ground to not make her look so short. "Can I get you some water?"

"No thanks. I won't take much of your time," Affird said, still standing, still wearing his shades.

Missy sat down on the couch, out of the way.

"When did you move here?" Affird asked Agnes.

"In 1981. I've loved it the entire time."

"I was looking at the records from the property appraiser's office. Lots of current residents bought units here when the building was constructed in the 1960s."

Agnes nodded.

"Those residents must be really old now," Affird said.

"Oh, we do have some oldsters here. But those who bought at the beginning were investing prior to retirement. Pre-construction prices are impossible to beat."

"Uh-huh. I did a little cross-checking of names and I found out some residents here bought property in the area even before Squid Tower existed. Leonard Schwartz, for instance, bought a bungalow in town in 1921. Which is odd. Even if he somehow bought it as a child, that would make him well over a hundred years old."

"I'm sure it's a different person by the same name," Agnes said.

"I checked public records, and it appears to be the same Schwartz—from Brooklyn, New York."

"It's probably his father or grandfather."

Affird ran a bony hand through this thick hair. "Don't think so, though I'd have to do more research to be sure. But there are more examples of other homeowners like him."

"Detective, please give me the courtesy of forthrightness. Why are you here today? Do you suspect a resident here of murdering the mayor's daughter?"

He frowned. "I can't comment on the investigation. But there's this impression we're only investigating the murder because it's the mayor's daughter. The fact is, there have been several victims and disappearances associated with this stretch of the beach and A1A. I've been investigating them all along. And I will be forthright with you. It's very odd that so many incidents have clustered around your community."

"Then you suspect one of us is a killer?"

Affird stared at Agnes for an uncomfortably long time, his eyes hidden behind the shades, his face unreadable.

"I do," he said. "Maybe more than one of you."

"I see," Agnes said. She sounded sincerely surprised, but Missy wasn't. Missy had feared the police were homing in on Squid Tower.

Agnes asked, "Is there someone in particular?"

"I can't divulge that. I've already said more than I meant to."

"I hope you've considered the possibility that a killer could have lured his victims here to cast suspicion on the residents instead of on himself," Missy said.

"But why Squid Tower?" Affird asked. "And why make the deaths look like a vampire did them?"

Missy wished she hadn't asked the question.

"Like I said before, I can't get my head around the odd hours you people keep here," Affird said. "You know, the department gets constant noise complaints late at night—"

"Regarding the people next door," Agnes said. "At Seaweed Manor. They're stuck in adolescence."

"Yes, I know about them. But we get complaints about here, too, from your neighbors on the other side. Horns honking all night, arguments on the pickleball courts, someone playing the bagpipes at four in the morning."

"That's Duncan," Agnes said to Missy. "Remind me to talk to him."

"Ms. Geberich," Affird said, frustration in his voice. "Why are your drapes closed at this time of day?"

"I have an eye condition. I'm overly sensitive to light."

"It's odd you'd live in the Sunshine State."

"I love the warmth."

He was at a loss for words. Then he reached into his shirt

and withdrew a crucifix on a chain. "This was my late wife's. I was having a debate with a friend about whether it's silver or platinum. What do you guys think?"

He removed it and offered it to Agnes, watching her closely.

Agnes held it in her hands, examining it. "Sterling silver, I'd say. It's beautiful."

Affird took it back, looking defeated. "Thanks. My friend was right." He moved to the door. "I won't waste any more of your time. Have a nice day."

After he left, Agnes said, "That man is becoming a big problem."

"Yes. He knows or suspects too much for comfort," Missy said. "I have a question. The crucifix? I thought—"

"Silly folklore. Why would being undead make you fear a symbol of any religion—Jewish, Muslim, Hindu, whatever? Just so you know, I converted to Christianity from paganism over fifteen hundred years ago, so don't you dare think a crucifix is going to scare me. And silver has never bothered me."

"So, what are we going to do about Affird?" Missy asked. "You realize he could arrest one of us at any moment?"

"One of *us*?"

"Just because I don't live here and I'm not a vampire doesn't mean I'm not part of this community," Missy said, trying to keep her eyes from tearing.

"And, indeed, you are, child. We depend on your medical care and all your support in so many ways. We are truly fond of you."

"Thank you. I wasn't begging for a compliment, but I am very worried things could go much worse than an arrest. There could be large-scale raids on this place. Then they would massacre everyone. Out of the public's eye, of course. And does anyone here have human relatives who are still alive who would try to find out why their great-grandma disappeared? I doubt it. This attack on us could happen any day now, any moment, if this case remains open. I'm not being hyperbolic."

"I know," Agnes said. "We need to give the police a reason to leave us alone."

"Yeah, by finding the actual killer."

When Missy left Squid Tower, she passed an SUV parked illegally on the shoulder of A1A. A man was using binoculars pointed toward Squid Tower.

It was Affird. And Missy believed he didn't care if he was seen.

22

OF LOVE LOST

Why did she feel such a protective instinct toward the vampires? She often asked herself that. A lot of it had to do with her grandmother being mistreated at the nursing home where she ultimately died. The vulnerability of seniors naturally made her want to protect them. Her mother was reaching the age of needing extra care. And not having any children, Missy knew she would be alone and in a precarious position when she herself reached advanced years.

But why vampires? She wasn't some goth vampire fetishist. But she did love a vampire once: her ex-husband.

Tom had bankrupted them, cheated on her, and then left her. She understood why on the latter two counts. He had been a closeted gay who was miserable in heterosexual matrimony. While their friendship had been fine, diving into romance and marriage was a serious mistake. And when he was turned into a vampire by the partner he was having an affair with, leaving her seemed to be the only thing to do.

Even after Tom left her, she couldn't bring herself to hate him. She knew he had truly loved her, and at first, he was eager in bed, leaving no clue that he was overcompensating. He was a physician's assistant to an orthopedic surgeon, and Missy met him at the hospital where she worked. He came from a very conservative family in a small town in Iowa and told her he had never even met an out gay person until he was in college. There, he said, he did some "experimenting," but had always been convinced he was straight.

Tom was hardworking, kind, and affectionate. He tried so hard to be the perfect husband. Sometimes she thought she saw the strain beneath his handsome, preppy face—the struggle to deny his true nature. But then, after a few years of marriage, as it often goes, he grew distant. On the night he finally admitted being unfaithful, and that he had been with men, he sobbed on her shoulder. He told her he didn't want to be like this and do what he had done. He promised he would stop and be a good husband.

Missy wanted to believe everything would return to normal. Happy ever after, and all that. She hoped he was just going through a phase. She blamed herself for gaining weight and not trying hard enough in bed. And, for a while, things were all right.

But then Tom met Carlos, and everything went off the rails.

Tom was in full romantic love for the first time in his life. He had the decency not to say this to Missy, but she could tell by his buoyant moods. His nighttime absences began again, yet now lasted all night.

She had no idea at first that Carlos was a vampire. She never met him, of course, and besides, she didn't believe in vampires back then. The drops of blood she found on Tom's collars and the adhesive bandages on his neck were presumably from shaving mishaps. As they continued to appear, she wondered if they were from overenthusiastic love bites. He didn't come home with wounds every time he disappeared for the night, but they started appearing more regularly, and his pale, haggard condition the next morning looked worse than hangovers or lack of sleep.

When Tom was turned, he disappeared for ten days. He didn't call or text once. She called his employer, fishing for information without it being obvious that she didn't know where he was. When the office manager acknowledged they hadn't heard from Tom, Missy invented a story about him having to leave town for a seriously ill relative. She didn't know if she was convincing at all.

Tom finally returned home before dawn on a Tuesday. She was in bed when the front door opened. The alarm keyboard beeped as it was disarmed, and his footsteps came down the hall. She was relieved he was back, but braced herself, expecting him to look like he'd come off a bender. He knocked lightly on the bedroom door as he opened it. She turned on the bedside lamp and took in his appearance. Her expectations were wrong.

He looked fantastic. He smiled at her, brushed a strand of blond hair from his forehead, then paused on his way to her side of the bed. His cheeks were slightly flushed, as if he had run home to her and his blue eyes glittered with happiness. He even seemed a bit taller and more muscular, but that made little sense. The clothes he wore were new.

His skin was remarkably pale, though not white in an unhealthy way. It was a whiteness glowing with health.

"I'm so sorry I did this to you," he said. "But I couldn't call you. Not just mentally—I physically was unable. I went through a horrible sickness."

"You look pretty well now."

"Yes. It was quite a transformation. Literally."

Tom came to her, bent down, and kissed her forehead. Then he told her Carlos was a vampire. And now he was, too.

"Don't play games with me," she said.

"You mean you've never wondered if they exist?"

"No. I'm a nurse. I deal with the science of the human body and the unpredictability of the human mind. Why would I believe in vampires? Or unicorns, for that matter?"

"I didn't either. Until I saw them with my own eyes and felt the effects in my own body."

He told her about Carlos and a small group of other vampires who lived in loft condominiums in the warehouse district. They partied at clubs, just like humans, but he soon observed them feeding on humans. Carlos began feeding on him, as well, but only in small amounts and as a gesture of intimacy.

"So what? They drank blood," Missy said. "Anyone can drink blood and say they're a vampire. Give me proof."

He was gone. She had been looking up at him as he stood over the bed, and then suddenly he wasn't there. He had simply vanished.

"Over here." He was standing on the other side of the bed.

"Okay," she said in a faint voice. "I believe in vampires now."

He smiled and continued with his story. Spending time with Carlos and the other vampires fascinated Tom. He was allured by the evidence of their heightened senses. He was fascinated by the thought of immortality. Although he didn't say it directly, he was blown away by vampire sex. He decided he wanted to be a vampire. Carlos at first resisted, but then, out of love, agreed to change him.

Tom skipped many of the details of being turned, but he admitted that after Carlos drank all his blood, Tom had died, at least clinically, until Carlos fed him with his own blood. This began the transformation, which was painful and psychologically harrowing. Tom said his body felt like it had the worst case of flu ever. His mind had careened from panic to ecstasy and back to panic. And he was roiled by strange thoughts and cravings. It took days before he could function. Even now, he struggled to make sense of his new reality.

"Have you fed on anyone yet?" Missy asked.

"No. Just animals. And don't worry, I promise you're safe with me."

"What are you going to do now?"

That's when he told her he was leaving her for good. Fighting his sexuality hadn't gone so well and trying to resist his new vampire instincts would be even more disastrous. Living here would be destructive to both.

She had seen the end coming already, and now it was undeniable. But still, her heart felt like it was crushed in a vise. She nodded, fighting back tears. He moved all his possessions out in two days.

She would never stop loving him. And she didn't think she could recover when she learned he died less than a year after he left. He never got to enjoy the immortality he craved.

She read the article in the newspaper and watched the brief segment on the local news, but it was Carlos who told her the true details when he visited her one night shortly afterwards. One of the neighborhoods of the nearby city was filled with cafes and bars popular with the LGBT community. Unfortunately, it also occasionally drew gangs of skinheads and neo-Nazis who liked to ambush individuals, then taunt and beat them. Carlos told Missy that he and Tom were several blocks away from the entertainment area, hunting along empty streets of shuttered stores when they were caught.

Carlos had sensed the presence of the gang lurking in a building under construction. He could have easily raced away before the thugs even got a good look at him. After all, he had preached to Tom that discretion was more important than anything else. Never fight, always flee. The existence of vampires must remain secret. But the Nazis, having seen the two men walking by, yelled anti-gay slurs at them.

Tom's anger got the best of him. He stopped and got into a fighting stance. He wanted to kill them all.

"Let's go," Carlos whispered. "Now!"

"I'm not running away from these punks," Tom said.

"You're a brand-new vampire. You have a lot of rage, and you haven't learned how to control it yet. Please, let's get out of here." He put his hand on Tom's shoulder. "*Please.*"

Tom appeared to shake off his anger and followed Carlos as they sprinted away before the Nazis, emerging from the building, could surround them. Some of them chased the two vampires, but there was no way they could catch up, even though the vampires weren't running their fastest, because Tom wasn't yet at his full strength.

A few blocks later, Carlos noticed he was alone. Tom had turned around and raced back to confront the thugs.

When Carlos arrived on the scene, Tom was already on the ground, getting stomped on by a dozen Nazis. A mere dozen men shouldn't have been able to get a healthy vampire of Tom's age on the ground. But Tom had yet to be fully adapted to his transformation. Perhaps his strength wasn't where it should be, or his coordination was unsteady.

Tom's face was covered with blood as the young Nazis kicked him, screaming obscenities about his sexuality. Every time he almost got to his feet, he was knocked down again.

Carlos grabbed the closest punk by the neck and threw him into a pile of concrete blocks. He slapped a second one in the back of his head, sending him tumbling. A third one pulled a pistol and aimed it at Carlos' head.

"C'mon, faggot," he said.

Carlos bared his fangs and snarled. The punk's face turned white, and he ran away. Carlos cursed himself for giving away his identity as a vampire. The last thing vampires needed was to give a hate group another target to attack.

Two, then two more police cars pulled up with lights flashing. Neo-Nazis scattered everywhere. The police officers, guns drawn, shouting orders for everyone to get on the ground, caught four of the punks. Carlos would have escaped, but he didn't want to leave Tom. One cop knelt beside Tom to examine his condition.

"Holy crap, it looks like his wounds are healing right in front of my eyes," the cop said. "No, I must be imagining it."

"These dudes are vampires," said the handcuffed punk who had run away from Carlos. "For real."

The senior cop, a sergeant, laughed. "You guys have been smoking too much meth. There's no such thing as vampires."

Carlos felt a malignant energy spread throughout the police. They packed the Nazis into two of the patrol cars, which left the scene. The sergeant and one other officer remained with Carlos and Tom.

"Follow me, sir, I need to ask you some questions," the sergeant said to Carlos, leading him to the street where they stopped beside one of the patrol cars. "Now, tell me your version of the events tonight."

As Carlos recounted the story, an alarm went off in his mind, a psychic warning. He glanced back at the construction site.

Where the other cop was kneeling beside Tom, driving a sharpened piece of rebar into his chest. Carlos' lover and vampire child writhed in the dirt, screaming in pain.

So quickly the cops probably didn't even see him, Carlos shot across the construction site, gathered Tom into his arms, and raced away into the night. He wanted to kill the cops, but that would only put the vampire population in more danger. And he had to get Tom to Harlan, a vampire friend who had healing skills, to save him.

But it was too late.

CARLOS SAT across from Missy at her kitchen table, a budding tear in one eye. He was slight and studious, with jet-black hair and a goatee. But he exuded strength.

"He died in my arms before I reached Harlan's apartment. I've only been a vampire for 50 years and I've never seen one die before. It was—I'm sorry. It's insensitive of me to even bring up that image."

She was in shock. "I appreciate your telling me."

"Vampires are in danger. I've heard rumors of the police summarily executing them, but I never believed the stories were true. Until now. They're treating us like vermin to be exterminated, without the public finding out we exist."

"Is this some sort of policy?" she asked.

"I don't think so. I think it's just rogue cops. The few that have actually come into contact with vampires or our prey. If the top brass know about us, I doubt they're saying anything about it."

"Well, Carlos, you're the only vampire I know now. I hope you have better luck than Tom did."

He gazed at her thoughtfully. She figured it had never dawned on him until now that Missy wouldn't have lost her husband except for him. Yeah, maybe he would have left her eventually, but he wouldn't have ended up dead.

"Again, I'm sorry for your loss," Carlos said.

She was silent.

"I want you to understand we're not murderers. Sometimes our prey dies, usually by accident. Sometimes they are humans. But, you know, humans kill humans more than we do—"

"Okay," she said in a firm voice. "I don't want to hear any more. I realize no one gets through this life as a saint, but Tom was pretty darn close. I just want to think about him tonight."

Carlos nodded, smiled grimly, and disappeared. She never heard a door open or close.

THAT WAS TEN YEARS AGO, and Missy hadn't fallen in love since. She dated now and then, but was reluctant to commit after experiencing betrayal and loss. What made it even harder to find love was a bit of magick that she taught herself to avoid being hurt again: a truth-telling spell.

Unlike the psychoactive drugs governments have used over the decades as truth serum, her spell didn't muddle the mind and make it open to suggestion. Her spell simply made those enchanted by it *want* to tell the truth.

She often used it on a second or third date if the man was clearly looking to escalate things and get her in bed. It was an easy spell. All she would do was sprinkle certain herbs on the floor beneath the restaurant table where the man couldn't see and chant a quick spell under her breath. And *voila*!

"Missy, you look so good tonight," a guy would say. "You remind me of the girl who just dumped me, and I want to use you to get her out of my system so I can then dump you and move on to better things."

They would always have a shocked look on their faces after they confessed.

"Check please," Missy would say before the man would plead, with a beet-colored face, that it had been a mere slip of the tongue and he hadn't meant it at all.

Yes, Missy knew she wasn't playing fair, but she wouldn't stop using the spell. The system itself wasn't fair, and women needed any help they could get. She only wished there was an easy way to use it on car salesmen.

23
CLOSING EARLY TONIGHT

When Matt pulled up to the gate at Seaweed Manor, he didn't know what to say without sounding suspicious. A different gate guard than the one he had talked to before came out of the booth. It was an obese white guy with no chin. He didn't greet Matt. He just stared at him.

"Hi," Matt said. "I'm here visiting a friend in A-305."

"Name?"

"Chainsaw."

"No, *your* name."

"Matt Rosen. Good ol' Chainy might have forgotten to put me on the guest list. He's such a knucklehead sometimes, that guy."

The guard studied his face for a moment. "There is no guest list," he said. "I'm just supposed to ask your name."

The guard returned to the booth and raised the gate. Matt

parked in the visitor lot and strolled up to the twin five-story buildings in the bright light of the full moon. Rock music blared from open windows. From one, incongruously, Neil Diamond crooned. It was like walking past dormitories on a college campus. Except for the howling of a wolf coming from some-where on the property, as if Matt had been suddenly trans-ported to Montana.

The entrance door to Building A was unlocked, and Matt took the elevator to the third floor. It smelled of spilled beer and Bengay ointment. The condos were accessed by open breezeways on the front of the building and a small sign outside the elevator told him to turn right for the lower-300's.

As he stepped out onto the breezeway, he was surprised to find a half-dozen people standing in line outside of a unit halfway down. It was a motley crew of mostly younger people in various states of disrepair. A couple of them looked insane, with wild, rolling eyes and mouths that snapped—the kind who would eat your face off for the fun of it. They shifted on their feet with anxiousness.

"Um, excuse me," Matt said. "Is this Chainsaw's place?"

The last guy in line nodded. He was young, pale, and looked like he was about to barf.

Matt kept silent as people left the condo, singly or in pairs, and the line moved forward. The herbal odor of marijuana drifted from the open door. Soon, Matt was next in line, standing in the doorway, waiting for the strung-out guy ahead of him to stuff a baggy in his pocket and practically sprint from the condo.

The lighting was dark in the living room, mostly supplied by a lava lamp and a couple of candles in puddles of wax on an ugly black coffee table. Matt walked in slowly, letting his eyes adjust to the near darkness.

A tall, skinny, bald man sat on the couch smoking a cigarette. He wore torn jeans, biker boots, and a tight AC/DC T-shirt. The ashtray overflowed. Next to it stood a giant blue bong.

"What do you want?" Chainsaw had a speech impediment of some sort.

"Do you have Reboot?" Matt asked.

"Who sent you?" he lisped.

"Kyle."

"Okay, but we have to hurry." Chainsaw glanced at the watch on his scarred and tattooed arm. "It's late. I'm running out of time."

The cause of the speech impediment was a pair of dentures that kept coming loose in Chainsaw's mouth. He also had a stud through his tongue, which didn't help matters. The man hadn't aged well. Matt guessed he was in his sixties, but it was hard to tell in someone who had obviously done a lot of hard living.

Chainsaw got up and looked out the front door, then shut and bolted it. Matt's pulse ratcheted up.

"Don't worry," Chainsaw said. "You're my last customer tonight. I don't want anyone else coming in. It's too late."

It was only 7:00 p.m., but Matt didn't mention it.

Chainsaw went into the adjoining dining nook, where the table held a scale and several piles of small plastic baggies with different substances in them. "How much do you want?"

Matt had no idea of how much Reboot someone would buy or even what measuring system was used for it.

"Uh, enough for one night. Just for me. And I'm a light user."

"Half a gram should be more than enough. Stay away from heights and if you think you can fly, don't do it. Oh, and if you have the urge to eat human flesh, choose a Snickers bar instead."

"Sounds like a plan," Matt said. "Hey, Chainsaw, do you mind if I ask a couple of questions? A friend of Kyle's and mine came by here recently. A pretty girl by the name of Taylor? Taylor Donovan?"

"I wouldn't remember."

"It was Saturday night last week. She came by very late to buy some Reboot." Her late-night visit made Matt question why Chainsaw was closing shop so early tonight.

The dealer handed Matt a tiny baggie of a light-brown powder that looked like dried, ground-up insects. "Forty bucks."

Matt handed him two twenties and took the baggie.

"You don't remember?"

"Nope. You saw tonight how busy I get."

"This is her." Matt showed Taylor's photo from the newspaper.

Chainsaw rubbed the scars on the top of his bald head. "I guess you're not a cop if you haven't arrested me already for drugs. Are you a private investigator or something?"

"I'm a reporter." Matt abandoned his subterfuge in case he wanted to use any quotes from Chainsaw. "I'm just trying to find out what happened to Taylor the night she died."

"She died? An overdose? I'm not responsible if anyone does anything stupid after they leave here."

"No. Murder," Matt said in a neutral tone, trying to read Chainsaw's reaction.

"Maybe I recognize the face. I usually remember pretty

girls." He glanced at his watch and grew agitated. "You gotta go now, man."

A wolf howled from the direction of the beach. Chainsaw rubbed his arms as if he were cold and ushered Matt to the door. Matt wondered if the dealer was having heroin withdrawals.

"One last thing," Matt said, stopping at the door. "She probably went straight to the beach after leaving here. Does that jog your memory?"

Chainsaw groaned with pain and raced toward the bedrooms. Painful coughs came from down the hallway. Matt expected to hear vomiting next.

Instead, there was moaning.

"Hey, are you okay in there?" Matt called.

No answer. Only a low groan, raw and throaty.

Do I check on him to see if I need to call 911, Matt thought, or just get the hell out of here?

He decided to be compassionate. He entered the dark hall connecting the bedrooms, went past the guest bathroom that smelled of mildew, and walked toward the master bedroom with a light on inside shining through a half-open door. A television played at low volume somewhere in the room, not visible behind the door.

"Hello?" Matt said outside the bedroom door. He peeked inside. There were piles of clothing on the floor. The bathroom door on the far wall was closed.

A deep, rumbling snarl came from behind him. He jumped in surprise and turned, heart pounding.

A massive form crouched in the shadows only a few feet away. The creature was too shrouded in darkness to make out more than fur covering massive muscles, as the creature prepared to spring. Eyes flickered in yellow, and claws gleamed in the reflected light.

"Don't kill me," Matt whispered.

A giant mouth opened in an angry growl that escalated into an ear-splitting roar.

And a set of upper dentures fell out, landing on Matt's shoes.

24
OF MIND AND MAGICK

When Missy got home, she practiced her telekinesis. Practicing strengthened this natural ability of hers, which could be combined with magick spells to powerful effect. If she could only get them right.

Every time she exercised her telekinesis, she found it difficult to begin. There's no ritual to put you in the right mindset— no changing into yoga pants and rolling out the mat. Meditation helped clear her mind, but to summon the kind of juice required to bend a fork or move a book across the room was no easy feat.

The fear-induced adrenaline that rushed through her when she dropped her phone the other day kicked her mind into the right gear to stop the phone before it smashed on the tile floor. She had then slowly eased it downward to rest upon the floor without damage. But she found it incredibly difficult to make the phone rise from the floor and return to her hand. In fact, it had taken nearly an hour of concentrating to accomplish this task. She feared it would bring on a migraine.

Her most impressive feat of telekinesis was clearing the table of dirty dishes and placing them in the sink last week. She had returned home from work and was angry to find she had accidentally left the dishes on the table when she left in a hurry for a patient appointment. She was so ticked off, the dishes seemed to sail across the kitchen on their own accord, as if they were scared of her. Too bad they hadn't washed themselves, too.

She hadn't even concentrated on making them do that. Clearly, emotion helped the power work.

Today, as the sunrise shined through the windows, her goal was to empty the dishwasher. Putting the dishes in the appropriate cupboards would probably be too hard, but for now, placing them on the kitchen counter would suffice.

She stood in front of the dishwasher and willed it to open. It was an ancient-looking model. Nowadays, the latest dishwashers had such advanced technology you could probably open them with your phone. But that was still not as cool as telekinesis.

Focus, Missy.

She tried to empty her mind of all thoughts except the vision of the latch clicking and the door swinging downward. A bird sang outside. She ignored it. Palm fronds scratched the window in the breeze. She forced herself to block all sensory input.

Concentrate.

There was only silence. There was only darkness. There was only emptiness. And in the center of it all, a dishwasher door slowly lowered itself until it rested in the horizontal position.

Missy opened her eyes. The door really was open now!

She took a deep breath and moved on to Step Two while she was still in the zone.

And the bottom dish rack, filled with clean dishes, rolled out a few seconds later. The process was getting easier now. Though the trickier operation came next: moving a plate from the rack and onto the counter.

This time, she didn't close her eyes because she needed to follow what was going on. She set her gaze on a white dinner plate all the way to the right, standing adjacent to the cutlery basket. She envisioned it lifting vertically until it rose above the counter, rotating to a horizontal position, moving over the counter, and slowly descending to rest on the laminate surface (no, she didn't have granite or quartz countertops, but don't judge).

She ushered all her strength and willpower. Finally, the plate began to ascend.

But not just the one plate—all the dishes in the lower rack rose into the air. In her confusion, her concentration faltered.

And all the dishes fell, clattering upon the dishwasher rack, half of them bouncing off and shattering upon the floor.

Okay, she thought, a little more practice is needed. But her head was aching from all the effort.

Instead of cleaning up the mess manually, she attempted one of the new spells she'd been working on. It was the very literally named Sweeper Spell. It wasn't the pure telekinesis she had used in her attempt to empty the dishwasher. Rather, it combined that ability with earth magick. She supposed most witches performed it without possessing any innate telekinetic abilities, but she wanted to hone her gifts and be better than most witches.

She focused, breathed deeply, and chanted the incantation. Simultaneously, she grasped a power charm in her hand and formed a mental image of the desired outcome.

And it worked. The pieces and shards of porcelain all began sliding across the floor, moving at the same speed, slowly at first and then faster. They slid toward each other, and the entire mass began swirling in a circle. Soon it rose from the floor like a miniature cyclone of broken plates and moved to the trash can a few feet away. The cyclone rose off the floor, hovered over the open can, and then dissipated. All the pieces of the plates dropped neatly into the trash.

Missy was thrilled. She was finally getting the knack of magick and harnessing her power. It was a waste of time, she realized, to attempt telekinesis alone when combining it with magick was so much more effective.

Rather than resting, she had some sleuthing to do. After microwaving a mug of water to make a quick cup of tea, she sat at the kitchen table with her laptop and looked online for stories about the mayor's daughter, Taylor Donovan. A nice, high-resolution photo was available of the pretty young woman smiling with every bit of charm she had.

Missy printed out the photo and drove back to the beach.

25
SUPPORT YOUR
LOCAL BUSINESSES

The Cone of Uncertainty was named after the feature on NOAA weather maps so familiar to Floridians: the possible path of a hurricane, becoming wider like a cone farther in time and distance from the present position. Locals jokingly referred to it as "the Cone of Death."

The Cone of Uncertainty was not a good name for an ice cream shop or any eating establishment, never mind the wordplay. The little restaurant decorated its walls with old newspaper clippings of hurricanes that hit Florida over the years and cheap reproductions of Winslow Homer shipwreck paintings. Each day, the shop featured a different "flavor of uncertainty" which you could buy at fifty percent off if you didn't mind not knowing what flavor you would get.

Missy arrived late in the afternoon and hoped the night crew had already begun their shift. She asked the pimply teenaged boy at the counter if he recognized the woman in the photo.

"I think I saw her on TV. Isn't she in the reality show with the naked people eating bugs?"

"Have you seen her here eating ice cream?"

"Um, I don't know."

You've got a great future ahead of you, sport, she thought. "Can I speak to your manager?"

A wispy young woman emerged from the back. She was not much older than the kid at the counter. Missy made her inquiries and showed the photo.

"Oh, yeah, Taylor, the mayor's daughter. It's so sad what happened to her. She was in here that night with her friends," the manager said. "It was late. They were kind of drunk."

"Have you ever noticed an old man hanging around in the parking lot? Really pale skin. Pot belly. His eyes were probably glowing a bit?"

"Yeah, the old pervert. Has he done something bad?"

"I don't know yet," Missy said. "Does he harass your customers?"

"No, he just stares at them creepily. It's weird, but he ignores them when they arrive and walk inside. But when they come out, he's like a horny hound dog. Especially if they're licking an ice cream cone. We've called the police a couple of times, but the old pervert is always gone when they get here."

"Did he follow Miss Donovan when she left?"

"No. Some scary-looking biker showed up, and she left with him."

"You saw her get on his motorcycle safely without being accosted by the pervert?"

"Yeah. I looked outside because the bike was so noisy when it drove off."

Missy thanked her and was about to leave when something bothered her like an itch.

"The guy on the motorcycle—have you ever seen him before?"

"No. And he didn't look like the type who hangs out in ice cream shops," the manager said. "What does he have to do with the pervert?"

"The old man isn't really a pervert. I'm friends with his daughter," Missy lied, "and she's afraid her father is considered a suspect in Taylor's murder. I'm just helping her out, asking some questions. Hopefully, her dad didn't do it."

"Okay, I get it."

The scary-looking biker concerned her. He could be the murderer after all, though she couldn't imagine why he would make the murder look like the work of a vampire, unless he was one of those vampire cultists. Or if he knew the secret of the vampires of Squid Tower and wanted to cast suspicion upon them rather than himself, just as the vampires were accusing the werewolves of doing.

"What about the friends who were with the mayor's daughter?" Missy asked. "Do you know who they were, or how I could find out? I really need to speak to them, just to ask a few questions."

"Sure. Taylor was with Ashley, and I can't remember the other one's name. I knew them from school. Ashley lives in a condo nearby. I can text her your number and if she's willing to talk to you, you'll hear from her."

Missy thanked her and left. The manager watched her, standing at the window next to the decorative hurricane flags.

The parking lot was full on this bright, sunny afternoon. An ocean breeze was picking up, slipping between the condo towers across the street. But just the thought of Schwartz lurking outside in an empty parking lot late at night made her feel uncomfortable.

MISSY MET Ashley at her condo the next day, after Ashley returned home from work, and just before Missy began the home visits of her elderly patients. It was a one-bedroom, not large, but luxurious. Light hardwood floors, stainless-steel appliances, quartz countertops, marble tiles in earth tones. The ocean view from the living areas was stunning.

"I love your place," Missy said. "Where did you say you work?"

"An event-planning agency. And yes, Daddy bought this place for me. As an investment." Ashley assessed Missy up and down. She wasn't overly impressed. "Now, what did you want to know about Taylor?"

Ashley had long, full auburn hair and vacant brown eyes. She looked like the typical twenty-something with rich parents: pretty, thin, expensive clothes, expensive hair, and the personality that goes with them. The kind of woman who would consider Missy not cool enough when Missy was her age.

"I want to know who killed her," Missy said, "and I don't trust the police. I hear she was last seen leaving with a guy on a motorcycle?"

"Yeah, Kyle. She met him when she was in recovery, and they had a fling. She's always been in love with an jerk named David who dumped her when she fell into addiction. On the night she was killed, she saw him at a party. He was with a girl-friend and Taylor took it badly. On our way to the ice cream shop after the party, I overhead her talking with Kyle on the phone, begging him to pick her up. She said something about getting some Reboot."

"What's that?"

"Some new synthetic drug that's been going around. Bad news. She was using it, among a lot of other stuff, before she went into recovery."

"Why would Kyle help her get it if he's in recovery?"

"Because he's a dirtbag. He never fully left the druggie world and now he's even dealing, I hear."

"If he's a dealer, why didn't he deliver the drugs to her? Why did he take her somewhere to get it?"

"Because there's only one guy in town who sells Reboot, according to Taylor. Even Kyle isn't bad-ass enough to handle the people who use that stuff. I'm guessing he brought her to the guy. He lives in Seaweed Manor just up the beach."

"And how do you know this?" Missy asked.

"Because I like to party now and then. The dude there sells everything, including pot and coke and stuff my friends like. He's like a retail store—you just show up whenever you want and buy what you want. The gate guards there never give you a hard time."

"Do you think Taylor went to visit this guy with Kyle?"

"That's what it sounded like based on what I overhead her say on the phone."

It was a good bet that Seaweed Manor was the last place Taylor went, Missy thought. After all, her body was found on the beach nearby. Missy didn't know the time of death like the police probably did. Taylor could have been killed at the drug dealer's condo and moved to the beach. She could have been killed right after she left by Kyle or by some other druggie. Or, she could have been hanging out on the beach doing her Reboot and been killed by just about anyone. But Missy had a gut feeling that Taylor's visit to the drug dealer had led to her demise one way or another.

"Just speculating here," Missy said, "but do you think Kyle killed Taylor?"

"He was the first person I thought of," Ashley said. "And Cindi thought so, too. I could see him wanting to get it on with Taylor for old times' sake and she says no because she hasn't gotten over David. So Kyle freaks out and kills her. Yeah, I could see it happening that way."

"Any reason he made it look like a vampire did it?"

"Vampire? What do you mean?"

Missy explained the exsanguination and the throat wounds.

Ashley snorted with contempt. "He probably stabbed her in the neck with a screwdriver or something and hit her jugular vein."

Missy didn't mention there was no blood found at the scene. She doubted Ashley would have a convincing theory about it.

"What's the dealer's name?" Missy asked.

"Chainsaw."

"How do I get in touch with him?"

"He's in A-305. Just show up. Cash only, of course. He's there most nights."

IT WAS NOT the best night to visit Seaweed Tower. Missy hadn't even realized it was a full moon until the howl of a wolf startled her when she got out of her car. Sure enough, a full moon shone low in the sky above the ocean, its long luminous reflection stretched across the churning water like an arrow pointing toward the condos.

Dark shapes slipped across the water's surface. She walked to the dune crossover to get a better view. Surfers—eight of them—wearing wetsuits, carving on the faces of five-foot-tall waves.

No, they weren't wearing wetsuits. They were naked and the dark material covering them was their fur. It was the werewolf surfing club. She recognized the Roarkes, who were actually pretty good surfers for people their age, as well as a few others whose names escaped her. One of them wiped out. The others rode the same wave with aplomb, howling with bravado, jumping off their boards as they slid to a stop in the shallows.

Missy quickly turned away. Even thick pelts of fur did not sufficiently cover saggy senior private parts.

She headed for Building A, but hesitated. Was it too risky to be here with werewolves running around? The owners' association had the same rule the vampires had about no hunting allowed on the property. But just in case, she grabbed her scrubs top, with its Acceptance Home Care logo, and slipped it on over her blouse. Even if any werewolves didn't recognize her, hopefully this would remind them not to eat the hired help.

The open breezeway leading to 305 was empty, shadows pooling between the yellow exterior lights. As she walked past each condo, the windows facing the breezeway had their blinds closed, but interior light seeped out. Hard rock blared from 303. The smell of fried hamburger and onions came from down the breezeway.

It wasn't just the noise and rowdiness that differentiated Seaweed Manor from Squid Tower—it was the cooking smells. There were never such smells where the vampires lived, of course. There were almost no scents at all, because the vampires' ultra-sensitive sense of smell led to rules outlawing strongly scented cleaning solutions. Even the chlorine in the pool was barely noticeable there.

She reached the door to 305, hesitated, and then rang the doorbell. Chimes to the tune of AC/DC's "Hells Bells" rang, but no one answered. She knocked. No answer.

Was that a voice inside?

She knocked again.

"Help me," someone cried faintly.

26
EAU DE WET DOG

Matt had been certain he was about to die.

The creature snarling in the shadows rose until it towered over him. The dentures that had fallen on Matt's shoe must have belonged to Chainsaw, but where was he? This creature must have killed him in the other bedroom. And now it was Matt's turn to die.

The creature lunged, its front paws punching Matt in the chest so hard he went flying backwards into the bedroom, landing on the bed. The mattress quivered like a bowl of Jell-O.

"A waterbed?" Matt said in amazement. "Really? People still use waterbeds?"

A tremendous roar like a stump grinder came from the doorway as the monster stepped into the light. It was a wolf with a vaguely hominid appearance standing on its hind legs, covered in black and silver hair, with very un-wolf-like genitalia. Actually, the creature looked a little like Chainsaw, just bigger, stronger, and much more dangerous. It even had a stud in its tongue like the drug dealer.

The monster came closer to the bed, its nostrils flaring as it took in Matt's scent. Matt took in the monster's scent, and it was bad—*eau de* wet dog and human armpit.

As Matt pushed himself away on the roiling waterbed, the creature leaned in, its face just a couple of feet from Matt's. The eyes below a bony ridge were bloodshot but looked human. The brown fur covering its head was thick, but graying around the mouth. Half a dozen long white whiskers stuck out from its slightly elongated muzzle that looked like a wolf's, but wasn't as long.

It snarled and bared its fangs—four canine teeth, but the rest of the mouth was toothless. It dawned on Matt that it was probably Chainsaw's mouth. The canine teeth had grown and pushed out the dentures that had replaced his other teeth.

The canine teeth by themselves, however, were more than capable of ripping out a human throat.

"Chainsaw, is that you? Are you a werewolf?" Matt asked.

Chainsaw growled at the stupid question and grabbed Matt's neck with both hands (or were they paws?), lifting him off the bed, squeezing as Matt dangled in the air.

Matt couldn't breathe. Spots swirled in front of his eyes. Then his vision narrowed, surrounded by a circle of darkness. He struggled to free himself, kicking the Chainsaw-creature.

The monster growled in frustration and tossed Matt against the wall, denting the drywall above the headboard. Matt collapsed onto the heaving sea of the waterbed, gasping for air.

Chainsaw stared at Matt, seeming to weigh a decision. He shook his hairy head in disgust and left the room. Before Matt could recover and get off the bed, the werewolf returned with a bicycle lock and cable. He wrapped the cable around Matt's neck and through an opening in the metal headboard between the post and a vertical slat.

During this operation, the monster's hairy torso pressed into Matt's face. Its feral, unclean stench singed Matt's nose. Chainsaw's paw-hands were surprisingly dexterous, despite having long claws instead of fingernails. The hands were covered with thick fur but were still human-like with opposable thumbs. They pulled the cable ends together and snapped the lock shut. Chainsaw patted him down, pricking him with the claws, and found the phone in his pocket, tossing it into the corner far from Matt.

The monster then slid the window open, howled with pent-up energy, and jumped out. The bedroom was on the beach side with no hallway outside and two stories below it. Why he didn't just walk out the front door would remain a mystery.

Matt lay there for hours. Or at least it felt like hours. He had no idea, since he didn't wear a watch and normally relied on his phone, which had ended up in the corner of the room, to check the time. He had plenty of it to wonder why Chainsaw hadn't killed him. And to study the interior design of the bedroom. It was illuminated by the single lamp with a bare bulb on the dresser and tastefully decorated with old posters of oiled-up, naked women on motorcycles hanging above the piles of dirty clothes on the floor.

Matt was thirsty and had to pee. Not to mention his throat and neck ached from his near strangulation, and he was sore in the upper chest where he'd been punched. He wondered if the *Journal* would give him a comp vacation day for all this trouble.

Too bad he hadn't told anyone where he was going tonight, as if visiting a drug dealer wasn't dangerous. Only Kyle knew he was probably coming here, but Kyle had surely forgotten by now after more tequila and Jagermeister shots. Why hadn't anyone warned him this drug dealer was a werewolf? Why hadn't he allowed Chainsaw to shoo him away when he closed shop early for the full moon?

Matt's phone vibrated with a text, jiggling on the cheap carpeting far out of reach. Maybe it was his ex saying she wanted to take him back. Or his mother telling him, one last time, that she loved him. Actually, it was probably his idiot friend, Taz, wanting to go out drinking with him. Taz would never know Matt was a prisoner here tonight, waiting to be slaughtered by a werewolf once it returned home from frolicking on the beach or eating disobedient children or whatever werewolves in Florida did on their Big Night each month.

No one would ever know how Matt died. Especially if Chainsaw devoured or otherwise disposed of every trace of him.

He imagined what the social media posts commemorating him would look like when the doorbell rang the notes of a song.

Isn't that AC/DC's "Hells Bells"? he wondered.

27
BAD MOON RISING

Missy tried the door to the condo. It was locked, of course.

The voice called for help again. It was a male voice that sounded familiar, but she couldn't quite place it. It was faint, as if it were coming from deep inside the condo. If it weren't for the poor insulation of the door, she wouldn't have heard it at all.

"What's wrong? Do you need me to call an ambulance?" Missy shouted at the door.

"I'm being held prisoner. Call the police."

Obviously, a drug deal that went bad.

"Please hurry," the voice said.

Finally, she recognized it: the reporter, Matt.

"Is that Matt?"

"Missy! It's you! Please get me out of here. I'm chained up."

He must be here investigating, she thought. Unless he's a druggie.

She reached into her back pocket for her phone when the elevator dinged, and a deep male voice uttering profanity echoed down the breezeway. Her gut told her to hide, so she hurried to the next doorway down along the breezeway, farther away from the elevator, and pressed herself into the space in which the front door was recessed.

Painful groaning and obscenities came closer. Missy dared a peek.

A tall, naked man slowly walked toward her, limping. He was in his early sixties and was in good shape, with a shaved head and ample tattoos and piercings, as well as bruises and scratches all over his body. He stopped at a fire extinguisher case halfway down the hall, opened the glass door, and withdrew a key. Then he walked to 305. She leaned back out of sight.

Well, hello Chainsaw, she thought.

The deadbolt clicked, the door opened, then shut, and the lock clicked again.

Missy knew she should call 911, but she first gamed out what would happen. All she could tell them was she heard someone calling for help. She hadn't seen any criminal act. When the cops showed up, Chainsaw might be able to talk his way out of it somehow. She wanted to at least ask him a few questions about Taylor. If she didn't, she would never get another chance if Chainsaw were arrested. She would lose that tool for protecting the vampires.

She rang the doorbell. Why not? Would he really take two captives on the same night?

She waited and rang the bell again. Maybe he was showering and getting dressed. Hopefully getting dressed. She waited some more, then pounded on the door. She sensed an eye on the other side of the peephole.

"What do you want?" Chainsaw said through the door. His voice had a bad lisp and was difficult to understand.

"I have an order," Missy said.

"I'm closed."

"Closed? It's only midnight."

"It's my night off. I'm binge-watching The Brady Bunch."

"I'm buying for a client willing to pay top dollar," she said. "And I mean top dollar."

The door opened a crack. "For what?"

He had put on clothes, but hadn't showered, which was quickly evident by his stench and the dirt on his face. She struggled to remember the name of the drug.

"Reboot. I need some."

"Make it quick," he said, opening the door. As soon as she entered, he closed it.

He had a gun in his hand. Her cocky self-assurance faded.

"How much do you need?" he asked. The hand not holding the gun slipped dentures into his mouth.

"The same amount Taylor Donovan bought."

His face darkened. She realized she'd made a mistake.

"Why is everyone asking me about that girl? Who are you?"

"A friend, I just wanted to know—"

"Shut the heck up. I'm sick of this."

He aimed the pistol at her face. It was only inches away, and she stared into the barrel. She smelled gun oil and rancid sweat.

"Leave her alone!" Matt shouted from somewhere in the condo. "I'm going to scream until the neighbors call the police."

Chainsaw cursed, grabbed Missy's arm, and yanked her behind him as he strode through the living room and into a hallway, turning right. He opened the door to a pigsty of a bedroom. Matt sat on the floor, leaning against the bed. A chain was wrapped around his neck and a slat of the headboard, joined by a bicycle lock.

"Good to see you again," Matt said, smiling. "Welcome to Chainsaw's bachelor pad."

Missy was shoved hard and collided with Matt, rolling off him onto the floor.

Chainsaw raised the gun, then hesitated. He looked like he was about to sneeze. He shuddered, shaking his head.

"You stupid people! You stressed me out and I'm really sensitive to stress. Dang it! Dang it!"

Chainsaw jerked with violent spasms. He alternated between looking like he was going into a seizure and simply fighting the urge to barf. He cursed under his breath and staggered into the bathroom.

Missy grabbed her phone and called 911 as she got to her feet.

"We're being held at gunpoint," she whispered and gave the address.

A long, painful moan followed by growling came from the bathroom.

"Run," Matt whispered to Missy. "Hurry. He's turning back into a werewolf."

"Do you know where he put the key to the bicycle lock?" She glanced around the room, as if Chainsaw would be stupid enough to leave the key lying in plain sight.

"It's a combination lock. You'd need bolt cutters to free me."

More growling. Then, for some reason, the sound of gargling. The scent of peppermint floated out of the bathroom. Missy tried to avoid imagining what was going on in there.

"Go, please," Matt said.

Missy left the bedroom but didn't leave the apartment. In the kitchen, she found a carving knife and plotted how she could prevent Chainsaw from killing Matt, or at least hold him off until the police arrived.

The front door shook from tremendous blows.

"Police! Open the door now."

She dropped the knife and ran toward the door, but before she traveled three steps, the door flew inward off its hinges. Two officers with a battering ram ducked out of the way while the rest of the team poured inside wearing armored vests, helmets, and other tactical combat gear. The first one pointed a semi-automatic rifle at her. She raised her hands in the air and pointed with her head toward the bedroom. They charged down the hall and into the room.

They screamed in a cacophony of voices to "get on the floor." They didn't yell anything about dropping a gun, so she assumed Chainsaw wasn't holding his at the time. Werewolves, after all, didn't need guns for killing.

A man and woman detective with vests bearing "Police" came into the apartment. The narcotics officers undoubtably had had Chainsaw on their radar for a while. They fanned out throughout the apartment, opening drawers and rummaging through cabinets, taking photos of a scale and piles of baggies on the dining-room table.

Missy tried to view what was going on in the bedroom, but there were too many people crammed in there. She did get a glimpse of a barefooted leg on the floor. It was not covered in fur. Chainsaw somehow had managed to transform back into his human form. An officer entered the apartment with long-handled bolt cutters and soon Matt came out of the bedroom, rubbing his bruised neck, and joined Missy standing in the living room.

"Did anyone see Chainsaw in his werewolf form?" Missy asked him.

"That's your first question? Not, 'Are you okay, Matt?'"

"You look okay to me. Now answer my question."

"The first guy in the door might have seen something, but Chainsaw transformed really quickly. I almost thought I had hallucinated it. But he left a lot of fur on the carpet. That guy is a real psycho, even when he's human. Actually, more so when he's human. I'll bet anything he killed Taylor Donovan. She was here the night she was murdered. He pretended not to know who she was, but I'll bet money he did it."

"I know."

"How?"

"You're not the only person who knows how to investigate."

Two plainclothes cops entered the apartment—Affird and a younger African-American woman. Affird was again wearing sunglasses at night. They conferred in the kitchen with the leader of the assault team, then the woman detective approached Missy and Matt.

"Say nothing about a werewolf," Missy whispered to Matt.

"But it's the most interesting part!"

"I'm serious."

"Hi, I'm Detective Ramirez," the woman detective said. "I'll need you two to give me your statements about what happened here tonight."

Affird sauntered into the bedroom as Matt explained to Ramirez how he had tracked down Chainsaw and about the drug dealer's erratic behavior. Missy strained to see what was going on in the bedroom. Shortly, the three officers who had remained in there left the room and closed the door.

That was odd.

"Why did you guys leave?" Missy asked.

The cops looked at her with annoyance. "The detective wanted to interrogate the suspect privately," one of them said.

She didn't like this. Matt droned on with his story as the detective took notes. Missy didn't listen. She wished she could hear what was said in the bedroom.

Two gunshots rang out. The door blew open.

"He attacked me and went for my gun!" Affird shouted.

The bedroom filled with cops again.

"His hands were handcuffed behind his back," Matt said. "How could he grab a gun?"

"Call an ambulance," one of the cops said.

"He's dead," another cop said.

Missy knew that in their human forms, werewolves were just as vulnerable to disease, injury, and death as humans. And she knew Chainsaw hadn't attacked Affird. The detective had summarily executed Chainsaw for being a werewolf.

Just like a cop had executed her ex-husband.

AFTER THE SHOOTING, two more detectives showed up at the condo. Missy guessed they were Internal Affairs or in a similar role. She and Matt had to endure more questioning before they were finally allowed to leave. It was nearly dawn and Missy was exhausted.

The two were awkwardly silent as they walked through the parking lot.

"We need to talk," Missy said.

"The last time a woman said that to me, I was kicked out of my apartment."

"This won't be as bad. But it depends on you."

"This isn't looking good."

"You saw a werewolf tonight," Missy said. "How do you feel about that?"

"I haven't had the chance to process it. I'm still getting used to almost dying and hearing someone being executed."

"Did you already believe in supernatural creatures before tonight?" Missy asked.

He stopped on the asphalt and looked at her. "Why are you asking?"

"I take care of the seniors in these two communities here. Most of them are, shall we say, 'special needs.' They deserve compassion and safety just like any seniors. They shouldn't have to suffer from discrimination."

"Werewolves and," Matt gestured toward Squid Tower, "vampires kill people."

"So do alligators and sharks. Should we wipe them all out, then?"

"I don't know what you're getting at."

"You're a reporter. Your job is to publish stories and uncover secrets. You know nothing about privacy and could destroy the lives of all these people I take care of. What I'm getting at is I need to know if you're an enemy."

He looked hurt. "You saved my butt tonight. I'm forever in your debt. And to be honest, I'm kind of fond of you. How would I be an enemy?"

"Like I said, by blowing the cover of all these people. And betraying me."

"I wouldn't—"

"Can you imagine what would happen to them if the world knew they were vampires and werewolves? Aside from being executed by the police?"

"I understand."

"Do you?" she pressed. "Can I trust you not to betray us in service of getting some stupid scoop?"

He paused. A bit too long.

"Yes," he said, "you can trust me. When I discovered Mr. Schwartz is a vampire, I didn't write about it. If I did a story about these creatures, my editors wouldn't believe me, and I'd lose my job. Or if it was published, it would a one-time scoop, a flash in the pan. It's too big a story for one person to own. And once it's out there, it would simply create unnecessary anxiety among the regular people. Nothing good could come of it."

"Exactly. If you're curious, like most reporters, join me as I learn more about these worlds. You won't get stupid articles out of it, but maybe someday you'll have a book's worth of material. Someday, when it's safe for these people to come out of the closet, for the lack of a better term."

"Okay," he said with a big grin. "I'll go along. If you share information with me."

"And you with me?"

"Deal."

"Deal."

"So, do you think this thing is solved?" Matt asked.

"What do you mean?"

"Was Chainsaw the one who killed Taylor and left all the dead bodies around here?"

"I think so. I hope that's the case," she said.

"Do the werewolves and vampires know about each other?"

"Yes. Why?"

"I'm not sure about Chainsaw's motive for all the murders, but it was probably something to do with drugs," Matt said. "Maybe all the victims were his customers. Maybe he's a serial killer who does it for fun. And making them look like vampire killings makes sense for deflecting blame onto the vampires."

"I'd already wondered if a werewolf was trying to frame them," she said.

"Well, it's beyond my skill set to prove it. Hopefully, the police can do it through forensics."

"And Affird would be extra motivated to do so, to help justify executing the guy."

"Yeah," Matt said. They reached her car. "If this whole thing is really over, will I ever see you again?"

"Of course. Remember, we promised to share new information about this world of monsters. Who knows what else is lurking out there?"

28
STAY VIGILANT

Before Missy had gone to bed after the tragic night, she texted Agnes. The 1,500-year-old vampire was fluent in texting, unlike Missy's mother, though she preferred old-fashioned face-to-face meetings.

A werewolf drug dealer in Seaweed Manor was killed by Det. Affird tonight. This dealer was my top pick for the person who murdered the mayor's daughter.

Agnes answered: *Thank you for the information. Hopefully, this is the end of it. But stay vigilant.*

This was the headline the next day in *The Jellyfish Beach Journal* online:

"Drug Dealer Killed in Police Raid."

Matt's byline wasn't on the story, even though he had told her he was writing a story. In fact, the story had no reference to Matt or even to the fact a *Journal* reporter had been involved and witnessed the entire thing. She suspected Matt's own story contained a bit too much truth and was vetoed by higher powers.

She was reminded of the violence the following day when it made the print edition. The newspaper had been tossed in its usual spot in Missy's driveway, where there was always a puddle. It had come in a plastic bag but was soggy, nevertheless. The story was on the front page, but she didn't bother reading it again.

Missy truly wanted to believe that this was the end of it.

MISSY WAS HAVING a hard time putting the horror of Chainsaw's execution behind her. A few nights later, after her last patient appointment, she went to the end of the Squid Tower dune crossover and sat on a bench to watch the sunrise and try to relax. The ocean was flecked with silver from the full moon, and where it met the sky, oranges and violets seeped into view in advance of the sun. The air was fresh and salty. And the crashing of the waves soothed her.

But then the spreading colors in the sky reminded her of a growing bloodstain.

She tried to turn off her imagination and empty her mind. But she kept hearing the gunshots from behind Chainsaw's bedroom door.

Why did Affird have to execute Chainsaw? He was the perfect suspect in the beach murders. Maybe they could have gotten him to confess. That would have been a huge feather in Affird's cap. Would they even investigate this angle now?

Why was the existence of werewolves and vampires such a threat to the members of law enforcement who knew about them? Were they afraid to bring attention to these creatures because, instead of leading to a slaughter as Missy feared, it would instead lead to the creatures' legal protection? Whatever the reason, this attitude imperiled all the residents of Seaweed Manor and Squid Tower, along with all the other freaks hiding on the fringes of society. It was an untenable situation.

She took a deep breath and tried again to relax. She stared at the empty beach and in the faint light could make out the curvy, dark line of seaweed and sargassum washed up by the tide. Most people didn't know about the tiny organisms that lived in the sargassum as it floated like a giant carpet miles offshore. Creatures not understood by humans were fated to die with indifference.

Movement caught her eye. Someone was walking up the beach from the south. As the person got closer, it became clear that it was a man. He was dressed in black but was easily visible in the fading darkness. He walked close to the sand dunes, studying them, looking for something.

Then he looked up and saw her. He made a beeline toward her.

The hairs on the back of her neck prickled. He picked up his pace as he approached. She couldn't make out his face, but he was definitely looking at her.

She got up from the bench and started walking down the dune crossover away from the man. She would get in her car, lock the doors, and get the heck away from here. As she reached the stairs on the inland end, she glanced back toward the beach.

The man was already on the crossover, walking quickly, almost jogging.

"Wait," he called. "I have a question."

She raced down the stairs and started down the winding,

landscaped path to the parking lot. Her car was too far away. She would have to enter the lobby and lock herself in the bathroom or a meeting room. She should try to stop the man with a binding spell, but she was too panicked to pull it off.

His footsteps thudded down the steps behind her.

Before she broke into a run, she had to at least try to stop him. She began building the spell in her mind. And turned toward him.

"Missy! I can't believe it's you."

He was so close now she could recognize him. It was ex-Father Marco Rivera Hernandez.

"Father, what are you doing here?"

"You can call me Marco," he said.

"Tell me what you're doing here!"

He stopped in his tracks with a shocked expression at her hostility. "I was searching for runaways or drug addicts sleeping on the beach. I do it all the time."

"Why?"

"I counsel them and try to find them a shelter. I did it when I was a priest, and I still do it now because of the murders. Getting them off the beach could save their lives."

She didn't know whether to believe him or not.

"I looked like a runaway or drug addict?" she asked with sarcasm.

He laughed. "Of course not, though I couldn't really tell at a distance. I talk to anyone I see alone at this hour, especially women. I want to make sure they're safe."

"Good," Missy said. "Do you know who's killing these people?"

"No idea," he said. "And for all I know, he could kill me, too."

"Be careful. But I'm going to go now. I'm a little shaken up."

"Sorry about that. Have a nice day."

"He wants to ask you out," a deep voice said.

"Don't listen to him," ex-Father Marco said. "He's the demon who possesses me."

"I'm telling her the truth," the deep voice said, "you horny toad."

"Don't embarrass me in front of my friend."

"She's not your friend. You freak her out."

"I freak her out because of you, you spawn of Satan. Why don't you leave me and possess someone else more interesting?"

"Making your life a living hell is actually pretty interesting."

Missy walked away and left the two to their argument. She didn't feel safe until her car was crossing the bridge over the Intracoastal Waterway.

2 9

ENTITIES MOST FOUL, PART TWO

Bernie stared at the bag of homemade cookies on the gatehouse desk and shook his head. He'd let them sit there all night, untouched. A note said they were from Philomena. It was just his luck.

He thought he'd made significant progress by being attracted to Missy, who was way older than the chicks he usually was into: the kind who posed in bikinis next to hotrods in the calendars you'd only find hanging in a mechanic's shop. Of course, chicks like them would never be interested in him, but they set the bar as far as he was concerned. A woman closer to his own age and with no bimbo factor was a good sign he had finally outgrown his adolescent libido. But, wouldn't you know it, Missy appeared to have no interest in him.

It was an insult added to injury that the only woman showing him any interest was almost old enough to be his mother. Philomena. Yes, *Philomena*.

At first, he hadn't realized she'd been flirting with him. The kissing of his cheek, the hugs, the handsy-ness were a Caribbean-culture thing, he had thought. The cookies and casseroles were just a motherly instinct.

Her patting him on the butt at shift change the previous night—that was when it finally dawned on him what she wanted. And now he felt dirty. He also felt under siege. Schwartz wanted to drain him of his blood and Philomena wanted to . . . he couldn't bring himself to think about it.

Unfortunately, he didn't have a choice. Near the end of his shift, he happened to glance out his window and saw Philomena smiling in at him.

He jumped to attention and opened the door. "Hey. What are you doing here so early? It's almost an hour before your shift. And I thought you'd never come here in the dark."

"I woke up early and couldn't get back to sleep," she said in her lilting island accent. "So, I thought I'd watch the sunrise over the ocean. Wanna join me? Two of us will be safer if a vampire comes along."

"Philomena, you know I can't leave my post except to go to the men's room."

"No one will know, man. Aren't they all in their condos now?"

"I'm not sure. The last thing I need is for Schwartz to catch me hanging out on the beach instead of doing my job."

"That bad vampire still bothering you?"

"I've told you he wants to kill me."

"He'll never do that."

"Or get me fired."

"Ah, *that* he might do."

"Put in a good word for me with Rudy, will you?" Bernie

asked. "I keep asking him to reassign me to another community, but he says it's too hard to find someone to take this shift here."

"No wonder."

"If Schwartz forces me out of here, do you think Rudy will put me somewhere else instead of just canning me? I can't afford to be out of work."

"I'll tell him you're a good man," she said, slipping in through the door and invading his personal space. She leaned against the wall with a forced casualness, stared at him with hunger, then moved right up against him.

"Now, show me how good you are," she whispered in his ear.

Bernie stumbled backward and fell into his chair. He realized Philomena didn't really come here to watch the sunrise.

"We've got some time to kill before the shift change," she said, sitting on his lap.

Missy's sandwich bag still sat on the windowsill, filled with secret ingredients to keep evil at bay. He was happy no one had thrown it out, but disappointed it didn't work on horny, older women.

"Don't worry 'bout the window," Philomena said, "no one will see us."

She kissed him hard on the mouth, and her hands roamed over his chest and down his stomach.

Gurglegurglegrrrrrrreeeeeeeoooooogggrrrr!

Good Lord, he thought, a historic seismic event was occurring in his bowels.

"What was that noise?" Philomena stopped what she was doing and looked at him in shock.

"Sorry. That's embarrassing."

Another loud gurgling and rumbling from below. And the

feeling that a massive force of nature was threatening to break free.

"Oh God, I'm sorry, Philomena, but something's wrong."

She got off his lap and backed away as if he were about to explode. In truth, he was.

"Must have been something I ate," he said.

"My cookies?"

"No. I haven't tried them yet. But I will."

More cartoonish sound effects echoed in his colon, and he felt the stirrings that warned the dam was about to break.

"Sorry," he said as he launched from the chair and shot out of the gatehouse, sprinting toward the bathroom just off the lobby. His trembling hands almost dropped the card key for the main building. He made it into the men's room stall with less than a second to spare.

When he emerged twenty minutes later, feeling as if he'd lost all his water weight, he limped back to the gatehouse in shame. Philomena had put on her uniform jacket and closed the door.

"You go home early and clean up," she said. She was frosty, as if she had hard feelings from the interrupted seduction attempt. "Drink lots of water and chicken broth. And stay away from whatever you had for dinner tonight."

WHEN PHILOMENA ARRIVED for her shift the next morning, she didn't say hello. She didn't even acknowledge him. It had been the same when he had relieved her at the start of his shift.

"Hey, I'm sorry about what happened the other day," Bernie said. "My stomach rarely acts up like that."

She pushed into the booth, swiped her ID card through the sensor, and sat down in his chair.

"I hope you didn't take it personally," he continued. "My bowels were really bad off. I know it sounds silly, but I think it had to do with a magic spell gone wrong. This chick who does a little witchcraft on the side created a spell to protect me from Schwartz. But I think it did something to my insides."

Philomena didn't say anything.

"When she was casting the spell, she said something like, 'Expel all entities most foul.' That would describe most of the food I eat."

Still no response.

"I'm sorry, Philomena. Won't you forgive me?"

She finally rotated her chair and looked up at him. "No," she said.

"Why not?"

"I disgust you. I'm an old hag. Kissing me makes you sick to your stomach."

"That's not true!" He considered kissing her, just to make her feel better.

But then his stomach rumbled. Loudly. She looked at him with a frown and an arched eyebrow. Pressure was building in his basement plumbing.

Bernie quickly swiped out with his card, mumbled an excuse, and headed for the bathroom before going home.

That evening, Philomena didn't say a word when he took over guard duty.

THE SCREAM RANG out about an hour before dawn. It sounded to Bernie like it came from the beach. He opened the window and strained to hear more. At this hour, there was almost no traffic on A1A, and the only sound was the irregular crashing of the surf on the other side of the dunes.

There it was again—a woman screaming for help.

He reached for the phone, then hesitated, remembering being lambasted by Rudy about secrecy. Chances were, the cause of the woman's distress was a human, but he couldn't risk calling the police if, in fact, Schwartz or another vampire was being careless and feeding so close to home. He would have to leave his post and go out to the beach himself to investigate.

He grabbed a flashlight and went outside, locking the gatehouse. He cut through the parking lot, past the precious handicapped spot Schwartz claimed, then walked along the paved footpath that skirted the building and led to the dune crossover. The path wound through shrubbery and patches of flowers, illuminated by small ground lights. He passed the shower for washing off sand and saltwater and climbed the wooden steps of the short boardwalk over the dunes.

He paused and listened. Nothing other than the soughing of the waves. His eyes adjusted to the darkness, and he moved to just before the stairs at the end of the crossover, looking up and down the beach. There was only a partial moon, and in its faint light he could make out the dark piles of seaweed washed up by the tide.

No one was in sight. He didn't want to use the flashlight and give himself away in case a predator was still around. He remained unmoving, staring up and down the beach as his pupils opened more and he could see better. No one was around. He really ought to get back to the guardhouse.

The wet slurping sounds came from beneath him.

Bernie froze, his heart hammering.

A faint moan, a rustling of cloth, a scratching of sand.

Right below him, under the dune crossover.

He turned on his flashlight and aimed it at the narrow gaps between the planking. Dark shapes moved beneath him. He couldn't tell what was going on except that a shape was moving toward him. Fast.

Pain ripped across his ankle, and it was wrenched sideways. Something gripped his ankle with vise-like force. He fell on his back, hitting the planks hard, and was pulled toward the edge of the crossover. As he slid toward the darkness, his free foot landed on the handrail post, and he pushed back against it.

Whatever gripped him let go, though he sensed from the tightness of the grip it had the strength to pull him off the structure if it had wanted to. He caught a glimpse of a bloody arm and fingers with pointed, curved nails shooting away, back under the walkway. His trousers had been slashed and blood oozed over the top of his shoe.

Burning red eyes rimmed with yellow flashed between the boards, and now they appeared on the side of the dune cross-over, rising above the floorboards. It wasn't finished with him.

He ran faster than he had since he tried out for, and didn't make, the high school track team. Despite the pain in his ankle, he made it to the stairs on the west side of the dune crossover and turned his head.

A large humanoid creature swung itself over the handrail onto the dune crossover behind him. It crouched and stared at him with those yellow-rimmed, coal-ember eyes. Bernie couldn't be sure it was a vampire, but it emanated coiled muscular power and malevolence. And hunger.

It began to move toward him.

Bernie leaped off the stairs, landing on the ground with a flare of pain in his wounded ankle. He didn't know if the guard-house would be safe, but he knew his car wouldn't start in time to make an escape, so he sprinted for the booth and collapsed inside, locking the door, and turning off the interior light.

Whatever that thing was, it wasn't Schwartz.

Bernie spent the rest of his shift kneeling on the floor, peering out of the windows, watching for the monster. It never came.

30

GREAT BALLS OF FIRE

att heard about it on his police scanner shortly
after dawn. More bodies had been found on the
beach. He drove there right away, but this time
the police presence was more robust, and he wasn't allowed
anywhere near the crime scene. Matt had to park at the nearest
public beach and walk about a mile until he reached the police
tape. Affird was already there, pacing around angrily. Even the
mayor showed up, surveying the scene from the dune crossover
like a goddess casting judgment upon the feckless mortals.

Two stretchers with body bags were carried up the stairs of
the dune crossover by the county medical examiner's staff.
They squeezed past the mayor, who watched impassively.

The dune crossover belonged to Squid Tower.

Matt's theory that Chainsaw had been the vampire-
imposter killer was now dashed to pieces. Unless this was a
copycat killer. Matt needed to find out if these victims had been

drained of blood. He was back to thinking a vampire was the culprit.

A tall, skinny old man was standing on the beach nearby, watching the police. He wore a wide-brimmed hat over long white hair and carried a water bottle. His skin was very pale. At first, Matt thought he was a vampire, then he remembered a vampire wouldn't be out here in daylight. Maybe the man was a werewolf. Or, most likely, he was simply an old man, however predatory he may be.

"Excuse me, sir," Matt said.

"Are you a cop?" the man asked with a Maine accent laced with lots of hostility.

"Actually, I'm a reporter."

"Not much better, in my opinion, when it comes to destroying a hardworking man's reputation."

Oh boy, Matt thought, this guy is carrying a lot of baggage.

"Do you know what happened here?" Matt asked, feigning ignorance.

"A young couple was murdered—that's what happened. I was power-walking up the beach like I do every morning before sunrise. I need to avoid too much sun because of skin cancer. Those expensive sunscreens aren't worth a dime, in my opinion. Seems like every month the dermatologist is taking a chunk of flesh out of me. And then you've got to go back to get the stitches out and it's a royal pain in the—"

"Please tell me what you saw." Matt needed to get the conversation back on track.

"Didn't see anything at first. I heard a scream. The wind was blowing, and I could barely hear the girl's voice. But I was approaching the spot up there where the cops are standing right now, and I saw three people—I think it was three—in an argument. I would have called 911, but I didn't have my phone with me because of all the darned robocalls I get. Can you believe Russia calls me five times a day? I block each number and they keep calling, anyway. What the heck does Russia want with me?"

"What happened?"

"I don't answer. The one time I did, they told me they would kill my wife if I didn't give them my bank account number, but my wife was already dead."

"I mean, what happened with the people on the beach?"

"What people? Oh, the dead people. I didn't see anyone anymore and didn't hear anything, so I thought they left. I kept walking down the beach until my usual turnaround point at the public beach. They have a water fountain and a bathroom, but the bathroom is always locked until dawn, which is really inconvenient for me since it's still dark when I'm there. I gotta admit I've taken a leak in the dunes now and then, because at my age the old bladder just isn't worth diddly anymore. Even though I'd probably get arrested if the cops saw me. And ruin my reputation all over again for a victimless crime that didn't hurt anyone. I've never hurt anyone. If you don't count people losing their life savings. At least they weren't physically hurt."

"But the murdered people?"

"Yes, I was getting to that. Don't be so impatient. Where was I? Oh yeah, drinking water at the fountain. I didn't pee this morning, mind you. It's a rare event, anyway. I don't want you to get the wrong impression of me. Anyway, I walked the return route and right there I saw two people sleeping on the beach. But I'm no idiot. They were on the spot where the argument took place before. Of course, this time I walk by much closer and they looked more like a couple of rag dolls tossed next to the dunes instead of people sleeping. I got closer and, sure enough, they looked pretty dead to me. Another walker was coming up the beach, and I called out for her to call 911. I guess she doesn't get robocalls from Russia because she did carry a phone."

"Was there any blood in the sand?" Matt asked.

"Some blood was smeared on their necks and arms, but that's it."

"Did you see anything else?"

"Not related to this. But there was the strangest thing: A shooting star went by, and it seemed so low in the sky it looked like a fireball. Really strange."

"You know, there have been other murders on this part of the beach," Matt said. "Have you ever observed anything else?"

"Nope. Except once I found a bunch of gear some shark fishermen left on the beach. A kayak, expensive-looking fishing rods, tackle boxes, coolers. Just lying on the beach unattended like the fishermen were beamed up by a UFO or something."

"Can I use your name in my story, please?"

"Nope," the man said. "Well, I've got to go." He gestured at the rising sun, bright in a cloudless sky. "This is a prime day for melanoma."

The man strode away north, hugging the edge of the surf to get around the crime scene. Matt combed through his memory and recalled an incident involving two fishermen found dead and drained among the sea grapes nearby.

"I had hoped Chainsaw really was the killer," Missy's voice behind him said.

She came up beside him, wearing her green Acceptance Home Care scrubs.

"I talked to a witness," Matt said. "He saw a third person in some sort of argument with the couple who were killed, but he didn't see the assailant clearly enough."

"It was a couple?"

"Yes, a man and woman."

"Did he see anything else?"

"Nothing useful." Matt thought about the earlier conversation. "He did mention a shooting star or fireball flying by overhead. It was strange enough to him that he brought it up to me."

"How odd," Missy said. "I have an idea: Is there a way to go through all the stories of similar murders committed here?"

"Yeah. You search the morgue at work—our slang for the archives. I already printed out all the stories that seemed relevant. Why?"

"I want to find out if any other witnesses mentioned a shooting star or a fireball."

"And what would that tell us?" Matt asked.

"It would tell us we would have to do some supernatural research."

THEY MET a couple of hours later for breakfast at a café on A1A, facing the public beach. Matt had run home to grab the printouts, and he placed them on the table in a thick manila envelope. The ocean was flat and shimmering in white-diamond sunlight, a prime melanoma day indeed. Joggers and cyclists passed by, absorbed in their workouts, listening to music and podcasts, totally oblivious to the deaths that had occurred only a mile or so up the beach. A faint breeze brought the scent of coconut and brine. It was a perfect day to do anything other than talk about murder.

"I ordered you a coffee," Matt said when Missy sat down. She had changed into a sundress and smelled like shampoo.

"Thanks. I prefer tea, though," she said. She wore a floppy hat and dark shades. "Sorry I'm late. The traffic was horrible. It turns out there was some crazy guy driving a riding lawnmower down A1A. He was drinking. And naked. Finally, the police pulled him over. Poor guy had a horrible sunburn in the kinds of places you don't want a sunburn."

"Ah, Lance Jenkins," Matt said. "He's out early today."

"It's early for me, too. I'm not used to being out in the sunlight these days. I feel like a vampire myself."

"Let's hope you don't become one."

"Don't worry. I take precautions."

After the server brought their coffees and took their orders, Matt opened the envelope.

"I had read all of these before, but wasn't looking for shooting star mentions, and if I did see any, they didn't stand out at the time." He handed her half of the pile. "We'll divvy them up to get through them faster."

"God, there are so many. That many murders?"

"A lot of these are multiple stories about the same murder."

"But still."

"Yeah, I've counted nearly thirty over the past couple of years," he said. "But there were probably many more—people found dead and assumed to be the result of overdoses or natural causes that never made the news. The interesting thing is many of the victims had bite marks not just on their necks, but also on their arms or feet. If you were found dead with wounds on one foot, it might not raise a flag."

They each read through the stories, picking at their food

without enjoyment when it arrived, even though they both had ordered beautiful-looking crepes.

"I haven't seen anything yet about orbs," Missy said.

"Unfortunately, if a witness mentioned that, it might have been edited out of the story as being too random and unrelated."

"Wait, I spoke too soon. A woman claims she saw a fiery UFO flying over the dunes. That's how she noticed the body of a teenaged runaway."

A few stories later, Matt grunted in recognition.

"Here's one. The witness said, 'A giant firefly flew by, bigger than I've ever seen in my life.'"

"We need to look into this angle," Missy said. "I've read some stuff on the internet, but I know someone we should speak to who can give us the real story."

MATT HAD NEVER BEEN in a botánica before. In fact, he had never known what a botánica was. Now that he was here at the Jellyfish Beach Mystical Mart, he recalled passing by the store before, unaware of what the narrow storefront with cryptic boxes and bags on display with Tarot Card-like labels was all about.

He followed Missy into the shop and through a cloud of incense. There were shelves covered with candles, bottles with ornately illustrated labels holding unknown potions, plastic bags with printed labels glued on, tons of statues and statuettes. For some reason, part of one shelf held insect repellant. The reason being Florida.

The proprietor approached them, a black woman wearing a blue scarf on her head.

"Ah, Missy, what brings you here today? And who is this *tipo guapo?*"

"Luisa, this is Matt, a friend of mine."

Being called a friend was pleasing to Matt.

"We've come to ask for your help in investigating a supernatural creature," Missy said.

"Uh-oh."

"Yes. Do you know of any creatures in Florida, besides vampires, that drink human blood?"

"Aside from the IRS, I know of a few," Luisa said. "From the legends, not personally, of course. They've come to Florida from elsewhere, like so many humans who live here."

"Are any associated with glowing orbs or fireballs?"

"Ah, yes, the soucouyant. Sometimes known as the loogaroo. They're found in the Caribbean, in islands with French heritage. Trinidad, Dominica, St. Lucia, Guadeloupe, Haiti, and others. They're descendants of Old-World French vampires that came with the original colonists to the islands. They're basically the Caribbean version of vampires."

"What's the deal with the fireballs?" Matt asked.

"That's how they move around," Luisa said.

"Okay. Of course," Matt said. "Who amongst us doesn't travel as a fireball?"

"I'm serious. Soucouyants are often old people in their human form, but not always. They appear to live normal lives and can go out and about in the daytime. When they transform into their monster form at night, they shed their human skin and store it in a container in their home, then fly around as a ball of light. They can go anywhere, slipping through cracks under doors into rooms. When they find a victim, they bite them and drink their blood just like a vampire."

"I'm surprised I've never heard of them," Missy said.

Luisa continued, "They've been known to infest small villages in the countryside of some of the poorer islands. Sometimes they simply drink from their victims sleeping in their beds, and the victims wake up feeling weak with bruises on their necks or wrists or feet. But sometimes they go all out and drain their victims, killing them. They'll feed upon pets and livestock as well."

"Sounds like human mosquitoes," Matt said. "But deadly."

"How do you stop them?" Missy asked.

"By killing them," Luisa said. "There are ways to do it, according to the legends. Usually, it involves burning them or letting the sunlight kill them."

"I don't want to hear the details," Missy said. "It feels a little hypocritical of me to protect one kind of bloodsucker by killing another."

"You think?" Matt said.

Missy glared at him.

"My patients don't kill people. As far as I know. But just in case, the communities where they live have strict rules against killing on their properties," she said. "And they deal harshly with anyone who breaks those rules. This soucouyant, whether it's a resident, a guest, or a trespasser, is subject to the same rules. But it's not up to me to decide or to carry it out. Besides, I'm a nurse. It would be difficult for me not to give medical aid to the soucouyant if it came to that."

"You sound very conflicted," Matt said, trying to keep any touch of sarcasm out of his voice.

"I am. I don't want harm to come to anyone, human or other creature."

"I doubt you'd feel obligated to give medical care to the soucouyant if it was trying to kill you."

"True," she said. "And I've accepted responsibility for helping to protect my patients and their neighbors. They come first. And this soucouyant, or whatever it is, is putting them at risk of being blamed for the murders. Not only could that destroy their privacy and protection, but it could also get them killed. You saw the other night what the police do to supernatural creatures."

"Yeah." Matt felt a knot in his stomach when he recalled the sound of the gunshots in Chainsaw's condo.

"I know of an obeah man from St. Vincent who could take care of the soucouyant for you," Luisa said.

"A *what*-man?" Matt asked.

"A practitioner of obeah, Caribbean black magic," Luisa said. "A witch of the dark arts. A sorcerer."

"He can defeat a soucouyant?" Missy asked.

"Oh yes. And he's also a realtor," Luisa said. "In case you want to put your house on the market."

31
TEAMWORK

After seeing her last patient and filling out a bunch of paperwork, Missy was late in leaving Squid Tower. The sun had already crested above the ocean. She was concerned that two police cars were leaving the parking lot.

"What happened?" she asked Philomena, the day gate guard. "Why were the police here?"

Philomena wiped a tear, and her lips quivered. "They arrested him."

"Who?"

"My friend, Bernie. It's all my fault."

"My God. Arrested him for what?"

"When I came to work yesterday morning, I found a credit card on the floor in here. I thought it was Bernie's." She stifled a sob. "When I picked it up, I see it has a woman's name on it. The mayor's murdered daughter."

Oh boy, Missy thought.

"So, I call the police, and they come by and pick it up and ask me more questions. And today they come, and they take Bernie. It's all my fault."

"Do they suspect Bernie murdered Taylor Donovan?"

Philomena nodded and smeared a tear with her thumb. "But I didn't tell them nothing."

Missy thanked her and told her not to blame herself. As she drove away, she pondered what to do. She felt almost certain a soucouyant was responsible for the murders. If someone—or something—else also committed some or all the murders, it was highly unlikely it was Bernie. She felt bad for him. He must be frightened out of his mind. But how could she tell the police she suspected a supernatural creature she had never heard of until recently?

At least Bernie didn't have to worry about Schwartz while he was behind bars.

Halfway home, she got an idea and pulled onto the shoulder. She texted Agnes, hoping she would still be awake.

Agnes answered that she was.

Bernie, the night gate guard, was taken in by the police this morning, Missy texted.

Oh no. For what? the ancient vampire texted back.

They think he murdered Taylor Donovan. Her credit card was found in the gatehouse after his shift.

Not good, Agnes texted.

I think it was planted. We need to contact the security company. I'm sure they capture video from the security cameras. We must do it fast before it's lost or recorded over.

LOL. Good luck getting Rudy to respond quickly.

Missy couldn't believe a 1,500-year-old vampire just used "LOL."

I'll go to his office in person, if necessary, Missy texted.

We need to wait until nightfall when Rudy gets to the office. He has humans working for him during the day, but they won't fulfill a request like this without his permission.

Bernie's with the police now.

You and I will visit Rudy tonight and we won't leave until we have video to give to the police.

BERNIE EXPECTED he'd be interrogated in one of those small rooms with the two-way mirrors he was familiar with from TV cop dramas. Apparently, the Jellyfish Beach Police Department did not have these. Instead, he found himself in a conference room with a long table surrounded by chairs, with a TV on one wall and corny motivational posters on the others.

Affird sat at the table on one side of him and a detective named Smallquist was on the other. Smallquist was not small. He looked almost seven feet tall and had a big gut. His too-short necktie barely made it over the crest of his belly. The pointy top of his shaved skull made the bald look backfire for him.

Bernie twisted in his chair. "Can I have a soda?"

"No," Affird said.

"I thought you'd be the 'good cop,' since you know me," Bernie said.

"In your case, we're both gonna be the 'bad cop,'" Smallquist said. "I'm going to ask you again to clarify that you stole Taylor Donovan's credit card when you killed her."

Bernie decided Smallquist was the rare giant of a man who was also a nerd.

"No, I didn't steal her credit card," Bernie said.

"But you did kill Ms. Donovan," Smallquist said.

"No! I told you I didn't kill her and didn't take her card."

"Then how did the card end up in your gatehouse?" Affird asked. He had his sunglasses on, even in here. "We spoke to the day and weekend guards, and no one saw the card anywhere until it was found this morning after your shift."

"Someone put it there to frame me." Bernie said, trying to sound confident. "You'll see my prints aren't on it."

"No one's prints are on it. It was wiped clean," Smallquist said. "Who would frame you and why?"

"My guess is Mr. Schwartz. He's been out to get me fired since I started working there. I think he even wants to kill me."

"A powerful accusation to throw around so lightly," Smallquist said.

Bernie stared at the wall. One poster was a giant photo of a swarm of ants attacking a caterpillar. The headline read, "Teamwork."

"I wasn't going to mention this," Bernie added, "but I saw him stalking customers at the ice cream shop."

"Do you think Schwartz killed Ms. Donovan?" Affird asked.

Bernie had to be careful. "I'm not supposed to say anything negative about our residents."

"Stop swinging your chair back and forth and answer the detective," Smallquist said.

"Do I think he killed her?" Bernie said while nodding frantically, looking at each detective and pointing to his own nodding head.

"We're recording this conversation with audio, not video," Affird said. "You need to state your answer out loud."

"I'm not supposed to *say* anything," Bernie replied.

"For the record, the suspect has been nodding like a bobble-head in response to my question about if he thought Leonard Schwartz killed Taylor Donovan," Affird said in a loud voice directed at the audio recorder on the table.

"Okay, tell us again everything you did on your shift last night," Smallquist said.

"Why? Was someone else killed? I've changed my mind. I think I should have an attorn—"

Smallquist's arm shot out like a rattlesnake strike and paused the recorder.

"No. Too late. You said you didn't need an attorney. Now answer my question," he said, switching the recorder back on.

"I got to work at the usual time, around 5:45 p.m. Talked to Philomena, but she ignored me. Took over the post at six. I worked twelve hours until Philomena relieved me. And still wouldn't talk to me."

"You surely weren't in the booth the entire twelve hours?"

"I left a few times to go to the bathroom. It was the only reason I left. I bring my dinner with me every night. We have a little fridge and microwave in the gatehouse, so I don't have to leave for food."

"A resident reported hearing strange sounds from the gatehouse early in the morning," Smallquist said.

"Um, well, I'm a musician. When things are slow, I play music on my tablet and sing. Do you want to hear some songs? I wrote a new one last night, as a matter of fact. You could call it Frank Sinatra meets Ozzy Osbourne."

"No," Affird said.

"You never left your post to patrol the grounds?" Smallquist asked.

"No. I'm supposed to stay in the gatehouse at all times to let cars in. We do a quick walk-around at shift changes. The HOA is too cheap to hire security guards."

Awkward silence while Smallquist scrawled notes on a legal pad and Affird stared at Bernie with a stone face. Bernie glanced at the wall. Another poster had the famous black-and-white photo of the airship *The Hindenburg* going down in flames. The headline said, "If you're afraid to fail, you'll never win." He didn't get it.

"Tell me more about Schwartz," Affird said. "He sounds like a really antisocial guy."

"You're telling me?" Bernie said before pulling back on his own reins. "He's on the board of directors. And very particular about things."

"What did you mean when you said he wanted to kill you?"

"It was just an expression, Detective Affird. I simply meant he was mad as heck."

"Stop swinging your chair back and forth," Smallquist said. Bernie stopped. "Sorry."

"Do you have a girlfriend?" Smallquist asked.

"What? Why are you asking?"

"Answer my question!"

"No, not really," Bernie said, scratching his ear.

"What does 'not really' mean? Do you play around with hookers?"

"God no! It didn't mean anything. The thing is, I almost had a girlfriend, but it wasn't meant to be."

"Because you killed her?"

"No! Because I had a bowel explosion. And between us guys, she was a little too old and weathered, if you know what I mean."

"You prefer young women?" Smallquist asked.

"Yeah, generally. Is that not normal?"

"So, Taylor Donovan is more your type," Smallquist said.

Bernie realized he'd walked into a trap. "I don't know what she looks like. I mean, looked like."

"Because it was too dark to see her face clearly," Smallquist said.

"No. Because I've never seen her at all. Not on that night and never."

"I know that's your story, but I don't believe it. Anytime you left the guardhouse allegedly to use the bathroom, you could have gone to the beach instead. Found Ms. Donovan there, intoxicated on drugs with her defenses down, and tried to have your way with her. When she resisted, you stabbed her in the neck."

"You're totally wrong," Bernie insisted. "We have security cameras. Didn't you check the recordings? When I went to the bathroom, I just went to the bathroom. I always need to hurry to get back to my post."

"At three in the morning? How busy can it be then?"

"Um, it just takes one person to complain."

"But there would actually be more than one person complaining, right Bernie?" Affird said. "Squid Towers is pretty busy in the middle of the night."

Bernie didn't know what he was getting tricked into. So he stayed silent.

"If you haven't figured it out yet, Detective Smallquist is certain you're the murderer," Affird said. "Me, I'm not so sure. I think the perp is one of the residents there. Do you really want to take a fall for some old geezer?"

"No."

"A geezer who might not even be human?"

"Fred, lay off the loony conspiracy crap," Smallquist said.

"Sometimes you have to take evidence at face value. The homicides looked like they were committed by vampires. I'm just saying."

"I don't believe in vampires," Bernie lied.

"If Schwartz gets you fired, are you going to continue to run interference for them?" Affird asked.

Bernie didn't answer. The detective had a point.

"Do you know where Schwartz was around three that morning?"

"No."

"Does he stay inside his condo all night?"

"No. He goes out sometimes."

"Does he like young women?"

"I wouldn't know."

"Why are you protecting him?" Affird asked, frustrated. "The guy wants to kill you."

Bernie didn't answer. He stared at the conference room wall. His eyes roved over the team portrait of the small police force, a photo of a K-9 German Shepherd posing with the chief, and then another poster.

It was a beautiful photo of a sunrise. The headline said, "Time to wake up."

Someone knocked at the door. Affird got up and opened the door a crack. He spoke in a low voice to someone not visible.

Affird picked up his coffee cup from the table. "I've got some new evidence to look at. You can wait here, Burdine, until we bring you to the county lockup."

"Lockup? Have I been charged with a crime?"

"You will be," Smallquist said. "We're going to nail you, Burdine. I guarantee it. Are you ready to tell me the truth now?"

"I already did."

Smallquist turned off the audio recorder.

"A few hours in the county jail will change your mind," the detective said before he ignored Bernie and began playing a game on his phone. Bernie couldn't tell what it was, but there were plenty of barnyard animal sounds.

32
OBEAH MAN

The obeah man's name was Carriacou Jack. (His realtor name was Jack Wilson of Trident Realty, call anytime for his latest listings.) He was an African-Caribbean man of late middle age, dark complexion, and short white hair. He wore rough brown work clothes and several amulets around his neck. Missy was pretty sure he didn't dress like this at home showings.

He and Missy were guests at the emergency board meeting at Squid Tower at 10:30 p.m. Matt was not allowed to attend because he wasn't a resident and, even worse, was a reporter. Missy and Carriacou Jack sat in folding chairs, the only two chairs set up where the homeowners usually sat. They faced the long table where the stern-faced board members presided with post-meal, ruddy glows.

Missy noticed Schwartz staring at her. Did he suspect she had spied on him?

"We have a quorum. Do we have a motion to proceed?" Agnes asked in her raspy voice.

"Move to proceed," said Schwartz.

"Seconded," said Bill.

"This emergency owners' association board meeting has come to order," Agnes said. "The reason we are here is that our beloved healthcare partner, Missy Mindle, came to me with information that the murderer who has put us all at risk might not be a human or vampire or werewolf pretending to be a vampire. It might be a different kind of supernatural creature I admit I was not familiar with."

"I told you jerks it wasn't me," Schwartz said.

"My money is still on you—you ornery old coot," said the director of the landscaping committee.

"Order, please," Agnes said. "The creature Missy suspects is called a soucouyant—"

"I knew it!" Bill exclaimed. "I mentioned that before. From the Caribbean. Yet another immigrant here in Florida."

"May I remind you we're all immigrants," Agnes said, "regardless of whether your family was here for more than one generation before you were turned."

"Get to the point," someone said over all the talking that was breaking out.

Agnes rapped a piece of wood on the table. Rather than use a gavel, she had a piece of a stake that had killed a resident many years ago, a vampire who had flaunted all the rules, not only killing prey on the property but, even worse, hanging non-approved holiday decorations on her front door. The stake fragment was meant to intimidate, and it did its job. The room fell quiet.

"The gentleman here with Missy is an obeah man and has experience with soucouyants," Agnes said.

Carriacou Jack stood and bowed to the board members. "What this lady says is true. I have killed two soucouyants in my lifetime."

"What the heck is an obeah man?" Schwartz said.

"Obeah is what we call magic in my country. I am a master at it. I come from a long line of obeah men, and learned from my papa who learned from his papa and so on."

"So, you're like a wizard?"

"I am an obeah man. I can make your livestock die or your legs shrivel up and become covered in sores. I can make people fall in love or become more virile. I can make your crops fail or riches come your way."

"You can make people more virile?" Schwartz asked. "Even old guys?"

Carriacou Jack nodded. "I know the spells and can make the potions to do so."

"Sounds like superstitious nonsense," Bill said.

"If you believe, the power will flow."

Someone growled disdainfully.

"And I have no fear of you vampires," Carriacou Jack said, clutching a cloth amulet hanging from his neck on a leather cord.

"How will you find and destroy the soucouyant?" Agnes asked.

"That is a secret of my trade I cannot share. Obeah men and women are very competitive, so we don't share our techniques. Sometimes we try to kill one another. And I don't want the soucouyant to know, either."

"You're not suggesting one of us is the soucouyant, are you?" Agnes appeared annoyed.

"No. I'm saying the soucouyants hunt close to home, so it might be around here often and could overhear conversations."

"Where would it live?" Agnes asked.

"Back in St. Vincent's, they were easier to find. You looked for an old person living on the edge of the village by the forest. Here, everyone is old, and there is no forest. But I have spells that will help me. I might need to live here, though, until I find it."

"I don't have any room for company," Schwartz said.

"I have a blanket. I can sleep in here," Carriacou Jack said.

"You can stay in the party lounge," Agnes said. "At least there's a couch in there. Is there anything else you need?"

"Someone to show me where the killings took place."

"I'll do it," Missy said.

"Motion to adjourn?" Agnes asked.

"I move to adjourn."

"Seconded."

"Hey, Mr. Jack, can I have one of your cards?" Schwartz asked. "I want to order a potion from you."

"I DON'T BELIEVE THAT MAN," Agnes said. "How much is he charging?"

"Five hundred a day," Henrietta said, stacking the folding chairs. "But he knows we'll pay it because we want to believe more than anything that the killer is not one of us."

"It's about time we faced the hard truth," Agnes said.

"We'll have to hold an inquisition. We can't keep our heads stuck in the sand any longer."

"Poor Leo. If he's innocent, this will cause a lot of suffering he doesn't deserve."

"But at least we'll know for sure then," Henrietta said. "And he's not the only one deserving scrutiny."

"Who else could there be?"

"Remember, we have many residents here who still hunt for their sustenance. Sometimes they get lazy and bend the rules. Sometimes they come upon prey that's easy pickings but a little too close to the neighborhood. I hear things, you know."

"Come now, Henrietta. We can't put someone through an inquisition based only on rumors."

"That's not what I'm suggesting. But there must be some form of discipline that is appropriate. We should issue fines at the least."

"Vampires get very upset at fines."

"Here's another situation: A vampire I will not name has mild dementia and occasionally gets lost when out hunting. This vampire has been caught by other residents at least once feeding too close to home. It was an honest mistake, but it could have serious consequences. What do we do about her?"

"I never considered that scenario."

"I'm not saying this individual killed the mayor's daughter or any of the other victims, but we need to be vigilant with everyone who hunts."

"I'll send out another letter to all the residents reminding them to participate in our neighborhood watch program and issue strict warnings to the vampires you're talking about."

"Is that enough?"

"What else can we do?" Agnes asked. "I personally patrol the grounds and adjacent areas whenever I can."

"We need to begin an inquisition of Schwartz. It will set an example."

Missy and the obeah man stood on the beach close to the dune crossover.

"The victims were found in other locations as well, but always near this spot. As if the soucouyant wanted to implicate one of the residents here," she said.

"Ah, I see," said Carriacou Jack. "This feels like a good place. A peaceful place. I sense no evil spirits anywhere near here. The victims did not have to be led here. No, they came willingly. They were enjoying a beautiful night on the beach when the soucouyant found them and attacked. The fiend likes to find victims who are asleep or relaxing, but not always."

"Someone who is drunk or on drugs?" Missy asked.

"Yes. Perfect. More difficult to defend themselves."

"What is your plan to stop it? I hear you have to burn it?"

"Yes. You can't kill it at night in its monster form. But since it takes its human skin off before it goes out to hunt, you cover the skin with salt. This shrinks it so it no longer fits, and it burns when the soucouyant tries to put it back on. Once dawn comes, the monster is defenseless. You douse it with hot tar, or sometimes the sunlight is enough to kill it when it is not wearing its skin."

"Do you have to kill this one?"

He looked at her like she was crazy. "How else are you going to stop it?"

"With magic?"

"If you know a way, you tell me. There ain't an obeah man or woman I've ever heard of who knows magic powerful enough to stop one of these evil creatures."

"Okay," Missy said. "How will you find this one's skin?"

"As I said before, I have spells that will assist me. And I have a good instinct for these things. You will help me, too."

"What can I do?"

"You will guard the beach tomorrow night. When you see the soucouyant, we will know its home is empty and the skin is unguarded. Then I will take care of it. Look for a potential victim here on the beach. Or maybe the soucouyant will come for you."

"I don't know about this."

He took a cloth pouch on a cord from his pocket. "Wear this. It will protect you. I see you already wear an amulet."

"To protect me from vampires, in case one of them is a little hungry and wants to take a bite of me."

He laughed and handed her the pouch. "Now you will be doubly protected."

"How do I let you know the soucouyant is here?"

"This obeah man has a magical tool for everything." He showed her his phone. "You call me on this."

33
FROM FRYING PAN TO FIRE

Bernie got into Rudy's BMW outside the police
department around 4:30 a.m. He was tired and dirty,
and felt like he'd just passed through the intestinal
tract of a goose that was under the influence of Missy's laxative
spell.

"The security camera footage did the trick, eh?" Rudy asked
as he put the car into gear. "You know, you smell like a septic
tank. You are killing my vampire's olfactory sensitivity."

"I mentioned there was a video, but the cops didn't say
anything about it. I was getting really worried. They were about
to take me to the county jail. Thank God they looked at the
footage."

"You should thank me for getting it to them promptly."

"Thank you. The detective said he couldn't believe you let
me go to the men's room so often during my shift, but the
footage proved it was the only place I went when I wasn't in the
gatehouse."

"How often do you go to the men's room? We pay you to guard the gate."

"I've been having irritable bowel syndrome lately. Cut me some slack," Bernie said.

"Okay. But don't expect to get paid for tonight."

"Are you serious?"

"I had to pay someone else to replace you," Rudy said, his eyes fixed on the road ahead.

"Who took my shift?"

"My brother-in-law. He wasn't happy about it."

"I want to know who put the credit card in the booth," Bernie said. "It had to have been Schwartz. A great way to get rid of me without killing me."

"You can't let anyone hear you accuse him of that. He's on the board and could make me fire you. Or he'll break the contract and fire my company."

"You never stand up for me," Bernie said.

"Have you noticed what car you're riding in right now? The one that belongs to the man who gave the security footage to the police."

"Yeah, I know, thank you. But how come you've never taken me seriously about Schwartz?"

"None of my people have been attacked by a vampire or werewolf," Rudy said. "At least not on the job. Aside from that one time when the guard had a bloody nose, and the vampire couldn't help himself."

"None of the guards have annoyed Schwartz as much as I have. And I told the cops all about him."

Rudy slammed on the brakes.

"Bro, I think you gave me whiplash," Bernie said.

"You told the cops about Schwartz? That he's a vampire?"

"Nah, not that he's a vampire. Though I was tempted to while sitting there in the interrogation room, thinking my life was over. I only mentioned he threatened me. And that I saw him lurking at the ice cream shop. And that maybe he killed the mayor's daughter and the others."

"You idiot! This better not get back to him or you're out of a job."

Bernie didn't answer. He sulked the rest of the way to Squid Tower and thought again about quitting. The piano lounges in Orlando were surely waiting for him.

AN HOUR into Bernie's next shift, the phone in the gatehouse rang. His heart practically leaped out of his throat. He let it ring five times and picked it up.

It was Schwartz. He said he was expecting company. A young lady friend. He wanted Bernie to let her through the gate.

Bernie choked out a yes and hung up. What was going on here? Schwartz never had visitors. Was he having a vampire friend over for tea?

More important, there was no trace of extra menace in Schwartz's voice, so hopefully he hadn't gotten wind of Bernie's big mouth at the police station.

He was falling asleep again when headlights suddenly flashed through the windows. A car pulled up, an old Camaro with fuzzy dice hanging from the rearview mirror. Bernie slid open the door of the gatehouse and stepped down to look inside the car.

"I'm here to visit a Leonard Schwartz. I'm his niece."

She had a huge mane of bleached-blond hair, pink plastic earrings and a tight purple top revealing a Grand Canyon of cleavage. She was binge-eating Snickers bars. A vampire she definitely was not. And the candy was not a good idea before meeting Schwartz.

"Sorry, miss, but I really don't think you should go up there."

"Why? The building's on fire or something?"

"Look, I'm not sure how to say this . . ." How *would* he say this? "I have reason to believe Mr. Schwartz has hurt some people before. Really hurt them."

"Oh, he didn't say he was into *that*," she said. "But I've been around long enough to be able to take care of myself. Now open the gate."

"I mean, I think he's killed people before. You shouldn't go up there."

She opened the door and got out. Bernie stepped back and tried not to look at her breasts.

"You really don't want me to go in, do you?" she asked. "You got an offer that's better?"

"You're not listening. He's a *vampire*. You're his dinner and he's having you delivered like a pizza."

"I'll play along with anything you want," she said.

"Just get out of here."

"C'mon, if I cancel this appointment, the service is going to be really mad at me."

"Please go now, or I'm calling the cops."

As she finally backed up and turned around, the gravity of what Bernie had done began to sink in. Why did he care about saving some stranger's life when he was putting his own at risk?

It wasn't long before he sensed an evil presence.

"What did I do to deserve a moron like you?"

Schwartz. He was standing in the open door of the gate-house, his pot belly protruding beneath a Panama shirt. His eyes glowed like beacons in the fog.

"I didn't tell anyone anything about you," Bernie blurted out. "Not a word."

Schwartz wasn't listening.

"The board of directors of the condominium association, they tell me to leave you alone," he said. "They say you're the only human stupid enough to work this job without causing trouble for us. I've been wanting to kill you ever since the oil stain. And this time, you pushed me too far. I was expecting an amorous evening, and now I'm hopping mad."

"Amorous? I thought you were going to feed on the young lady and possibly kill her."

"You have a problem with an old man being with a hooker? You think my parts aren't in working order?"

"No, I . . . so you wanted the hooker just to be a hooker?"

"That's it. I've had enough of your idiocy," Schwartz said, moving into the booth.

He's coming inside, Bernie thought with panic. So, Missy's protection spell was truly only a laxative spell.

"Please don't make me a vampire." Bernie knew it was a dumb thing to say, but he was too scared to be witty.

"I'm not making you a vampire. What, and have to put up with you for centuries? No, I'm just going to kill you."

He bared his fangs. Bernie hadn't realized they made fang dentures, but now he knew.

Schwartz's body tensed, about to spring at his prey. But he paused.

His shoulders slumped, and he deflated with disappointment. His eyes were glued to Bernie's chest.

Where his amulet hung from its leather cord. His vampire repellant, courtesy of Missy. At least this protection worked.

The one thing vampires don't expect is for their prey to run towards them. Bernie bolted for the door, somehow slipped past Schwartz, and almost got caught as his shirt snagged on the door latch. He pushed through and sprinted across the parking lot toward the beach. As he climbed the dune cross-over, he looked back. He couldn't believe Schwartz wasn't following. The charm must have truly freaked him out.

But something felt wrong. He patted his chest and the back of his neck. The amulet was missing. The cord must have gotten caught on the gatehouse door latch and broke. He couldn't go back for it now. In fact, he couldn't go back ever again. His career guarding Squid Tower was effectively over.

He kept running as far as he could down the beach with no clue of how he would get to his apartment. A few miles later, he collapsed exhausted and out of breath, not far from a lady combing the beach for shells.

As Bernie watched the elderly lady hunting for shells walk in his direction, something about her was familiar. Yet as she got closer, he couldn't recognize the shadowy face. From this distance, it seemed hideous. He stood up. The woman came closer.

The face was like a giant festering wound. Blood, pus, and raw flesh barely covered the bone. Her hands were the same. As was the rest of her body, unclothed and skinned.

"Hello, Bernie," said the woman in a voice he instantly recognized.

"Philomena?" It couldn't be her—not this zombie-like hag. Icy fear trickled into his stomach.

"It's me. Do you like what you see?"

She came closer, and he smelled blood, sulfur, and dank rot. She had no skin, just the exposed flesh as if she'd been flayed alive.

"Um, did you forget your makeup tonight?" he asked.

"I left my skin behind as I always do when I hunt."

"My god, are you a vampire like the rest of them?"

She was uncomfortably close to him now, and the stench was making him nauseous.

"I am a soucouyant, what we call vampires in my homeland."

"Are you . . . are you the one who's been killing the people near Squid Tower?"

She smiled. A row of needle-like rat teeth appeared beneath her oozing mouth.

"Why did you do it?" he asked.

"Because I was hungry." She laughed. "I have to eat, no? But I did all my hunting there because those vampires are such snobs. They deserve to be blamed, man. Since I work days, I only deal with them when I come early or stay late, but every time they treat me rudely. They think they're better than me because I'm from Martinique and they're from New York."

"New York rocks!"

"Shut up, you idiot. You rejected me."

"Are you the one who put the woman's credit card in the gatehouse?"

"I wanted to punish you. No one rejects me."

"I didn't reject you. I—"

Bernie tried to scream as Philomena jumped on him, smothering his mouth with hers—the foul, oozing, gaping wound of a mouth. Her needle teeth punctured his lips, his tongue, his throat.

Then she shoved him, sending him careening into the sand behind a dune, the wind knocked out of him. She pounced upon him, biting his hands, face, neck, ankles, and thighs. She moaned and slurped.

He felt too weak to struggle. Spots swam across his eyes.

And then it went dark.

HE WOKE UP, not knowing how long he'd been out. Every inch of his body burned with pain and his mouth was filled with blood.

Something was different. All his senses were off kilter. He didn't feel like himself. Was he dead?

"I drank too much of you," Philomena whispered in his ear. "Couldn't stop myself. I was so hungry and you're too tasty. But instead of leaving you dead, I made a soucouyant out of you. As a male, you won't be able to fly. You're basically an ordinary vampire. But you will live forever now and be my mate until the end of time."

Bernie howled in horror. A vampire was bad enough, but her mate? *Forever?*

He ran away from her, back up the beach, in the vain attempt to return to a life that was forever gone.

34
DELAYING ACTION

As she walked to the front of the building, Missy noticed the gatehouse was empty and its door left hanging open. Missy assumed Bernie had gone to the men's room, but after several minutes went by, she sensed something was wrong. When she spotted the amulet she had given Bernie dangling with a broken cord from the door latch, she was certain. She unhooked the amulet so she could return it to him.

"Can you believe that dolt has been away from his post for over an hour?" Schwartz said as he approached from the shadows.

"I'm worried about him," Missy said.

"Did you know he was arrested last night? There were almost two hours without a guard here until they found a replacement."

Missy pretended to be shocked. "I didn't know."

"The day guard found a credit card belonging to the mayor's

daughter, and they figured maybe Burdine was the one who killed her. The security service had footage that gave him an alibi, though. Too bad."

"Who put the credit card there?" Missy asked, wondering if it was Schwartz.

"How would I know? Now, that little coward better get his butt back here."

"Coward?"

"Yes, well, I, uh, had a little confrontation with him earlier, and he got scared and ran away."

"Did you attack him, Mr. Schwartz?"

"Verbally is all. And maybe I threatened him a bit. But he's supposed to be a guard. He needs to have a backbone. Can't let some old man's words make you abandon your post."

"Did you threaten to kill him?" she asked in a low voice.

"Maybe. In a metaphorical sense. But c'mon, he had to know I wasn't being literal."

"Which way did he run?"

"To the beach. Like a frightened little rabbit. And a rabbit has more brains than Burdine."

"I'm going to look for him," Missy said, heading for the dune crossover stairs.

"You're crazy," Schwartz muttered.

THE BEACH WAS DESERTED, and the light from a mere sliver of crescent moon was dim. After she crossed over the dunes, Missy didn't know which way to go. On nothing more than a gut feeling, she went south toward the public beach. If she believed she was being chased by a vampire, a more public area is where she would go.

The wind was steady from the southeast and she didn't see a single soul on the beach ahead of her as she trudged along in the soft sand near the dunes.

A man's scream was carried to her by the wind. Oh no, she thought, was that Bernie?

The beach curved inland slightly, then seaward again, and at the far side there was movement. A figure detaching itself from the shadows of the sea grapes covering the dunes, stumbling along the beach toward her.

And a flare rising from the same spot on the dunes, flying rapidly towards her. It looked like it was coming right at her, but passed several feet above and took a slow turn away from the beach and toward the west.

It was a ball of fire. And within it she thought she could make out a human face.

The ball of fire could only be the soucouyant. If the monster was heading back to its home, Missy had to delay it. Carriacou Jack and Matt were on their way to find its skin, and she couldn't allow the monster to beat them to it.

There was no time to think of a spell. Missy could only try to stop the fireball's motion, hoping her telekinesis would work once again. She focused on the ball as it sped away from her, envisioning it stopping, willing it to stop. But it was moving away too quickly, like a fireworks rocket. And now, a tiny fire-fly, it grew ever smaller until it finally disappeared.

No, it appeared again. And now it was growing larger. And larger.

It was coming back toward her. Was it because of her? Did her telekinesis truly work? She was thrilled.

But only for a moment. Now she was getting concerned. Problem was, getting the soucouyant to return wasn't what she had hoped to accomplish. She had simply wanted to stop it. She had no idea what to do now, but she had to think quickly.

She ran toward the nearest dune crossover belonging to an unfamiliar building. The gate at the bottom of the steps was unlocked and she scrambled up to the boardwalk, somehow feeling safer here than on the open beach.

A binding spell—that's what she needed. She had begun learning one but had no confidence it would work. She had to try anyway. As the ball of fire sped toward her, she summoned what power she could from within her and held the power charm in her pocket to add more. She spun the power into invisible strands of steel-like strength and then wove them into an imaginary net she suspended in the path of the fireball.

The fireball neared her. The soucouyant's face inside it stared at her with angry eyes and a gaping maw of needle-like teeth. Its face was female and the essence of raw hunger. The ball was seconds away from consuming her.

Missy dropped to her knees on the dune crossover, trembling, trying to marshal her strength.

Then the fireball struck the net, only a few yards away from her. The net would be invisible to others, but Missy could see it flex as the fireball slowed, like a baseball hitting the foul-ball netting protecting the stands. The net wrapped around the fireball as Missy had intended. The fireball darted erratically, like a panicked bee.

The soucouyant shrieked a jagged, ear-splitting sound that could probably shatter windows up and down the coast if they weren't impact-resistant hurricane windows.

The fireball strained against the binding spell's net, dropped back, then slammed into the net over and over. Missy worried that it wouldn't hold. Could the monster's fire somehow burn through the strands of magick power?

The fireball plunged forward again, pushing closer than before. The net strained to hold together and not break. Inside the ball, the face fixed its eyes on Missy and snapped its jaws, eager to tear her apart.

Missy wondered what she needed to do now. And perhaps it was her brief moment of indecision that created the weakness, allowing her spell to falter. Suddenly, strands of invisible steel wire hit and wrapped around her, a fragment of the net she had spun, still hot from the fireball. She was yanked into the air and knocked off the crossover. Part of the net attached itself to the railing, and she ended up hanging over the dunes below, suspended upside down like a bug in a spider web.

The soucouyant's fireball made a sharp turn and headed inland, quickly disappearing from her upside-down view.

This is embarrassing, she thought. The expression, "hoisted with her own petard," came to mind.

At least the soucouyant was more anxious to get home than to kill her. Maybe the web of the binding spell protected her, even as it was wrapped around her.

She freed one hand enough to pull her phone from her pocket and called Carriacou Jack to warn him. She told him to text her with his location when he found the soucouyant's home.

Then she tried to figure out how to dismantle her spell before any early risers wandered by to find—

A little dog yapped at her from the dune crossover. Its owner, a shriveled old man with a coffee mug in hand, stared at her curiously.

Okay, too late to dismantle the spell before an early riser wandered by to find an incompetent witch dangling helplessly below him.

"Um, I was wondering how you managed to hang in mid-air like that," the man said.

"Magick," Missy said, because she couldn't think of a believable lie.

"Ah, you mean you do magic shows like the ones in Vegas? This is just an illusion? I think I saw a trick like this before."

"Exactly."

"I bet you're using fishing line that's invisible in this early morning light."

"Something like that."

"You look like you need someone to cut your lines for you."

"No thanks. I'll be fine," she said, though she wasn't sure if she would be.

35
INTO THE LAIR

Matt had the distinct impression Carriacou Jack resented having him tag along. Matt didn't care. Reporters had to have thick hides, and when Missy had called and told him to hurry to Squid Tower before Jack left, Matt decided there was no way he was going to miss this. He didn't mind that when they left the car to continue on foot, Jack forced him to carry the twenty-pound paper sack of salt and ten-pound plastic bag of rice.

First, Carriacou Jack had performed some magic ceremony on the seating area at the beach end of the dune crossover. He lit several multi-colored candles that almost died out in the sea breeze and burned a strange-smelling powder in a copper dish. The wind succeeded in blowing the burning powder out of the dish and straight into Matt's face. He had to smack his own face to put out the fire in his beard.

Then, the obeah man chanted in an unfamiliar language for, it seemed, an eternity. He had painted stones in his hands, which he rubbed between his palms. The chanting picked up in intensity. And then his eyes rolled up in his head until only the whites were showing.

"Um, dude, are you okay?" Matt asked.

"Man, seriously?" The eyeballs were normal again and glared at Matt with anger. "I'm trying to get my obeah on."

He began chanting again, eventually dropping into a trance again. When his eyes rolled up, Matt remained silent.

Carriacou Jack's body quivered and shook. It looked as if he were about to levitate. Then he growled like an animal and Matt had an unpleasant reminder of Chainsaw.

Finally, the obeah man grew quiet, and his body sagged. His eyes popped open, alert and excited.

"It lives not far from here," he said. "Come on, I'll drive."

Carriacou Jack's car was a beat-up Honda that was in even worse condition than Matt's pickup truck. The interior reeked of incense and burning motor oil.

"I thought realtors are legally mandated to drive luxury cars," Matt joked.

"But obeah men aren't. The Jaguar is at home in my garage."

They drove, the muffler roaring, over the Intracoastal bridge, through the mainland part of Jellyfish Beach, then headed west into the not-so-nice part of town before the suburbs began. Carriacou Jack turned into a street parallel to the railroad tracks with run-down apartment complexes and empty lots filled with giant banyan trees, trash, and discarded shopping carts.

He entered the parking lot of a dark, one-story building that resembled a motel. Few outdoor lights were on to pierce the dark shadows created by a sprawling banyan tree. Only a few units had their interior lights glowing behind tattered mini blinds.

"The spirits tell me it lives here," the obeah man said, parking the car on asphalt buckled by banyan roots. "But I don't know which apartment. Bring the rice and salt. I need to get closer."

They got out of the car as a large dog barked inside one of the units. Matt took the bags from the trunk. Carriacou Jack paced around the building's exterior. He stopped suddenly, and went directly to one of the doors, placing his palms and the top of his head against it. He chanted something indecipherable to Matt.

"This is not it," Carriacou Jack said with frustration. "They just have an illegal cable box." He continued his pacing.

The dog's barking became louder and more desperate. Matt hoped the dog's apartment wasn't the one they were looking for.

Carriacou Jack's phone rang, adding to the anxiety in the air.

"Yes? Okay. No, we're not ready. Thanks for letting me know." The obeah man put his phone back in his pocket. "Missy had an encounter with the soucouyant. She tried to delay it, but she last saw it flying west. It could be on its way back here. We need to hurry. How do I send Missy our location?"

"Let me do it," Matt said, opening a map app on his phone.,

"After you're done, spread the rice on the ground."

"Yeah, I've been meaning to ask you about the rice. What's it for?"

"If we can't find the skin, this is Plan B. The legend says soucouyants are obsessive-compulsive. When they see the rice, they must count how many grains there are. They can't resist the urge to do it. Of course, counting these thousands of grains would take so long the soucouyant would be trapped in the sunrise and die."

"And it would ignore us while we're out here standing around watching?" Matt asked. "I don't think so. I'll spread the dang rice after we get inside her apartment."

He strode to the nearest apartment with lights glowing inside and knocked at the door. A tall black man answered.

"Is there a soucouyant living here?" Matt asked.

"Apartment Three," the man said with a Caribbean accent. He closed the door.

Matt smiled at Carriacou Jack. "Reporter magic," he said.

They went to Apartment Three, two doors away. Matt tried the door, and of course, it was locked. Carriacou Jack pulled a small leather case from his pocket, extracted a tool with a long, knife-like blade, and stuck it in the lock, probing, sliding it in and out, twisting.

The door popped open.

"Realtor magic," Carriacou Jack said.

"Realtors know how to pick locks? Why? You have those lock boxes with keys inside on the doors of houses for sale."

"Not on unoccupied houses you want to rent out fraudulently. Big business down in Miami."

It was a small one-bedroom that reeked of strange incense. It was furnished sparsely with nondescript pieces and every flat surface held a fat burning candle.

"A monster really does live here. Who else would leave candles burning when they're not at home?" Matt muttered.

Though the occupant's interior design aesthetic left a lot to be desired, there were touches that showed a woman lived here, at least to Matt, whose own coffee table was a wooden door perched on concrete blocks. All the candles, for one example, pointed to a woman. The fact that the pillows on the sofa matched the throw rug. Vases—how many men had vases?

Maybe it was true about soucouyants being obsessive-compulsive, Matt thought, because the apartment was obsessively clean, as well. The cheap furniture had been carefully dusted and the old, industrial-grade carpeting didn't have a single speck of dirt. It was excessively clean to Matt, but he was the kind of guy whose vacuum rarely left his closet.

There were also creepy touches, too. Jars on the kitchen counter were filled with leaves, grasses, small bones, and dried pieces of flesh from God-knows-what. On the wall above the sofa, was a painting of a large tree with a buttressed trunk and a dark figure with glowing red eyes peering from a gap in the tree.

"That be the demon Bazil. He gives the soucouyants their power."

The two men explored the apartment separately and quietly. They both knew the soucouyant could arrive at any moment. In fact, Matt felt as if the creature were watching them explore its lair. The pressure in his stomach increased with every minute he spent in the apartment.

The kitchen was ordinary, small but clean, with a narrow pass-through bar to the living room. The bedroom held only a bed and dresser. Matt slid open the closet door, revealing bright blouses and several uniforms hanging in dry-cleaning bags. He slid the hangers apart to study one of the uniforms. It was light blue and vaguely police-like with patches that said: Eternal Security Service. The company name sounded familiar, but he couldn't remember where he'd seen it.

He looked in the bathroom and turned on the light. It was

small and clean, with candles everywhere, but at least they weren't burning. As he opened the door to get a better look, an object tapped against the inside of the door, something hanging from the inside doorknob. It was a heavy plastic ID card attached to a lanyard. He lifted it for a better look.

It had the Eternal Security logo and a name: Philomena Toulard. On the left was her photo. He recognized her.

The day gate guard at Squid Tower. The one he had spoken to.

"Hey," Carriacou Jack called from the living room.

Matt jumped at the sudden noise.

"I found the skin!"

Matt rushed out of the bedroom.

36
WHERE SHE HID HER HIDE

The Obeah Man slid a large grey plastic storage container from the coat closet near the front door. It was the type sold in big-box chains for storing clothing.

"In the Caribbean, the soucouyants store their skin in large clay jars," he said. "In America they use Tupperware."

He opened the clips at each end and took off the lid. The smell of blood and sulfur struck Matt's nose. A folded, wrinkled, dark-brown material filled the container. It looked like the top of a tray of baked brownies with black hair beneath it. Only when he peered closer, did he truly realize it was skin—the entire hide, not just the epidermis.

"Get the salt," Carriacou Jack said.

Matt glanced around. He must have left it outside with the rice.

"Be right back," he said, opening the door.

He never made it outside.

With a howl louder than a category-five hurricane leaking through a damaged shutter, something big blew inside and bowled him over onto the floor. As he struggled to his feet, a kick bashed his chest, and he flew backwards into the wall, almost being knocked out.

The soucouyant stood in the living room facing Carriacou Jack, who, to his credit, wasn't cowering in fear. Matt, on the other hand, was cowering like a baby, his heart pounding like a jackhammer.

The creature was a bloody mess of tissue with muscles, tendons, and blood vessels exposed to the air. It reeked like the box of skin but stronger, with the smell of other body fluids mixed in. She wasn't tall or bulky, but she looked strong. Her muscles were taut as she prepared to spring.

"Did you kill all those people on the beach?" Carriacou Jack asked, thrusting his shoulders back, acting confident in the face of the monster.

"Yeah, I did. Made it so the vampires where I work would get blamed. Now, you're next. You gonna die, obeah man," she said, baring a bloody mouth filled with rows of rat-like fangs.

Carriacou Jack looked at Matt and nodded toward the container of skin. Then he sprinted into the bedroom and slammed the door behind him.

The shrieks of the soucouyant filled Matt's ears as she slammed her body against the bedroom door and wrestled with the locked doorknob. Matt slipped out the front door. The bag of salt was two doors down where he had left it. As he grabbed it and raced back, he tripped on the bag of rice. His foot went right through the plastic and the grains slipped out atop the walkway. He didn't care. The situation had progressed long past the point when the rice would have helped them.

Back inside the apartment, the door to the bedroom had been broken open and sounds of banging against the locked bathroom door spilled out.

Carriacou Jack probably couldn't hold her off much longer, Matt thought as he quickly ripped open the paper sack of salt and poured a big pile on the skin. Since the skin was folded, he would have to expose more of it to the salt. Trying to keep from getting sick, he grabbed the hide and pulled some of it from the box. It felt cool and clammy. He poured copious amounts of salt on it.

A loud bang came from inside the bedroom as the bathroom door broke open and slammed against the wall.

Carriacou Jack screamed in pure panic.

Matt grabbed the half-empty bag of salt and ran into the bedroom as the sound of bodies crashing into the wall came from the bathroom.

The soucouyant bent over the obeah man as he lay sprawled across the toilet. She was gnawing at his thigh. Blood soaked through his trousers as she chewed with needle-like teeth.

She sensed Matt's presence and looked up. Her teeth dripped with blood.

"Your turn," she said with a growl.

Matt didn't hesitate. He swung the bag underhanded and sent a spray of salt upon the soucouyant, sinking into her exposed flesh.

She howled in pain and dropped to the floor, writhing.

But she didn't dissolve like a slug on a patio. Nor did she go up in smoke like a monster in a horror film.

Instead, she fixed her eyes upon Matt and snarled. She was really, really mad. Matt couldn't exactly blame her.

He ran.

Her footsteps were right behind him, the clutch of claws in the cheap carpeting. He darted from the bedroom and entered the kitchen. A knife was what he needed. He yanked open the closest drawer. Nothing but candles. Another drawer held incense sticks. He ran past the sink and opened another drawer. It was filled with locks of hair tied with ribbons.

"Doesn't this woman cook?" he mumbled aloud. But then he realized the answer to his question.

No, idiot, she doesn't cook. She drinks blood.

"I do bake cookies for the humans," she said in a wet, phlegmy voice.

She stood in the doorway to the kitchen about ten feet away, blocking his escape.

"Maybe I'll cook your eyeballs after I kill you," she said.

Matt glanced behind him. There was no other exit, no window. He was trapped. Hopeless, he opened one last drawer. He pulled out a wooden rolling pin.

Then she pounced.

She crossed the distance between them so fast he could only raise his arms in defense. Her fangs sank into his left forearm while her bloody arms wrapped around his neck and shoulders, pulling him close to her.

With his right arm, he swung the rolling pin and hit her on the back of the head. He hit her again and again and kicked her to free himself.

She pulled her teeth from his arm and lunged at his face.

He jabbed the rolling pin, thrusting it into her open mouth.

In her short moment of hesitation, he pushed away from her and flung himself at the opening of the pass-through bar, squirming across the counter and falling into the living room.

He scrambled to his feet and headed toward the front door.

Piercing pain shot through his left ankle as it was seized. He fell face-first in the living room, the rug burning his face as she slid him toward her.

Immediately, she was on his back. Claws sliced through his clothing and skin. She was even stronger than before. Being crazed will do that to you. He twisted and tried to worm his way out of her grasp, but the claws had dug too deeply and even as he tried to get away from the flaring pain, he couldn't free himself.

He shot his right arm backwards, and his elbow landed on her face with a wet thud. She growled just behind his ears.

Snapping his upper body backwards, he slammed the back of his head into her face, resulting in searing pain from her teeth slicing his scalp. But he felt her hold upon him loosen slightly, briefly, and he wriggled out from under her. He crawled across the floor and struggled to get back on his feet.

Again, she caught him by the foot, his right this time. But as he fell, he managed to twist so he landed on his butt. And, as she lunged toward him, he nailed her with a solid kick with his left leg to her windpipe. She hesitated, clutching her throat, her breath coming in loud rasps.

Matt made it through the apartment door, the monster close behind him. She never even stopped to examine her pile of salt-covered skin by the closet.

Just as he broke into a sprint, he slipped on the spilled rice, falling again, this time on the asphalt parking lot between two cars. He braced for her onslaught.

But she stopped suddenly, distracted by the rice. She stared at it for a moment in fascination. She looked at Matt, her yellow-rimmed eyes fixating on him within the bloody maw of her face. Then her concentration flickered, and she was staring at the rice again. She struggled with herself, shaking her head, looking up at Matt again, and down at the rice.

Her body relaxed as if a conflict had been settled.

She squatted down and began counting the rice, whispering each number. Matt crawled backward away from her, avoiding any sudden movements that would divert her attention. He made it past the cars into a shadowy part of the lot behind a tree.

The soucouyant continued her census of the rice, stooped over, pointing at one grain after another, counting aloud in Creole French.

He crouched behind the tree, getting his wind back. The pain from all his wounds throbbed with more intensity. Could he stay here and wait until dawn, or would she finish counting and come after him? He risked a look at her. She was still deeply engrossed in counting the rice grains. Would she notice if he ran away?

But just then, headlights swept over him and the creature as a car pulled into the parking lot.

Uh-oh, Matt thought, that's going to distract her from counting.

A car door opened and closed. The soucouyant continued with her task. Someone came up behind him and he jumped.

It was Missy. "My God," she said, staring at the monster. "Do you know who it is?"

"One of the gate guards from Squid Tower," Matt said. "Her name is Philomena Toulard."

"What is she doing?"

"This is one of the ways to stop a soucouyant, Carriacou Jack told me. According to the lore, if you spread rice on the ground, they can't help but obsessively count each grain."

"Wow," Missy said. "And I thought I was bad about obsessive stuff like that." She took a closer look at Matt. "You look horrible."

"Thank you. I had a little tussle with the soucouyant. Carriacou Jack is pretty messed up, too. I guess we're lucky she can't mesmerize her prey like vampires do."

"Is she definitely the murderer?"

"She admitted it," Matt replied.

"Remind me to look at your wounds later," Missy said.

Then she abruptly walked over to the monster, gone before Matt could stop her. She walked right up to it, pulled a bag from her pocket, and sprinkled some sort of powder on the ground. It didn't interfere with the rice-counting. Missy murmured something in a low voice and pulled out her phone, shooting video of the soucouyant.

"Don't get so close to her," Matt whispered.

"I need it to look like a selfie."

She said to the creature in a calm voice full of authority, "Tell me who you are and how many people you have killed in Jellyfish Beach."

It looked up at her slowly and began speaking in an entranced manner.

"I am Philomena Toulard. I have been a soucouyant since 1843. At night, I leave my skin behind and hunt along the beach near where I work during the day. I have killed forty-two people since I took this job. Lately, I have been careful to make my feeding look like it was done by the residents where I work. The last one I attacked, I did not kill, though. I made him a soucouyant so he could be my lover for eternity." She cackled.

"The first one I killed here was a young girl, a runaway, who was sleeping on the beach. Then I killed a man who was urinating on the sea oats. It was very rude of him to do that. Then I killed a man in the car in front of me who made me miss a green light because he was too busy texting . . ."

Matt actually sympathized with her on that one.

"Then I killed a young couple on the beach who were high on some drug. There have been many like them. They are easy prey, but the drug makes their blood taste strange. Then I killed a pizza deliveryman who . . ."

Carriacou Jack staggered out of the apartment like a zombie, covered in blood. He muttered to himself in Creole as he walked right past where the soucouyant squatted. She paid him no mind, deeply engrossed in confessing to Missy, methodically listing every murder.

Matt slipped around the rear of a parked car where he hoped to hide until Carriacou Jack started his car. Then he would run over and jump inside. But how long was Missy going to record the confession? He glanced at the sky. It looked the slightest bit lighter, but there was no sign of dawn yet. The sunlight was their only hope of destroying the monster, if her obsession with counting the grains of rice would keep her occupied until then, after her endless litany of people she'd killed ended.

A car trunk opened, then slammed shut with a hollow, metallic *clunk*. Footsteps slapped across the asphalt, getting closer.

The obeah man walked up to the soucouyant, carrying a red, plastic gasoline can. Missy put her phone away and retreated to where Matt was hiding.

Not until the soucouyant was doused with gasoline did her concentration break and her confession cut off. She looked up at him and her eyes widened in horror as she realized what was happening.

She screamed.

"Stupid, evil creature," the obeah man said as he lit a candle and tossed it at her.

She was engulfed in a blazing pyre that sucked the air from around them. Matt couldn't help but pity her, though it was over almost instantly. Instead of writhing in agony, she was consumed in a couple of seconds like a paper doll.

"She be hundreds of years old and alive only by the grace of Bazil's evil power," said Carriacou Jack. "Ain't that much of her to burn, really."

"She seemed pretty strong to me," Matt said, wincing at the pain from her bites and claws.

"She was as strong as the Devil himself."

"I can't believe she stopped to count the rice," Matt said. "That sounded like a stupid bit of folklore to entertain kids. Not something real."

"I thought it was just a legend, too. I killed two soucouyants before her, but I never tried using the rice until tonight. Man, OCD is a really bad thing to have, no?"

"And it was nuts for you to shoot video of her," Matt said to Missy. "What if she had attacked you?"

"I saw how engrossed she was with the rice-counting. And I knew my truth-telling spell was strong enough to control her. I didn't expect her to go into so much detail, though. If you can help me get the video to the police in an untraceable manner, it could really help convince Affird to leave the vampires alone."

"That truth-telling spell is awesome," Matt said.

"Yeah. I've never used it against a monster before. Unless you count some of my dates."

"You never told me you could do magic."

"I didn't?"

"No. I mean, I figured you were into occult stuff since you work part time in a botánica. Are you a witch or something?"

"That's a topic for discussion on another day," she said with a smile.

37

EXTRAJUDICIAL

When Missy returned to Squid Tower, she pulled her car up to the gatehouse to find Schwartz standing in the doorway.

"Bernie's not back?" she asked.

"Do you think I'd be sitting here doing his job if he was?" Schwartz said. He looked beyond annoyed. "I called the security company, and that crook Rudy can't get anyone out here for another hour. Where did you go? I thought you were looking for Burdine?"

"I was, but something else came up. We were dealing with the soucouyant mentioned in the board meeting. It confessed to preying on people around the community."

"Ha! And all those jerks thought it was me," Schwartz said with a gloating expression.

She wanted to tell him she knew his hands weren't exactly clean but decided against it.

"It turns out it was Philomena, one of the day gate guards," she said.

"Wait, are you telling me we're short a gate guard tomorrow, too? Someone has to tell Rudy."

A large SUV pulled up behind her. It honked its horn after only a few seconds of waiting.

"Hold on," Schwartz shouted at the driver. "Our guard ran away. I gotta figure out how to open this thing."

Schwartz went into the gatehouse. Guttural cursing came from inside. The SUV honked again. Missy turned around and resisted the urge to give the driver a one-finger salute. Finally, the gate arm rose.

Missy pulled through and parked nearby in the visitor lot. As she was locking her car, she noticed the SUV had stopped just inside the gate. The driver stepped out of the vehicle. It was Affird.

"Mr. Schwartz," Affird said. "I need a moment of your time."

Affird reached into the SUV and pulled out a wooden pole with a sharpened end.

Missy froze. Oh God, he's going to execute Schwartz.

She ran toward the gatehouse, her heart racing. She didn't know how to stop him, because she couldn't assault a cop.

Unless she could stop him with a spell. Not Florida Cracker folk magick, not a simple truth-telling spell, but a strong, force-projecting spell drawing upon telekinetic power within her, like the binding spell. But it had to be faster and stronger.

And this time, she couldn't fail.

EVERYTHING SEEMED to slow down until it was as if she were watching a video frame by frame. Affird stepped toward the gatehouse and raised the wooden pole. He moved closer to the open door.

Missy stopped, took a deep breath, and focused with all her will, picturing Affird hit by an invisible force that would knock him over like a giant ocean wave.

Of course, nothing happened. Affird began moving into the doorway, his head turning to locate Schwartz.

She kept concentrating with all her mind and soul, adding the urgency of her panic to the strength of her conjuring.

Affird stopped in the doorway, his shoulders squaring off as he braced himself, holding the pole with two hands like a medieval pike.

Schwartz cowered beneath the gatehouse desk, looking up at his executioner, frozen in terror.

Time was up. This was Missy's only chance. She imagined her mind shooting laser beams, invisible and aimed right at Affird's back.

Nothing happened. Affird would thrust his stake any second now.

She kept drawing from whatever power she had inside herself. She drank from the emotions she had felt when she heard the story of her husband tormented by the neo-Nazi thugs, and then, when the police who should have saved him arrived, being executed by the evil cop.

She imagined with brutal clarity the cop unexpectedly thrusting the rebar into her husband's chest, forcing it through his shirt and his skin, between his ribs, and into his heart.

The anger and sadness swirled through her chest and up into her brain. Her head felt like it was going to explode.

She remembered jumping at the *BAM-BAM* reverberating in Chainsaw's bedroom as Affird killed the biker, illegally, unfeelingly, immorally.

Righteous rage hummed within her. It sang beneath her temples and along the edges of her ears.

And then it was gone, released from her in an instant, leaving her lightheaded and dizzy.

Affird's back appeared to collapse inward as he went flying sideways in the gatehouse, smashing through a window and out into the approach lanes. His stake skipped across the asphalt and into a hedge.

She did this. Her mind did it all by itself.

She ran the rest of the way to the gatehouse. Inside, Schwartz was still beneath the desk, his face even paler than a vampire's, which is saying a lot. He quivered with fear.

"What, what, what," he mumbled.

"You were remarkable." Agnes had somehow shown up. "You've finally discovered your power. I've always known you had it."

"I have a lot of work still to do," Missy said. "I was lucky tonight."

"You weren't lucky. You were *strong.*"

Missy and Agnes went around to the front of the gatehouse and bent over to examine Affird's body sprawled face-down in the residents' lane. Missy touched his neck and felt a pulse. She didn't see any serious wounds.

"He's alive," Missy said. "But what are we going to do now? He needs medical attention. And once he wakes up, he'll call a plague of cops upon our community."

Agnes said, "I'll mesmerize him. It'll make him forget what happened here tonight. Then, we'll move him and his vehicle off the property, and call nine-one-one from where we drop him."

"Good," Missy said. "But he didn't come here to kill Schwartz on a whim. There must have been some physical evidence or a tip from someone. He'll come across it again in his office and be reminded about why he was here."

"This is the best we can do for now." Agnes crouched beside the prone detective and touched the back of his neck. "You will wake up and accept my commands. Do you hear me?"

"Yes," Affird said in a sleepy voice, his face pressed against the asphalt.

"Why are you persecuting our residents?"

"Because I hate monsters, all of you. A werewolf killed my wife."

Agnes looked at Missy with concern in her eyes. "You can't mesmerize hate away," she whispered.

Missy nodded.

"You will not remember what happened tonight and have no memory that you came here at all," Agnes continued, intoning to Affird. "You won't remember why you wanted to come here, or even what you did earlier today. It is all permanently erased from your memory."

"I'll make a complaint," Schwartz said, venturing out from the gatehouse. "Police brutality."

"That's not a good idea, Leo," Agnes said. "None of us can acknowledge seeing the detective here tonight."

"I have to look for Bernie," Missy said. "He could be in danger."

"Of tripping over his own shoelaces, the moron," Schwartz muttered.

Missy thought that after narrowly escaping death, Schwartz would be a little more charitable. But she was wrong.

38
WE'RE IN THIS TOGETHER

Missy nibbled at her toast while Matt dumped hot sauce on his scrambled eggs. The ocean dazzled with the rising sun. They were the first customers at the beachside café, which had become a regular meeting place for them with their opposing schedules. A sparrow hopped around on the patio searching for crumbs. It gave Missy an unpleasant memory of the rice grains and the soucouyant.

"Do you want me to look at any of your wounds?" she asked. "Something tells me soucouyant bites would be a serious risk of infection."

"Thanks, but I stopped by the E.R. and they patched me up. Gave me a bunch of nasty shots, too."

She took a sip of tea, sweet with honey. "So, how does this end?"

He looked startled. "I hope you aren't talking about you and me?"

"No, silly. How does the murder investigation end, and how do we get the police to leave us alone? We know the killer is dead. We sent the confession video to the police. But how can we be sure they believe the video was legit? Would they actually accept that she was a Caribbean vampire and killed all those people?"

"I'm hoping we don't have to do anything. A friend of mine, a detective on the force, told me they received a video purportedly of the killer, but he wouldn't say anything other than she was a nutcase who claimed she was a vampire. But they had already started looking into her."

"Really?"

"Yeah. Philomena Toulard called to report finding a credit card on the floor of the gatehouse. It belonged to the mayor's daughter. So, the cops brought in the night guard—"

"Bernie."

"Yes. But security footage showed he never left the property on the night of the murder. The cops now suspect Philomena was trying to frame him. And there's more. It turns out she had dirt in her past."

Missy asked, her curiosity on fire, "Ties to other murders?"

"That's what it sounds like. My friend said Philomena had moved around a lot in South Florida and had been a person of interest in more than one murder case. The video might not be so far-fetched for them. I mean, the killing part. Not necessarily the soucouyant part."

"Are they looking for her?"

"Yeah. But as far as anyone knows, she skipped town, leaving her car and her possessions behind," Matt said. "You, Carriacou Jack, and I are the only ones who know what really happened to her."

"Are you certain none of her neighbors saw anything?"

"I'm pretty sure, unless someone was peeking out between their blinds. But the people in that building are not the types to talk to police."

Matt took a big gulp from his glass of tomato juice, and Missy shuddered. Ever since she began caring for vampires, she lost her love of Bloody Marys and ketchup. Even spaghetti sauce made her blanch a bit.

"Then what do we do now?" she asked.

"Make sure the vampires and werewolves are on their best behavior," he said. "The cops will still have their eye on them, especially if there are any reports of more drugs at Seaweed Manor. Aside from that, let's just wait and see. I assume there won't be any more killings near their properties and then, hopefully, the police will lose interest."

"Speaking of losing interest, I'm concerned about you."

"About me?" Matt asked. "Why?"

"You'll move on to other stories, but you know more about my patients than any outsider should know. Do you promise to keep all of this secret?"

"Yes, I promise. I'll honor our agreement."

"And if supernatural creatures pop up on your radar, do you promise to let me know?"

"You want to be involved?"

"I do. We have to be a team."

He smiled. "Agreed."

"And remember, I have a pretty good truth-telling spell, so don't try to B.S. me."

"I know. I hope you'll only use it on monsters, not on me."

Missy arrived at Squid Tower for her first patient appointment of the night at 8:00 p.m. The gate opened for her the moment she approached on A1A and signaled to turn into the entrance. Bernie, back on the job, was much more responsive thanks to his new vampire senses. However, she heard he still had the habit of dropping the gate arm too soon and clipping the rear ends of cars.

He smiled at her when she passed the gatehouse. Being a vampire only made him creepier than he had already been. At least he appeared to be happier now.

The Blood Bus had just arrived, and residents were pouring out of the building, heading for where it sat at the edge of the property. With their arthritic gaits, they looked more like a pack of zombies than vampires.

"Hey, Missy," Bill said, waving to her. "Can't wait to read you my new story at the next class. It's about vampire commandos."

"I look forward to it," she said.

Then Agnes with her quad cane, and Henrietta on her scooter, exited the building. They smiled at Missy and said hello, each of them giving her a little hug. She didn't worry one bit about having her exposed neck so close to their jaws.

She waited in the lobby for the elevator and admired the soft earth tones of the ultra-modern furniture, the walls, and decor. As much as the vampires complained about their HOA fees, they put a lot of effort into making sure the building looked great. The colors were always muted because of the residents' overly sensitive color senses.

The elevator opened, and Vicky emerged. She wasn't using her walker.

"I'm feeling so much better now, Missy," said the seventy-year-old who'd been a vampire for only two years. "Your advice to take extra platelets with my meals really helped with my knees. Thank you so much, dear."

She gave Missy a pat on the arm before Missy got on the elevator and pressed the button for the eighth floor. She hadn't felt like she belonged anywhere since she left her job at the hospital. And now in this community with residents decades older than her in appearance, and, in many cases, centuries older in age, she felt a kinship of shared purpose. With a few of the vampires, she even had a friendship. She wasn't like them, but as her powers grew, she was less like other humans.

She was more inclined to think of herself now as a witch—not as a mere hobbyist, but as a core part of her identity. Maybe being a witch would become more important to her self-image than being a nurse. The problem was, she was raised in a household where even talking about witchcraft was forbidden.

A candid conversation with her mother about this would have to happen soon. Missy had eventually learned that the sensitivity about witchcraft was because her birth parents were witches. She'd never known anything about this until when her mother let it slip when Missy was staying with her after her father's funeral.

Her mother also revealed then that Missy's birth parents had been murdered. Did their deaths have something to do with witchcraft? Missy needed to find out about that if she was going to wholeheartedly pursue being a witch.

In the meantime, it seemed that she had finally found a

group where she belonged—a family of sorts. A family that would never grow old and die on her.

39
THE NIGHTHAWK

Bernie liked his job much more now. The night had become his solace, and the tunes he sang, delicate songs of darkness, came from some part of him he never knew existed. Among his heightened senses was the ability to sing without slipping off key so often. This could do wonders for his musical career. Be sure to look for him playing acoustic guitar at the touristy seafood joints on weekend nights.

At the same time, he felt a greater responsibility to protect his vampire brethren at Squid Tower.

Schwartz was extremely unhappy that Bernie had kept his job, but the condominium association not only insisted that he stay but also gave him a subsidy to rent a condo of his own at Squid Tower.

Bernie learned some members were prejudiced against him because he was created by another kind of supernatural creature, but they were persuaded in the end that a bloodsucker was a bloodsucker, and that the soucouyant who created him was, in reality, just a vampire by another name—simply a female vampire from the Caribbean. And Bernie, unable to fly around as a ball of fire because of his gender, was more or less simply a male vampire from Long Island.

Schwartz didn't buy it. But Bernie very politely reminded him that he knew about his habit of having hookers delivered. The board would not be happy to learn about this, nor to have law enforcement digging around at the community again. Schwartz got the message.

Bernie was proud to say that Squid Tower now had the lowest crime rate of any condominium community in South Florida. In fact, there hadn't been any theft or vandalism at all since he started patrolling the parking lot on his nights off and during slow periods of his shift. Car burglars made a delicious meal. It seemed the board was occasionally willing to overlook the rule against hunting on the property when the prey was someone who had just smashed a window of a board member's Mercedes.

There was one downside. You could never get a plumber to come out to Squid Tower at night. Not for all the overtime in the world.

THE END

PLEASE LEAVE A REVIEW

Dear reader, thank you in advance:
Please give my book a better chance.
Success and sales depend on you,
So kindly post a book review.

COMING NEXT IN FREAKY FLORIDA

Gators. Pythons. Dragons?
Why not? It's Florida.

When Missy Mindle, witch and nurse to elderly vampires, goes to the Everglades in search of ingredients for a potion, she finds something she didn't expect. A young dragon with a broken wing. There are many bizarre creatures in the Everglades, native and non-native, but who knew dragons were among them? The dragons hide from humans in the massive wetlands while guarding a magic portal there to prevent entities from entering from other worlds.

And this isn't just any baby dragon. This is a dragon prophesied to restore the species to greatness. That's why an evil, ancient god wants to destroy it, and an almost-as-evil CEO tries to capture it. Missy has to protect the dragon while it heals (and snacks on the iguanas in her neighborhood). Her only weapon is her not-always-dependable magick, but she is learning that she has inherited more power than she realized. Too bad she also has her hands full with her vampire patients, including the always-annoying Schwartz. He needs to be rescued from jail after bringing werewolf blood through Customs. (It's like Viagra for vampires. Don't ask.)

Order *Invasive Species*, Freaky Florida Book 2 at your favorite online bookstore or visit wardparker.com

GET A FREE E-BOOK

Sign up for my newsletter and get a free novella. If you join, you'll get news, fun articles, and lots of free book promotions, delivered only a couple of times a month. No spam at all, and you can unsubscribe at any time. Sign up at wardparker.com

ENJOY THIS BOOK? PLEASE LEAVE A REVIEW

The number of reviews readers leave can make or break a book. I would be very grateful if you could spend just a few minutes and write a fair and honest review. It can be as short or long as you wish. Please visit the *Snowbirds of Prey* page on the online bookstore where you bought this. Thank you!

ABOUT THE AUTHOR

Ward is the author of the Memory Guild midlife paranormal mystery thrillers and its urban fantasy sequel series, The Goddess's Daughter, as well as the Freaky Florida series, set in the same world as Monsters of Jellyfish Beach, with Missy, Matt, Agnes, and many other familiar characters.

Ward lives in Florida with his wife, several cats, and a demon who wishes to remain anonymous.

Connect with him on social media: Bluesky, Facebook (wardparkerauthor), BookBub, Goodreads, and Pinterest, or check out his books at wardparker.com.

PARANORMAL BOOKS BY WARD PARKER

Freaky Florida Humorous Paranormal Novels
Snowbirds of Prey
Invasive Species
Fate Is a Witch
Gnome Coming
Going Batty
Dirty Old Manatee
Gazillions of Reptilians
Hangry as Hell (novella)
Books 1-3 Box Set

The Memory Guild Midlife Paranormal Mystery Thrillers

A Magic Touch (also available in audio)
The Psychic Touch (also available in audio)
A Wicked Touch (also available in audio)
A Haunting Touch
The Wizard's Touch
A Witchy Touch
A Faerie's Touch
The Goddess's Touch
The Vampire's Touch
An Angel's Touch
A Ghostly Touch (novella)
Books 1-3 Box Set (also available in audio)

The Goddess's Daughter Urban Fantasy Trilogy

(Sequel to the Memory Guild Series.)
Of Envy and Empaths
Of Fear and Fae
Of Vampires and Valor

Monsters of Jellyfish Beach Paranormal Mystery Adventures

The Golden Ghouls
Fiends With Benefits
Get Ogre Yourself
My Funny Frankenstein
Werewolf Art Thou?
In Sprite of Herself
Worms of Endearment